Dyslexia
Friendly

Cleaning Spells Before Courtship

Cleaning Spells Before Courtship

A Queer Historical Romance

Fae & Human Relations Book 4

Sarah Wallace & S.O. Callahan

For those seeking magic in others, we sincerely hope you find it.

Content Warning

Cleaning Spells Before Courtship is a cozy historical fantasy set in a queernormative world. As such, we hope our readers will find it a soft and light read.

But please note that this book will contain some on-page sex scenes.

Content Warning

Cleaning Spells Before Courtship is a **cozy** historical fantasy set in a queernormative world. As such, we hope our readers will find it a soft and light read.

But please note that this book will contain some on-page sex scenes.

Content Warning

Cleaning Spells Before Courtship is a cozy historical fantasy set in a queernormative world. As such, we hope our readers will find it a soft and light read.

But please note that this book will contain some on-page sex scenes.

Forthwith! Delicate sensibilities beware:

45. Bucolic delight, verdant and pristine;
A more magnificent expanse you have never seen.
Silk and silhouette, pay a visit to the modiste;
Couturier, spare no expense and give me your finest, I must insist.

46. Upon a horse, a mount, a stallion, or steed
One may find this action pleasing indeed
But with the dragon's foe, one might hesitate
Unless, of course, one lies in state.

47. A creature so grisly and so grim
So two become one as daylight doth dim,
But lo! The sight may well astound
For one too many appendages abound.

48. All matters continental and Gallic I respect
Be they culinary, sartorial, or aesthetic.
But epistoles and missives I appreciate the most,
Although of pressing news this type is unlikely to boast.

49. Not father, nor brother, nor sister, nay
But the doting matriarch to whom we pray.
Not of a few, or some, but more,
She looks upon heroes of mythical lore.

50. We are feeling magnanimous indeed,
For here are two hints for the first word of three:
Think first of a point of a dagger or sword,
If that does not suit, imagine pouring something onto the floor.
But there is one item that you need not fear should fall,
It is of soft and heavy drape, be it used on rod, or dress, or curtain call.

45. Green garment 46. Riding St. George 47. Beast with Two Backs 48. French letters 49. Mother of All Saints 50. Tripping the velvet

Chapter 1
Sage

There was nothing Sage Ravenwing detested more than travel.

Leaving the comforts of home for an extended period of time, only to arrive at a place that provided less familiar entertainment and less surety about oneself, was the last thing he wanted to do. This was especially true in the hot summer months, when the multiple layers and fine fabrics of his preferred wardrobe became more of a nuisance than a form of self-expression. Sage had always taken great pride in his appearance. Not even the weather could force him out of his coat or encourage him to undo a couple of buttons on his well-fitted waistcoat.

Sage was exceedingly aware of the perspiration gathered inside his shoes and on his upper lip. He was focused hard on ignoring it when his carriage rocked wildly after hitting yet another rut in the dirt road. The fan he'd been using flew out of his grip; he used both hands on his seat to stop his entire body from following it to the floorboards. With a curse, he leaned forward to pick it up and immediately began waving it at his face again, grateful that his head had not bounced against the window this time, at least.

"Do take care!" he shouted.

There came no response. He was unsure if the coachman hadn't heard him, or had simply stopped listening, but it made him feel better to voice his displeasure regardless.

The ride had been treacherous. Sage was beginning to wonder if they'd started aiming for the tracks and trenches in the worn country roads rather than trying to avoid them. With a grimace, he adjusted his shoulders and stretched his back, working out the tightness in them the best he could. The only reward was one satisfying *pop*, at which he let out a soft grunt.

His first order of business upon arrival at the estate would be to request a hot bath and a tonic strong enough to ease his aches from the journey. With any luck, it would put him right to sleep and he could be a much better version of himself before he addressed the real matter at hand: why in the blazes had he been invited to Wyndham and Roger Wrenwhistle's home?

With a heavy, irritated sigh, Sage set his fan down across his thighs and reached into his breast pocket to retrieve the letter. Naturally, it had been written on the finest stationery available. When it'd been brought to him on the footman's silver tray, he nearly mistook it for a royal missive. Upon further inspection, however, he discovered that the wax seal was instead stamped with a scrolling W that instantly set him on edge.

Sage eyed the letter in his hand again, just as critically as he'd done when it first arrived. He had known straight away that the handwriting did not belong to Wyndham. It was far too small and hurried. The name signed at the bottom confirmed that it had been sent instead by Roger Wrenwhistle, Wyndham's husband. Sage decided he would've been less surprised if it really had come from the palace.

Aside from still existing in the same social circles, there had been no contact between Sage and any member of the Wrenwhistle family since Wyndham and Roger's wedding nine months prior. Wyndham's last words that night were to inform Sage that, without an apology to Roger for what he had done, there would be no forgiveness granted on his part.

Sage had not apologized to Roger. In truth, he found the whole thing to be overly dramatic and unnecessary. Why should he be remorseful for what he said when *he* was the one hurting? Roger had single-handedly taken everything Sage ever wanted.

The man he loved—the man who always claimed he would never marry—had been swept up into a whirlwind romance. Wyndham displayed his love for all the world to see with a wedding spell so unbelievable that it left every witness to it forever changed. Meanwhile, Sage got to watch it all happen right in front of him, completely helpless to stop it or the cleaving of his heart. Roger had not offered an apology for that, had he?

So, he was left to wonder.

The letter itself was very brief as far as explaining why Roger was requesting his presence at their home outside of London. The Season had ended, and all the best residents of the ton had dispersed to their summer homes, Sage's family included. He'd only just finished settling at the Ravenwing estate when he got the invitation. It would've been far too convenient to get the letter beforehand and travel there directly from the city, of course, so instead he'd been so fortunate as to have all of his belongings packed twice within a fortnight and trundled across the countryside. His mother reminded him that he likely did not need to bring everything he owned for a short stay with friends. Sage had suggested that perhaps she go find someone else to bother.

The Wrenwhistles were not his friends. This was something else that Wyndham had made perfectly clear.

Sage could still feel the sting of each rejection the man had given him, some more painful than others. They had eventually settled into a routine Sage could live with, if only to remain close. He worked for years to earn the spot as Wyndham's favorite plaything. Each time he was requested at a party, or even on a random lonely night, it filled Sage with hope that maybe this would be the time Wyndham wanted to speak with him after their intimate encounter. This would be the time Wyndham looked at him as though he meant something. This would be the time that Wyndham confessed he was secretly in love with him, too.

But it never happened.

He knew he was a fool for accepting the invitation. Whatever was to come of this visit, certainly it would not be found without the pain of unresolved feelings and questions that Sage likely did not even want the answers to. His first instinct upon reading the letter had been to tear it to pieces and push it out of his mind completely. Instead, he went to his desk, ordered one of the footmen to hurry up and unpack his pen and paper, and had his answer sent out immediately.

When they came to an abrupt stop a short time later, Sage assumed the coachman had finally done irreversible damage to the carriage after such rough treatment. The thought of being forced to walk the rest of the way, however far it might be, instantly made his magic swirl with outrage in his chest. He drew in a breath as the door was opened, ready to let the footman know precisely how unhappy he was with the whole experience, but he was not given the chance.

"The Wrenwhistle estate, sir."

Sage allowed himself to be helped out of the carriage. His previous lack of attention to his surroundings meant he was forced to take in everything at once. As his gaze swept over the immaculate shrubbery and bright flowers, the stone walkway without a speck of mud to be found, and the pristine facade of a tremendous country house, his indignation took on new life with a scowl.

It was everything he always imagined it would be. Wyndham had described it to him once. But to see it in person was something else entirely. This was the house he had dreamed of sharing with the man he loved, and now it belonged to someone else. More than that, it had been crafted into a home. Sage could feel it spilling from the place; every detail, every bloom, all a reflection of the family inside.

Sage shook his head. What had he been thinking by coming here?

A member of the staff opened the door. "Mr. Ravenwing, welcome."

"I beg to differ," Sage responded flatly. The man, who was dressed as a valet would be, did not falter.

"Mr. Roger Wrenwhistle has been eagerly awaiting your arrival. I was instructed to take you to him in his study without delay. If you would please follow me."

The tonic and bath would have to wait, then. Without another glance at the house or the second carriage carrying all of his belongings, Sage followed the man inside. It was equally as perfect as the outside, decorated in the latest style with no expense spared. The scent of citrus and mint in the air was fresh and welcoming, as was the slight breeze flowing across the entrance hall as they approached the stairs. If he was preparing to meet anyone else, Sage might've wished to linger for a moment and allow the romantic aroma to help cover the stench of travel seeping from his pores. Roger would be lucky if he did not remove his shoes and prop his rancid feet on his desk for good measure.

As they paused outside a closed door, Sage was suddenly filled with a wash of uncertainty. Was Wyndham with him? Did Wyndham even know he was coming? Roger was the only one to sign the invitation, and he had made no mention of his husband in the letter at all. The valet knocked on the door before he opened it and stood back to allow Sage into the room.

"Mr. Ravenwing!"

Sage was not surprised to learn that Roger did not stand on ceremony and allow his valet to provide a proper introduction. He stood from the chair behind his desk and held a hand out to another on the opposite side.

"Please, have a seat. Notley, if you would be so kind as to shut the door."

Cautiously, Sage stepped farther into the room as the door closed behind him. The perimeter was lined entirely with shelves covered in books, though it appeared some also held a variety of jars and small canisters. A sleeping hearth took up a large part of one wall; before it sat an elegant, yet comfortable, chaise lounge and a small table. The desk was the focus of the space. It was enormous and completely covered with books, magical ingredients, and more papers than he could even begin to count. A trio of candles burned on one corner.

Sage finally brought his attention back to the man standing behind the desk. Roger appeared at ease in this space that had clearly been built just for him. His hands were clasped in front of him, and he wore a friendly smile that almost hid the pinched lines of worry between his brows. He sat again only after Sage had settled in his own chair.

"I trust that your journey was an uneventful one?" Roger glanced over his shoulder out the one window behind him that was propped open and not covered by thick drapes. "The weather has been fair for travel."

"Only if you enjoy being trapped in a sweltering carriage and perspiring through multiple layers of clothing for several days," Sage returned cheekily.

Roger's bright grin faded a little. "Oh dear. The heat can be as unpredictable as the rain this time of year, I'm afraid. I'll see to it that a bath is drawn for you at once, and that you are provided with a chilled pitcher of water to drink. I hope you'll be most comfortable now that you are here."

Sage fought the urge to roll his eyes. Of course Roger would run a most welcoming household with cool drinks and nice smells and beautiful flowers.

"Why am I here?" he asked, fishing the letter out of his pocket once again and tossing it onto Roger's desk. He did not want to keep it, so returning it to the sender served him just as well.

Roger picked up the letter and stared at it for a moment before he set it aside on a stack of papers to his right. He seemed to consider the question as though he'd been wondering the same thing. Roger placed both of his hands flat against the top of his desk and appeared pensive before he met Sage's stare across the desk.

"I realize that you have reasons to dislike me," he began carefully. Sage huffed out a laugh, but remained quiet otherwise, too interested to hear what he was going to say to interrupt. "I think you know that I could easily say the same. But part of my reason for inviting you was to see if we might be able to...to settle our differences somehow."

"I do not see how that is possible." The answer was simple.

Roger winced, but went on. "I can imagine that you are still hurting from—"

"Do not pretend to know that you understand how I feel," Sage snapped.

This conversation was about to be over before it truly began. Sage gripped the arms of his chair and moved to stand. He was not going to sit and be lectured on his own broken heart by the man who helped make it happen.

"I would never," Roger said in a rush, his hands coming up defensively.

Sage paused.

"Please," Roger went on, "just let me say what it is that you've come all this way to hear."

With a steadying breath, Sage leaned back and remained in his seat.

"Thank you," Roger said on a breath of his own; an exhale of relief. He pushed his spectacles up his nose and then laced his fingers in front of him on the desk. "I know that Wyn said the only way things could be resolved between the two of you is if you offer me an apology."

"No, what he said was that you must accept my apology," Sage corrected tersely. "Then he would be willing to consider our issues settled."

To his surprise, this made Roger laugh.

"Yes, that does sound more like him, doesn't it?"

Sage did not join in his amusement. Roger quickly sobered and continued.

"I will never be able to understand how you feel. But I want you to know that I do understand why you said the things you did. I consider myself most fortunate to be close to Wyn, and if I thought I was going to lose him, I would be trying everything I could think of to prevent it, too."

Sage curled his lip. "How lucky you were to be favored in that endeavor."

Roger pressed his lips together in a rueful grin. There was no use in either of them denying it. Sage found it almost respectable that he did not try.

"You said there was another reason my presence was required? I hope it's a rather good one, for your sake. If I came all this way for you to offer condolences on my loss after so many months—"

"Yes!"

Roger was out of his chair again, coming around the desk to lean against it, leaving very little room between them. Sage turned his legs out of the way, brows furrowed with confusion as to why the man needed to be so terribly close. Roger looked around the room and then gave one final long glance at the closed door before he leaned in even more.

"I need your help with something," he whispered.

"I'm sure I can't imagine why," Sage replied at normal volume.

Roger went on in a hushed tone. "As this is our first summer in the house, it only made sense for us to spend time hosting. Wyn said I could invite some of my friends, and I have, but perhaps a few more than he was expecting."

Sage's expression shifted from confusion to curiosity, though it was still guarded. "You're having a party, then."

Roger brightened, but held a finger to his lips to indicate that Sage should lower his voice. He peered at the closed door again. "Exactly."

"A secret party," Sage amended.

"Shhh," Roger urged. "Yes, a surprise party. For Wyn's birthday."

Sage snorted. "This should be interesting."

If he knew one thing about Wyndham better than most, it was how much he despised being the center of attention at any social gathering. For a long time, Sage had wondered if he used it as an excuse for them to wander away from a party earlier to hasten their more private moments. Eventually, he decided it was a genuine discomfort that made him wish to leave as quickly as possible. They had never talked about it, of course, but Sage could feel it.

"Wyn has been working so hard on everything for

the Council since the beginning of the year. I want to show him how much we all appreciate his dedication to the project we've just finished, and make him feel as special as he is for a night, surrounded by all the people who love him."

Sage gave him a long, level look. "And you wanted me to be a part of this?"

"I want you to be a part of this, yes," Roger corrected with a nod.

"Why?"

"You've known him for a long time. Far longer than I have, on a personal level. I want your help to make sure he will enjoy this night as much as possible."

After a pause, one corner of Sage's mouth curled into a smirk. His eyes flickered over Roger's form on instinct, before he met the man's gaze again. He leaned in this time and finally lowered his voice to a murmur.

"Mr. Wrenwhistle, did you invite me here to fuck your husband?"

Roger's reaction to his question was worth every miserable moment of the journey he'd just taken. His eyes went wide as he sputtered over his attempt to speak, until finally he managed to choke out a strangled, "No!"

Sage sat back and gave a small shrug. "More's the pity."

Once recovered, Roger promptly returned to his own chair and sat. He adjusted his spectacles again and straightened the sad excuse of a knot in his cravat before he spoke.

"Mr. Ravenwing. You would not be here if you did not still care about Wyn. I believe my letter could've said just about anything, and you would still be sitting exactly where you are right now. I am attempting to do what you have yet to try: apologizing. I do not wish to live my life avoiding people at social gatherings or wondering what other horrid things someone has said about me without my knowledge. Therefore, I have invited you to our home in the hopes that you might find it in yourself to also rise above, mend the rift, and rejoin the life of a man you still hold dearly in your heart as a true friend. If that is not what you wish, then of course you are welcome to stay as long as you need and be on your way. But if I am correct, then my offer still stands."

Sage's magic was a storm in his chest. He had never felt so angry at someone who was being kind to him before. He wanted to argue; he wanted to laugh at the ridiculousness of it all. In the end, all he did was gesture vaguely with a loose turn of his wrist.

"Show me to my room."

Torquil's Tribune

THURSDAY 15 JULY, 1814

Greetings, roaming readers,

Alas, it is time to bid the Season farewell. Most of London has already fled the humid streets of the city to take refuge in the comfortable country air. As such, you can expect to hear from this modest writer very little in the coming months.

But before we leave you to your idle summers, we wish to provide some final tidbits to take away with you in your carriages:

Mr. Keelan Cricket was recently married to Mr. Silas Rook-Worth. The two met during the Council's recent project studying Fae-Human magic. It would seem Mr. Cricket was interested in studying far more about a certain fae-human. We wish them both well.

Speaking of Mr. Silas Rook-Worth, he and Miss Anise Gloucester-Stone have joined the

Council as the newest fae-human members. This brings the total Council number to eight. Word is that the search remains to fill the third human position. It would seem that few meet the necessary qualifications, although this writer finds it hard to believe that such a feat is so very difficult. All the Council needs is a human who can do magic, is open-minded, flexible, looking to the future, and wanting to improve matters for the generations whothat follow. Then again, perhaps we can understand their difficulty. Any interested parties should direct their inquiries to Councilmember Barnes. He has assured this paper that he will welcome any messages pertaining to the matter while he is away in the country.

The relative quiet of the city fills many with an unquenchable curiosity. What romances are budding out of town?

Will Mrs. Pimpernel and Mrs. Iris Wrenwhistle finally confirm what all of the ton has already guessed? Will Mr. Gerald Irving return to London? Will Mr. Benedict Brooks join the ranks of married fae gentlemen soon? Will Miss Lydia Stanton prove herself to be a diamond of the first water? Will Mx. Fern Hillcrest, Miss Harriet Thackeray, and Mr. Cyril Thompson make any declaration to appease the titillated public? Will Mr. Sage Ravenwing finally find someone worthy of his attention? If so, who could such a person be? Since no one in London has appeared to

Cleaning Spells Before Courtship

steal the gentleman's heart, we must assume that the right person for Mr. Ravenwing resides beyond our city borders.

We can but hope.

In the meantime, we remain,

Your winsome writer,

Sal Bailey

Chapter 2
Conrad

Conrad Moore did not look his best. After traveling several days by post from Bristol, he was covered with dust, his clothes were fully wrinkled, and now that he was traipsing through the countryside, his boots and the bottom of his trousers were getting more and more gradually caked with mud. When a light rain started to fall, he had to laugh. It was, quite possibly, the worst first impression he could make. But Conrad had learned through years of practice that where looks could fail him, a positive attitude, a bit of confidence, an uptilted chin, and a well-placed smile could work wonders. He was fully prepared to utilize all of those tools to his benefit as soon as he arrived.

He consulted his map, idly brushing raindrops from the paper, and checked against his surroundings. By his reckoning, the Wrenwhistle estate was another hour or so's walk from where he stood. He smiled to himself and folded up his map. He pocketed it and continued at a brisk pace, delighted that his trip would be over so soon. The small piece of luggage he was hefting had felt heavier with each passing leg of his trip; but now that he was drawing nearer to his destination, the bag felt light and his spirits were high.

When he arrived, he looked, frankly, even worse, as he could now add bedraggled to his overall appearance. The mud was dripping down the bottom of his trousers and raindrops were still slipping down the brim of his hat. He carefully wiped his shoes, set down his bag, and knocked on the door. He straightened, pulled back his shoulders, lifted his chin, and had a smile ready before the door even opened.

He was not surprised by the butler's look of mild horror, nor the slight curl of the lip, nor the directions for where the servant's entry could be found. He widened his smile and stepped forward, "I am here to speak with Councilmembers Wrenwhistle," he said. "It is a matter of Council business."

The butler gave him another look up and down. "Whom may I say is calling?"

"Mr. Conrad Moore, if you please."

Begrudgingly, the butler stepped aside and Conrad grabbed his bag and hurried in. As he waited for the butler to deliver news of his arrival, he looked around the space eagerly. Everything was impossibly elegant. He kept both hands clasped around his bag handle in order to avoid the temptation to touch the gilt candelabra or pair of delicate porcelain birds sitting atop a small table nearby. He spun in place, trying to keep his facial expression neutral as he admired the artwork in ornate frames; it would not do to look like an awestruck bumpkin.

The butler returned, took Conrad's hat and coat, directed him to leave his bag by the door, and then indicated for him to follow. He was led into another lavish space, a small sitting room. There was a whole wall of open windows that kept the space bright and cheery, despite the overcast skies. There were several chairs, settees, and tables. Conrad saw the two occupants on one of the settees, who were both watching him enter with curious expressions on their faces. He privately cheered; curiosity was much easier to deal with than disdain. The other two stood as he came to stand in front of them.

One of them, a young man who was a little taller than Conrad, with a round body, spectacles, light brown skin, and dark hair, smiled at him, bowed, and said, "Good afternoon, Mr. Moore. I am Roger Wrenwhistle. My husband is...busy at the moment, but Torquil here was kind enough to join me in meeting you. May I present Mx. Torquil Pimpernel-Smith?"

He gestured at his companion, another person of average height, who was thin, with pale skin, sharp features, and dark hair that fell around their face in unruly curls. Conrad could hardly believe his luck. Roger Wrenwhistle and Torquil Pimpernel-Smith? He'd been following both of their work for months now. He tried to hide his giddiness as he returned the smile and the bow. "It is an honor to meet you both."

"Won't you sit?" Councilmember Wrenwhistle said, gesturing to a chair opposite.

Conrad paused. "I fear I may leave a watermark on the seat."

"Oh," Councilmember Wrenwhistle said. His eyes trailed down briefly over Conrad's figure. "Oh," he repeated quietly. "Dear me, it looks like you've had quite a dreadful journey."

"Not dreadful," Conrad assured him. "It was long, though. And I'm afraid I got caught in the rain on my walk here."

"You walked here?" Councilmember Pimpernel-Smith asked.

"It was only about five or six miles from the posting station," Conrad said.

Councilmember Pimpernel-Smith looked amused. Councilmember Wrenwhistle's eyes were wide. "My word," he said. "Don't worry about a water spot. We can see that it's set right later. Would you like some tea? I'm sure I would need some after walking that far."

"Tea would be lovely," Conrad said. "But I don't wish to impose."

"No imposition at all, Mr. Moore," Councilmember Wrenwhistle said, ringing a small bell pull before taking his seat beside Councilmember Pimpernel-Smith. "Now," he said as Conrad perched himself on the edge of the chair. "How can we help you?"

Conrad carefully adjusted his posture and said, "I am

here to inquire about the position on the Council. As I understand it, the third human position is still unfilled."

The other two exchanged a look. Councilmember Wrenwhistle pushed his spectacles farther up his nose. "I see," he said. "I'm afraid you may have mistaken me for my father, Mr. Barnes? He is the Head of the Council on the human side. He would be the one to appoint the third member."

"I am most certainly eager to meet your father, but I came here first with the intention of meeting you."

Councilmember Wrenwhistle gave a surprised little smile. "Really?"

Conrad nodded with a grin. "I've been following both of your careers for some time. The projects you've been helming have been so clever. I'd love to be a part of it. I have many ideas—" He broke off. It wouldn't do to speak too long too soon. "And as I know you are a person with many ideas as well, I thought you might be my best first contact. And, if you thought I might suit, then I could travel to your father with your recommendation."

He was relieved that the words had flowed more smoothly than in his multiple private rehearsals.

Councilmember Pimpernel-Smith turned to Councilmember Wrenwhistle. "It is a rather clever approach."

"Yes," Councilmember Wrenwhistle murmured. "What sort of ideas do you have in mind?"

"Any number of them," Conrad replied easily. "I've

been outlining some strategies for launching your new rubrics. And I've been trying to find some ways to weave some of your recent findings, in terms of performing different forms of magic at the same time, together with the rubrics or how we might train more adults to cast together."

"Really?" Councilmember Wrenwhistle asked, brightening. He scooted forward. "What would you suggest?"

"Well, for the second item, I'd really love to have some people trained to show others. I think we might do well to set up a sort of course that travels around the country and teaches others. It's one thing to improve relations between fae and humans in London; it's another matter entirely to spread that attitude across a bigger scope."

"Fascinating," Councilmember Wrenwhistle replied. "And do you—"

Councilmember Pimpernel-Smith stopped him with a hand on his arm. "Forgive me for interrupting you, Roger," they said quietly. "But I'm wondering if it might be advisable to have Mr. Moore stay the night, or perhaps even a few days. I imagine the two of you could go on for hours at this rate," they added with a smile. "And it would be good to take advantage of Silas' presence here so both he and Wyndham can talk to Mr. Moore. If our new friend can approach your father with four recommendations, it will definitely further his goal. And if there are any challenges in terms of getting along with any of us, we would do well to discover that now rather than in the Council chambers."

Conrad's heart lifted. This was the best scenario he had imagined—it was actually much, *much* better than he had imagined. Never in his wildest dreams could he have anticipated his visit would garner him introductions to four councilmembers at once! But it wouldn't do to look like he was angling for a free stay, so he stayed silent and kept his expression hopeful.

Councilmember Wrenwhistle seemed pleased by the suggestion as well. But almost as soon as his face brightened with agreement, it fell as well. "Oh dear. We have no more rooms." He turned to Conrad with an apologetic look. "We're having some friends over at present. So we're a bit at capacity, you see."

"I don't wish to inconvenience you," Conrad said. "I am happy to stay in the servant's quarters or take a room in the village."

The gentleman looked horrified. "The village is miles away! And, good heavens, I will not house a guest in the servants quarters. It really is perfect that so many of us are here at once; I just wish we had a little more space."

Councilmember Pimpernel-Smith seemed thoughtful. "I wonder if Mr. Ravenwing might be persuaded to share his room."

Conrad didn't know how Councilmember Wrenwhistle looked even more scandalized, but he managed it. "He might, but—" he glanced at Conrad and then turned back to his friend and said in a low voice, "I'm not sure that's a good idea."

Councilmember Pimpernel-Smith shrugged. "It's worth asking him."

Councilmember Wrenwhistle wrung his hands together. "How old are you, if you don't mind my asking, Mr. Moore?"

"Thirty-five," Conrad answered, mystified.

The gentleman looked a little more at ease. "Well, you're of age, at least. You see, there's one room with only one occupant, but...well, he's fae, and I don't wish to put you in an uncomfortable position."

Conrad couldn't have planned this conversation to go better if he'd tried. He was getting the opportunity to stay overnight, talk with multiple councilmembers, and he'd get the chance to prove he could get along well with fae? He beamed. "I assure you, I won't be in the least bit uncomfortable. If your friend is amenable to the idea, I would be happy to share the space during my stay."

Councilmember Wrenwhistle relaxed. Councilmember Pimpernel-Smith looked like they wanted to laugh. "Perhaps I should go and ask him while you have tea with Mr. Moore."

"What an excellent idea," Councilmember Wrenwhistle said. "Thank you, Torquil."

Councilmember Pimpernel-Smith gave their friend a little wink, gave Conrad a bow, and left the room. A few moments later, the tea was brought in and Conrad spent a lovely half hour talking to his host about his journey, how he'd come to learn about the

position, and all of the things that Council had
achieved recently that he was most impressed by. By
the time Councilmember Pimpernel-Smith returned to
say that Mr. Ravenwing had agreed to the
arrangement, Conrad was calling Councilmember
Wrenwhistle by his first name, and he had never felt
prouder for concocting such a bold scheme.
Everything was working out beautifully.

· ·. ·. .·

After his room had been arranged, Roger ordered a
bath for Conrad. The mysterious Ravenwing fellow
sharing the room was not present and had clearly
not anticipated compromising on his space at all. His
things were spread out across the bedroom. Conrad
took his bag to the side of the bed with the least
amount of items on it and began laying out his
clothes. While the servants prepared the bath,
Conrad decided which of his clothes was the most
presentable for dinner. Thankfully, among the three
outfits he had packed, he had included his best coat.
He knew it would be nothing compared to the rest of
the guests', but he was here to apply for a position;
it was best if they knew exactly who he was and
what his station was. A dockworker from Bristol was
not apt to have elegant attire, but that did not mean
he didn't have sound ideas. If anything, the class
differences would be a point in his favor, offer a
variety of viewpoints. He felt cheered as he folded
the clothes he wasn't wearing and returned them to

his bag. The wardrobe was fully stuffed with clothing, so Conrad didn't bother attempting to squeeze his things in. He didn't wish to make a bad first impression on Mr. Ravenwing by combining their clothing prematurely.

As he got into the bath, he began speculating on how to approach meeting the others at dinner. He had prepared himself for an interview of sorts with the Wrenwhistles, but he was not at all sure what to do at a house party. He scrubbed himself clean with lavender-scented soap, fascinated by the opulence. Then he dressed himself for dinner and strode back downstairs, following the sounds of voices until he reached a large sitting room where a dozen people milled about and chatted.

Roger noticed him first, although Conrad suspected the man had been keeping an eye out for him. He beckoned him forward and wasted no time in introducing the gentleman at his side.

"Conrad, this is my husband, Wyndham Wrenwhistle. Wyn, this is the fellow I was telling you about, who wants to join the Council."

Councilmember Wyndham Wrenwhistle was tall, slender, and elegant, with pale skin and golden brown, shoulder-length hair that was tucked behind his pointed ears. He gave Conrad a smirk. "Ah, yes. The one staying in Sage's room. Hopefully that experience doesn't send you scurrying back to your home come morning."

Roger shushed his husband. "Don't say that," he whispered.

Conrad laughed. "I doubt it, sir. And I do appreciate your hospitality, especially considering how unexpected I was."

The gentleman shrugged in response. "What's another person more or less at a house party? And you can call me Wyndham. If we get along, it will reduce confusion. So many Wrenwhistles in residence right now. If we don't get along, I doubt we'll see much of each other for it to make a difference."

Conrad beamed at him. "A pleasure, Wyndham. And do call me Conrad."

"Why don't I introduce you to the rest of our guests?" Roger said, taking Conrad's arm. Wyndham sauntered towards a quieter part of the room as soon as his husband was no longer at his side. "Now you already know Torquil," Roger said as he led Conrad to one of the couples watching him with curiosity. "This is their husband, Mr. Emrys Wrenwhistle. Emrys, this is Mr. Moore."

Mr. Wrenwhistle was a little shorter than Wyndham, though still quite tall, and a little broader around the shoulders. His hair was shorter and his expression was much friendlier. Although he seemed just as proud of the spouse on his arm as Wyndham had been of Roger.

"You're the one who walked here?" he said. "You must have really wanted to meet Roger. I'm sure I'd have given up before walking from the posting station."

"I'm on my feet a great deal with my work. It was no trouble."

"What is your work, Mr. Moore?" someone said beside him.

Conrad turned to see another tall individual, this one with a muscular build, dark brown skin, and short black hair. His accent was less polished than either of the Wrenwhistle brothers, which instantly put Conrad at a little more ease.

"I've been working in the shipyards. I'm from Bristol."

"I see," the other man said. "You're the one wanting to work in the Council?"

"Yes," Roger said. "Conrad, this is Silas Rook-Worth and his husband, Mr. Keelan Rook-Worth. Silas works on the Council as well."

Conrad nodded at both men. Mr. Keelan Rook-Worth was of equal height to his husband, though of a trimmer build. He had dark blond hair and a smile that hinted at a cheerful disposition. Councilmember Rook-Worth shook Conrad's hand.

"You can call me Silas," he said. "It would be nice to have another person from a similar background to myself on the Council."

Conrad felt a thrill at the endorsement. He bounced a little on his toes—a habit that he was trying to quell, but had difficulty quashing when he was excited. "That is wonderful to hear, Silas. Thank you."

Roger led him to a small cluster of people conversing in one corner of the room. "Conrad, this is Lady Anthea Fitzhugh, Lady Imogen Fitzhugh, Miss Harriet Thackeray, Mx. Fern Hillcrest, and Mr. Cyril

Thompson," he rattled off, pointing to each person in turn.

"You don't need to be so formal," Lady Anthea Fitzhugh said with a kind smile. "I think I can speak for all of us when I say you can use our first names." She was a human with a brown complexion and tightly-coiled ringlets. Her wife was a bit taller and wore trousers and a suit. The lady's short blonde hairstyle barely reached the back of her jaw. She also seemed friendly, although a little less warm in her greeting than her wife.

"Thank you," Conrad said, relieved. "And do call me Conrad."

"Where are you from, Conrad?" Fern asked. They had dark, straight hair that fell neatly around their pointed ears. Even the way they'd inclined their head in greeting seemed graceful and elegant.

"Bristol. Just arrived this afternoon."

"That must have been quite a long trip," Imogen said, looking sympathetic.

"It was. Traveled by post mostly. I'm sure I looked a fright when I arrived," he added, with a sidelong glance at Roger.

"Oh, my word, the poor man was soaked to the skin from the rain," Roger put in.

Cyril—a slim gentleman with impeccable attire and dark eyes—crooked a grin at Conrad before giving his outfit a brief, assessing once-over. "It appears as though you've recovered rather quickly, old chap."

Conrad chuckled. "I don't mind a little rain."

"Ooh, I like him," Harriet said, with a bounce on

her toes that made Conrad immediately like her as a twin in habit. The lady was as short as he was, with a curvy figure, bronze-colored skin, and bountiful black chignon at the back of her head. "You should stay for the whole party."

"I don't wish to impose on my hosts' generosity, but I will be pleased to stay for as long as they wish. Or as short," he added with a wink. "How long will you all be staying?"

Roger quickly glanced over his shoulder. Conrad followed his gaze over to Wyndham, who was still in his corner, sipping wine.

"And now I'd better introduce you to our final guest," Roger said, taking Conrad's arm again and leading him to another man sitting by himself in a corner. "Conrad, this is Mr. Ravenwing. Mr. Ravenwing, please allow me to introduce Mr. Moore."

Chapter 3
Sage

Sage had been silently observing the interloper from the moment he entered the sitting room. He had already been introduced to the rest of the guests that he was not at least somewhat familiar with as they arrived throughout the remainder of the day, so Sage knew *this* must be the man he would be sharing his room with for a night.

When Torquil interrupted his bath earlier to ask if he would be amenable to the idea, Sage had given pause in sliding the lathered sponge along his leg. The tub was offensively small compared to the one he used at home; with his heel propped on the edge, his knee was pressed firmly against his shoulder. First, he'd been beckoned halfway across the country to aid in a party for his ex-lover, and now he was expected to share a room? He gave an indignant huff and agreed. He was no stranger to sharing a bed with men he did not know.

Cleaning Spells Before Courtship

There was so much hesitation in Roger's face and posture as he approached with the man on his arm that he looked as though he was guiding a lamb into a lion's den.

"Conrad, this is Mr. Ravenwing," Roger said. "Mr. Ravenwing, please allow me to introduce Mr. Moore."

Sage did not stand from his chair as he let his gaze roam sedately over Mr. Moore. Remarkably, he was even shorter than Roger. His eyes were the same shade of brown as his hair, which now that he was closer, Sage could see had obviously been styled with nothing but his fingers and was still damp from a bath. Rounded, human ears peeked from beneath the wet strands. The smile he wore was eager and confident, but it did nothing to mask the thirst for approval simmering just below the surface.

After a sip of wine from his glass, Sage turned his attention away from them and he focused on nothing in particular across the room. "I was not aware I'd be sharing my bed with a schoolboy."

Roger let out a sharp, startled sort of laugh.

"I assure you, Conrad is of age."

Mr. Moore was not deterred. He spoke up for himself easily. "I will not make any trouble for you, Mr. Ravenwing. You'll hardly know I'm here."

Sage looked him up and down again, faster this time.

"I daresay you might be right."

When dinner was announced, everyone wandered to the dining room in high spirits. Sage was not surprised to discover that he had been seated at the far end of the table—with as much distance between Wyndham and himself as possible. The premise of Roger's invitation was still absurd, but the man was not as witless as he seemed.

Instead, he found himself situated between the Ladies Fitzhugh, dividing two groups of people who obviously knew each other quite well. Their conversations were easy and dotted with laughter. Before long, Sage felt like a lame horse in the middle of a busy London street, clearly in the way but ultimately something that could be worked around. Even if they had been paying him any mind, he had little interest in conversing, so instead he settled for more quiet observations over the rim of his wine glass.

Wyndham was as beautiful as ever. Seeing him poised at the head of his own table and dressed down just enough to fit with life in the country stirred a fantasy within Sage that he'd spent months trying to forget. He would have been willing to travel for this, to follow Wyndham anywhere if it meant seeing him so at peace. But that relaxed smile was not for him. It was for Roger. The two of them exchanged several glances throughout the meal, each more tender than the last. Sage finally forced himself to look away.

Everyone was endlessly curious about the man who had wandered up to the house like a stray animal. Roger filled Mr. Moore's plate three times as he answered questions about his life, his family, his work, and his desire in earning a position on the

Council. Sage was barely listening to begin with, but he lost interest entirely after that.

The Council for Fae & Human Magical Relations was designed to bring both sides of society closer together. For over a century, they had been working to manage and better understand the similarities and differences between fae and human magic. On occasion, radical minds approached the Council to share ideas of their own. Roger had been one of them.

Within a couple of months, he and Wyndham had worked together to change policies that had been in place for decades. Shortly after, Torquil became involved to represent the "dramatically underserved" fae-humans of society. The entire thing had been highly controversial. It was all anyone could talk about at social events or read about in the papers. The unprecedented shifts in the Council left everyone stunned, and they were seemingly far from over.

To Sage's limited understanding, there remained only one human spot open on the Council, and Mr. Moore was after it. He wanted it so desperately that he had reduced himself to the likes of a twine-wrapped parcel and journeyed for days at the mere chance that he might be given the opportunity to speak with the newest members of the Council and prove himself worthy.

Sage rolled his eyes and drained the last of his wine.

When dinner was over, Roger invited everyone to return to the sitting room to allow their meal to settle in continued good company. One of the ladies offered to play a couple of songs for everyone on the pianoforte, which got several delighted responses. Sage cast one last look in Wyndham's direction and left the room without speaking to anyone.

The faint sounds of music and laughter carried up the stairs. Sage's attention was drawn to the bedroom door when it opened and closed, allowing the noise in for a moment. He watched in the reflection of the dressing table mirror as Mr. Moore walked silently across the room in the direction of the bed. His smile was still brave, but the rest of him looked like he wished he'd been asleep hours ago. Without so much as an abashed request for privacy, or even a glance of acknowledgement, Mr. Moore began to undress.

Sage arched a brow and resumed applying his favorite blend of rose water and sweet almond oil to his face, methodically working it into his skin. When he finished with his neck and moved to his chest, he turned slowly on the ottoman in time to see Mr. Moore stepping out of his trousers. The resulting view was less than exciting. The man was so short that his shirttail reached his knees.

"Do all humans in Bristol lack propriety?" Sage purred.

Mr. Moore chuckled at that, but did not look up from folding his abandoned garments into a neat stack. "Only me, I'm afraid, much to my mother's dismay."

Sage rubbed the last of his oil into his hands and forearms as Mr. Moore produced a small bag from underneath the side of the bed he was standing next to. His expression shifted to one of disbelief as the man stuffed his clothes inside with little care. Was that where he planned to keep them? Worse yet, did all of his clothes fit in one piece of luggage? Sage eyed the wardrobe in the corner of the room. It had barely been able to contain what he'd brought.

"I hope that won't be a problem."

There was no time for Sage to answer if it was or not. Mr. Moore reached behind his head and grabbed his shirt in one fist, pulling it forward and off in one swift motion.

Now that, Sage decided, was a view.

Hidden beneath his clothes, Mr. Moore was muscled in every way that a man could be. Sage remembered faintly that he did some sort of physical work for a living. It was quite evident. He tilted his head slightly and did not look away as Mr. Moore folded his shirt and put it in the bag, too. Perhaps this was what all human men looked like naked? He had never seen one before.

Sage stood lithely from the ottoman as a smirk curled at the corner of his lips. This was certainly an unexpected surprise. It took little effort for the silk of his banyan to slide from his bare shoulders and all the way to the floor. He stepped out of the puddle of fabric and left it there.

"No problem at all," he confirmed airily.

Sage had given up wearing nightclothes the moment he was old enough to protest them. The convenience of such a decision only became more apparent with time and a more mature shift in his nighttime activities.

As a drunk might reach for their tankard, Sage took a half-step back and reached for a smaller jar of oil than the one he'd been using before. The scrape of glass against the polished wood of the dressing table as he picked it up finally made Mr. Moore look at him, but only briefly, as he climbed under the covers they were about to share.

Anticipation of something—someone—new had Sage's pulse fluttering a bit more than he might've expected. Certainly he had not come all this way thinking he might actually get what he truly wanted, but he had learned long ago to never be unprepared.

Sage made a small show of peeling the sheets back. He placed one knee on the mattress, slowly shifted to the other, and then reclined onto his hip and elbow facing Mr. Moore. With a coy smirk, he held the jar out for him to take. Most men were plenty happy to allow him to apply the oil, but he always liked to offer.

Mr. Moore glanced at the jar and then flicked a small but polite grin at Sage.

"Oh, no thank you. It smells lovely, though. Roses always do."

Sage huffed out a breath of a laugh. So that's how it was going to be, then.

He was not opposed to games. With the right partner, a little teasing could be quite enjoyable. Just as Sage opened his mouth to say as much, Mr. Moore leaned in the opposite direction, nearly so far that he might've toppled out of the bed, and blew out the candle on his side table with a sharp puff of an exhale. Then, he turned fully onto his side, bunched up his pillow, and let out a content sigh as he relaxed into it.

Sage remained perfectly still for a moment, staring at the man's back.

He was...going to sleep?

Sage's surprise melted into outrage. With a heavy scoff, he shifted his weight off his elbow and collapsed back against his own pillow for a few seconds. Then, with hot, jerky movements to match his foul mood, he sat up, set the jar of oil on his side table with a smack, and blew out his own candle.

In his effort to wrench the covers up over himself, he caused Mr. Moore to stir and resettle beside him, entirely unbothered by all the commotion. Sage's jaw clenched as he drew in a deep breath.

His heart seized.

The smell of lavender soap—the same kind Wyndham always used—hit him with force. He glared over at Mr. Moore in the dark. Of course the man would've had to borrow soap to bathe with. With a sob of frustration, Sage rolled onto his opposite side and squeezed his eyes shut.

Chapter 4
Conrad

Conrad had never slept in a more comfortable bed in his life. After such an exhausting journey and walking for miles across unfamiliar countryside—which was very different from walking back and forth around the docks—he had felt tired in every part of his body as he'd sunk into bed.

When the sun peeked through the lace curtains, he woke up, feeling deliciously refreshed. The first thing he noticed was that his body was still sore from his journey, but not appallingly so.

The second thing he noticed was that Mr. Ravenwing had, over the course of the night, curled his body around Conrad's. Their legs were now tangled together and one of Mr. Ravenwing's arms was slung over Conrad's stomach. His dark hair tickled against Conrad's cheek from where the man had snuggled close, his face pressed against Conrad's shoulder. Conrad smiled to himself. It was rather sweet. He had always enjoyed that form of affection, although he happened upon it rarely.

He thought back to the evening before. Roger had seemed particularly anxious about introducing Conrad to Mr. Ravenwing. And very few of the guests seemed to include him in the conversation. In fact, his first impression of the man, sitting alone in a corner, had seemed to be the standard. Some aspects of the situation he was beginning to piece together, like the way Mr. Ravenwing's gaze seemed drawn to Roger's husband, and the way the gentleman's lip seemed so often curled in a disdainful smirk. But there had been other aspects that mystified him, like the way Mr. Ravenwing had offered to let Conrad use his rose oil before bed. Conrad couldn't fail to notice the precise way the man had used the oil over his body; it was clearly very important to him. The small gesture of generosity had been unexpected but still...sweet.

Conrad shifted carefully so that he was lying on his back. Mr. Ravenwing did not seem to mind as he snuggled even closer. He had been so focused on getting into the house and meeting the councilmembers that he'd barely given himself time to figure out what he would do afterwards. He had no idea how long he was going to stay. But each time it'd been brought up in conversation at dinner, neither of his hosts had jumped in to explain that Conrad could only stay for a day or two. So now he had to figure out how to make sure he was still a welcome guest and how to make the best use of his opportunity. One thing he was sure of was that it would be good to arrive downstairs early, and ensure he maintained a good impression. He was fairly sure the upper crust did not make a habit of being early risers, but he had learned the night before that several of the house's occupants were closer to Conrad's class than the Wrenwhistles. The trouble was how he ought to get downstairs when his legs were tangled together with someone else's.

He turned his face to look at the other man. He hated to wake him. Mr. Ravenwing looked relaxed, his features softened with sleep. Conrad heaved a sigh and decided his ambitions would just have to wait until the gentleman woke up. He began to mentally compose a list of topics he'd like to discuss with Roger and the other members, started trying to determine how and when he ought to clean his clothes, what he would do when he did finally leave the Wrenwhistle home.

It was over an hour before Mr. Ravenwing stirred. He woke up slowly, pulling Conrad closer and nuzzling into his skin before he seemed to realize he was doing so. Conrad could feel the moment the other man noticed his presence in his arms. Mr. Ravenwing stiffened and drew away slowly. The cold and indifferent expression shifted back into place like a mask as he locked eyes with Conrad. Soon their legs were no longer tangled, the arm slipped off his stomach, and Mr. Ravenwing had curled over on his side with his back to him.

"My apologies," he said in a clipped tone.

42

"I don't mind," Conrad assured him. "It was rather companionable." He heard a scoff in response.

Now that his obstruction was removed, he got out of bed, retrieved his bag, and began laying out his clothes for the day. He heard Mr. Ravenwing shift on the bed and could tell the man was watching him over his shoulder.

Mr. Ravenwing was the first to break the silence. "Are you going downstairs? At this hour of the morning?"

Conrad shrugged as he peered into the looking glass and got his hair into some semblance of respectability. "I'm awake. I'm sure others must be, too."

"I'm sure they're not," Mr. Ravenwing retorted.

"Well, then I'll be the first at breakfast," he said, turning and giving him a bright smile. "Wouldn't be the first time and won't be the last, I'll wager."

Mr. Ravenwing scowled in reply. He seemed about to say something, but instead flopped back onto the pillow, effectively ending the conversation.

Conrad went downstairs and was pleased to find that he had been correct: Roger and Torquil were both at the breakfast table. They greeted him as he walked in.

"How did you sleep?" Torquil asked as he helped himself to food and sat down opposite.

"Like a wee babe," he replied with a laugh. "The bed was marvelously comfortable. I cannot thank you enough."

Roger beamed, but then his expression swiftly

dropped in concern. He leaned forward. "Was Sage—
that is, Mr. Ravenwing—I hope he didn't make you
uncomfortable."

"Not at all. We got along quite well."

Roger's eyebrows went up. "Oh. Y-you did? I was
worried because you're human...and he's fae...and
there are different views on...intimacy between the
two cultures. I hated to throw you into it like that. So
I hope nothing untoward happened."

Conrad laughed as he thought of the other man
nuzzling against his shoulder. "I suppose one might
say it was untoward, but I found it rather pleasant.
And underneath it all, I suspect the gentleman is of a
sweeter nature than he appears."

Roger's eyes widened and he blushed. "Oh! I...I
see."

Torquil looked very amused. They took a sip of
tea. "Roger and I were discussing that you seemed to
get along so well with everyone last night, that it
might be nice if you stayed for the whole of the
party—if you're amenable—and get to know all of us
better."

Conrad couldn't help the grin that took over. "How
marvelous! Thank you very much. I would be
delighted."

Torquil chuckled. "Good. Our primary concern was
the bedroom situation. But it sounds as though we
needn't worry overmuch on that matter."

"You needn't worry at all."

"That's certainly a relief," Roger admitted. "And
it's good to see how well you get along with other

fae—not that I had any doubt after our interactions last night. Still, it is good to see that you really do value our diverse parts of society being more amicable."

He could hardly believe his luck! It had been quite a gamble to leave his home and everything he knew behind. He was relieved it was already paying off. At the very least, he would have a comfortable place to stay for a week or so. He was confident he had Roger's approval already. Now all he had to do was work on getting the others'.

Mr. Keelan Rook-Worth showed up just as Torquil was asking Conrad about his thoughts on the rubrics. Conrad allowed the topic to shift away from Council affairs as the other two asked after Mr. Rook-Worth's sleep and overall wellbeing. The gentleman seemed cheerful and easygoing in nature and it didn't take long for Conrad to decide he liked him a great deal. By the time others began trickling into the room, the four of them had struck up an engaging conversation and were getting along beautifully. Everything was going even better than he had planned it. It hardly seemed possible. Conrad relaxed in his seat, allowing himself to simply enjoy the others' company.

Chapter 5
Sage

After tossing and turning for entirely too long, Sage gave up on trying to find sleep again. He was flustered. With a groan of irritation, he slid his wrist from where he had it draped across his eyes and flung his arm out against the empty side of the bed where Mr. Moore had slept.

The silent rejection had been bad enough. There was only one other man who'd ever denied him, and Sage was completely lost on how to handle it. His shock and frustration somehow faded into lavender dreams about Wyndham. When he woke, reality shattered over him like broken glass as he realized that a different man was in his arms smelling like fond memories. Sage had braced himself to be shoved away, just as Wyndham had always done when he'd had enough, but somehow Mr. Moore's reaction was worse. He was *nice* about it.

Understanding, even. Sage couldn't wrap his mind around it.

Reluctantly, he got out of bed. The only option he had was to face the situation. There was no choice but to see Wyndham living the life he'd made for himself and accept that he was not a part of it. As he dampened a sponge in the basin to wash his face, Roger's words came back to him. The whole idea of this was for Sage to be a part of Wyndham's life again. As much as he had longed for Wyndham to be his everything, he'd wished equally as much just to be his friend. This was his chance. But was he capable of it? Was something truly better than nothing?

These thoughts and more like it whirled as Sage dressed himself. He was already unaccustomed to the task, and combined with everything else, he did not realize until he was walking out the door of the bedroom that he'd unconsciously selected a soft purple waistcoat from the wardrobe.

When he looked up, he locked eyes with Wyndham.

"Mr. Ravenwing," he said, just as he had a thousand times before.

"Mr. Wrenwhistle," Sage managed.

Wyndham smoothed a hand down the front of his waistcoat before he gestured for Sage to take the lead down the stairs. He could hear the familiar noises of what sounded like a pleasant breakfast and several voices talking at once. Wyndham did not want to speak to him alone. Given their history, it was a fair request. Sage dipped his head in understanding, biting back all the things he wished to say, and placed a light touch on the bannister as he took the stairs down first. Start small, he told himself. There would be time to talk later.

Sage and Wyndham were the last two to make an appearance. When they walked in the room, a few heads turned his way, but mostly everyone was smiling at and greeting the man who had come in after him. Wyndham did not respond to anyone; he went directly to Roger, pressed a hand to his chest, and kissed his temple. The warmth of the grin it pulled from his husband could've rivaled the sun. Sage turned away silently to fill his plate.

After taking a seat, Sage soon realized that there were not many safe places to look. All around the table, hands were being held, arms were around shoulders. He could only assume what was going on out of view. What he'd already seen proof of the night before became even more abundantly clear in the soft morning light: this was a party full of sickeningly happy couples.

Was this the real reason Roger had invited him here? To show off how happy he was? To force Sage to look at all of the perfection happening around him and remind him that he was miserable and alone?

If that was the case, he could've saved everyone the trouble and stayed at home. His mother had been determined to see him married by the end of the last Season. After finding a suitable spouse for all of his older siblings, she'd become quite skilled in her matchmaking, but Sage wanted no part of it.

Fortunately, it wasn't all for naught. He'd escorted each gentleman she presented to bed before he informed her that the match was no good.

Sage glanced at Mr. Moore as he spread butter onto a piece of bread. If possible, the man seemed even more vivacious than he had the previous day, moving his hands excitedly as he spoke to Roger. Sage turned his attention back to his breakfast with a mild look of distaste. Apparently he had lost his skills in seduction, as well. Now he would have no choice but to marry a man of his mother's choosing come next Season. She would be thrilled.

"Heard you had a pleasant night like the rest of us, Ravenwing."

Emrys Wrenwhistle was grinning at him. The statement was plain enough, but nearly everything the man said was laced with a smirk or came in the form of lighthearted banter. It was difficult to tell if he was trying to get a reaction out of Sage or not. He had his arm around Torquil's waist, but they were busy listening to the conversation at the other end of the table. To save himself from more embarrassment, he decided to feign innocence as best he could. There was no way to know what Mr. Moore had told them all.

"I slept as well as anyone might hope to, what with all of the cacophonous noise happening downstairs into the early morning." The piano playing had continued for hours. With the addition of loud, tuneless singing and even more laughter, it had been difficult to ignore as Sage struggled to fall asleep.

Emrys laughed. "Your companion did not seem to mind it."

Sage's gaze traveled up the table again to Mr. Moore.

"Fatigue will do that to a man," he muttered.

Emrys' grin turned sly. "I suppose it's easier to overlook small irritations when you're not sure how much time you've got with someone." He tugged Torquil closer against his side, which finally pulled their attention away from whatever it was Mr. Moore and the other councilmembers were so busy discussing. They offered Emrys a calm grin, which was met with a kiss. "Now that Conrad is staying a bit longer, perhaps he will go easier on you tonight."

It was Torquil's turn to offer a look of amusement, now that Emrys had pulled them into the conversation.

"Mr. Moore is staying on?" Sage asked with as little interest as he could manage. He picked at the pastry on his plate for good measure.

"Yes," Torquil said. "We've asked him to stay so we can all get to know him better. He's made a fantastic first impression, wouldn't you say?"

"Oh, he has certainly made an impression."

"It seems you've left one on him, as well," Torquil went on easily.

Sage's brow furrowed, still wary of what was said before he came down for breakfast. Emrys' insinuations were rather clear, but why? Nothing had happened between them. Mr. Moore did not strike him as the sort of man who would lie. Then again, they had only met him less than a day ago. What did they know of him at all? He'd clearly come with a goal in mind. Perhaps he was the sort of person to say or do whatever was necessary to get what they wanted.

"I'm sure I don't know what you mean," Sage told them.

Torquil leaned forward a bit in their chair as they reached for their tea. In a voice only meant for the three of them to hear, they said, "Mr. Moore referred to you as *sweet*."

Sage's jaw dropped, thoroughly scandalized. So he'd told them all about what had happened in the morning, then. The way Sage had—

"Sweet?" Emrys said it so loudly that every person at the table turned to look before returning to what they'd been saying before. "Impossible." He tipped his chin up across the table. "*Keelan* is sweet. What did you do, Sage, hold his hand after?"

"I did no such thing," he protested. *And there was no after*, he wanted to add.

"There's nothing wrong with showing affection," Torquil said after their last sip of tea. They used their empty cup to gesture at the rest of the party sitting around the table before they set it down. "You see we are all apt to agree here."

Gentle touches. Tender looks. Those were things Sage had never experienced before. He stopped himself before he could look at Wyndham. He'd given them out, on occasion, but they were never returned.

Emrys hummed thoughtfully. "Perhaps you're right," he told Torquil, pulling them close again so he could press an exaggerated kiss to their cheek. "Maybe that is exactly what Mr. Ravenwing needs. A chance to soften that stony exterior of his."

Sage glared at both of them as he stood from his chair. He left his half-eaten breakfast where it sat and breezed out of the room.

Chapter 6
Conrad

Conrad thoroughly enjoyed his first full day at the Wrenwhistles' home. True, there was an expected awkwardness to being a stranger in a house full of friends. Inside jokes were bandied about, references to past shared experiences were dropped casually. But for the most part, Conrad could tell there was an effort to make him feel included. Breakfast stretched on for a couple of hours, as no one seemed in a hurry to leave the table—although Conrad did notice that Mr. Ravenwing's presence in the room was short. Then Roger and Wyndham took Conrad on a tour of the house. Roger took great pride in showing off the study his husband had designed for his use. Conrad was fairly sure his own enthusiastic praise of the room improved Wyndham's opinion of him, but it was hard to tell.

The gentleman had reclined on the chaise lounge in the center of the room to watch Roger explain how his specially-designed desk worked. Then Roger and Conrad began comparing favorite magical theory books. Roger had a far more impressive collection than Conrad could ever claim; he felt a small pang at the few titles he had owned previously that he'd sold to help pay for his journey. He ran a hand over some of the spines.

"It is truly impressive," he murmured.

"You're welcome to borrow any of them while you are here," Roger said.

Conrad felt warmth burst within him. "Thank you," he said earnestly.

"Well, don't thank me too much yet," Roger went on. "I'll probably ask you to cast some spells while you're here, too. And then Wyn will likely want to see how your magic blends with others'. And if we have time, I'd be curious about your thoughts on the rubric we put together."

"I would be delighted!"

"Better to wait a bit though," Wyndham said. "Give you time to rest from your journey."

"Oh, I don't mind," Conrad assured him. "I'm eager to show you whatever you'd like, or to help in any way I can. Even if I don't get the position, it would be marvelous to assist you."

Roger beamed—and then promptly ignored what his husband had just said, encouraging Conrad to cast an assortment of spells for several hours.

Lunch was another unhurried affair, after which Conrad found himself in deep discussion with Torquil and Silas, learning all about how fae-human magic worked.

By dinner, he was feeling prodigiously pleased with himself, having managed to speak to all of the councilmembers for at least some period of time. He was seated next to Wyndham, who was curious about the different spells Conrad used in his work, and whether he had ever performed magic with a fae before. Conrad had a feeling that Wyndham was only moderately interested in what he had to say, but he noticed the gentleman exchange a few smiles with Roger across the table. If he received Wyndham's approval merely because of his budding friendship with Roger, that was enough for him.

After dinner, time passed similarly to how it had the evening before. A handful of people started a card game, but Conrad was unfamiliar with the game in question, so he sat to the side and chatted with Silas and Torquil. Wyndham joined them after some time, as well.

As much as he wanted to stay up with the rest of the group, Conrad was unaccustomed to such late hours, so he regretfully bid everyone good evening when his eyes started to itch with fatigue. Mr. Ravenwing was already inside the room, just as he had been the previous night, dressed only in a silk robe and applying oil fastidiously about his person.

This time, however, he seemed to be in a different sort of mood. No sooner had Conrad taken off his jacket, the gentleman whirled around on his ottoman and glared at him.

"I don't know what you're playing at, Mr. Moore, but I assure you, you can leave me out of your games."

Conrad blinked at him. "I'm sorry?"

Mr. Ravenwing scoffed. "It's bad enough to have to be here. It's even worse to have everyone teasing me for pleasure I didn't even experience."

Conrad frowned, his confusion growing. "I'm afraid I don't—"

"Why did you tell everyone that we slept together?"

"We *did* sleep together."

Mr. Ravenwing made a frustrated sound at the back of his throat. "Why did you tell everyone that we fucked last night?"

Conrad was fully taken aback. "What? I never said that."

He rolled his eyes. "You must have said something. I've had no end of teasing from Emrys, Torquil, Keelan..."

Conrad thought back to all of his conversations throughout the day.

"You told Torquil I was *sweet*," the gentleman spat. "Does that help jog your memory?"

"Oh!" Conrad laughed. "Roger and Torquil asked how last night went and I told them it was fine." He paused, trying to remember. "One of them asked if anything untoward had happened. I assumed they were referring to the way we woke up together, so I said I found it rather pleasant. Which was true," he added.

Mr. Ravenwing gave him a long and irritable look. "That was not what they were referring to, you... half-wit human."

Conrad held his jacket close to his chest. "I'm sorry. I didn't mean to damage your reputation. I'll clarify things with our host first thing in the morning."

The other man heaved a sigh. "You didn't damage —quite frankly, clarifying things would be worse. Don't bother. Just try not to make it more of a mess, if you please."

Conrad nodded. "Right." He folded his jacket and then paused. "If they ask again tomorrow, what would you like me to tell them?"

Mr. Ravenwing's lips pinched together. "I suppose what's done is done. At least I know now what everyone was getting at. But you should know that anything you say to anyone here will get around to the entire house within a matter of hours."

"Thank you. It is very kind of you to warn me. I'll keep that in mind."

The fae scoffed and turned back to his looking glass. Conrad continued to undress, relieved that the conversation had ended on a congenial note. He looked at the last outfit in his bag with some wariness; he'd need to do a cleaning spell the next day if he wanted to avoid wearing dirty clothes. Perhaps Roger would lend him some of his supplies. He shoved the bag back under the bed and climbed under the covers, leaving his candle lit as Mr. Ravenwing was still busy applying oil.

He watched with some fascination as the man massaged it into his skin in a languid fashion. He'd been too tired the night before to pay it much mind. Mr. Ravenwing caught his eye in the looking glass and smirked.

"Like what you see?"

Conrad sat up a little in bed. "You're very methodical. Do you do that every night?"

"Most nights, yes."

"Hm. I suppose that explains why your skin is so soft."

Mr. Ravenwing lifted an eyebrow. "Noticing my skin, Mr. Moore?"

Conrad laughed. "Well, I did feel it against my own for quite some time this morning." He crossed his arms behind his head and leaned back against the pillow. "Do all fae share a preference for floral scents?"

Mr. Ravenwing paused in the act of rubbing his chest. "What do you mean?"

"Well, I was given lavender soap for my bath yesterday, which I've noticed is what Wyndham uses as well. You use rose oil every night. Back home, most of the humans I know use soap that is much plainer in scent. So I've been wondering if it's an aspect of fae culture."

Mr. Ravenwing's expression clouded a little as he frowned in a thoughtful way. "I can't speak for all fae," he said at last. "But Wyndham and I have always shared that preference for scents."

"Have you known him a long time, then?"

"Yes."

The response was curt and in a tone that suggested he did not want to discuss the matter further.

"Thank you for satisfying my curiosity," Conrad said. "If I can ever return the favor, do let me know."

Mr. Ravenwing didn't respond as he put the lid on his bottle of oil and stood sedately from the ottoman. His robe slipped off his shoulders in a fluid movement and pooled to the ground.

Assuming the conversation was over, Conrad leaned on his elbow to blow his candle out, but was paused by a fingertip grazing his arm.

"Are all humans as muscular as you?"

The question was asked softly, in a voice as silky as the robe that was now on the floor. Conrad turned and smiled at him over his shoulder.

"No, these were hard-earned. I've worked on the shipyards for over half my life, carting crates and boxes over the docks. It's heavy work. But I suppose I'll lose some of the muscles if I get this position. I imagine there won't be as much lifting and moving about in the Council."

"Pity."

Conrad chuckled. "I suppose it might be, in a way. But I like to think of it as a phase in my life that I'm moving on from. Besides, if all goes well, I'll be dressing more like Cyril or Silas and then no one would notice my body anyway."

Mr. Ravenwing pulled his hand away and his brow furrowed. "Who?"

"Cyril? He's one of Roger's friends, one of the humans. Very pleasant chap. I think you'd like him. He's very impressed with your fashion sense, you know."

Mr. Ravenwing gave a little huff. "There are too many people here to keep track of."

"It is a lot to remember. But at least they're all nice. I was very worried I'd be thrown out on my ear when I arrived. It never occurred to me that I might be invited to stay for any length of time." He turned back to the candle and blew it out before lying down on his back. "So I daresay I'll get used to the crowd."

The gentleman beside him made a non-commital noise before blowing out his own candle and curling up on his side with a long sigh.

··˙·.·

The next morning, Conrad woke with the sunlight dappling on the covers, and Mr. Ravenwing pressed up against him. This time, the man's head was on Conrad's pillow, with one arm flung across Conrad's chest, and their legs tangled under the sheets. Conrad smiled to himself and breathed in deep. The scent of rose oil surrounded him and Mr. Ravenwing's body was slight and warm against his.

It occurred to him that he ought to keep one of Roger's books by his bedside in the future, if he was going to always be so delayed in getting out of bed. He sighed a little and made more lists in his head: what ingredients he needed to request for his cleaning spells, the best methods for traveling to Roger's father, the best methods for traveling to London, and a to-do list for when he got to London (assuming he had the position).

Like the previous morning, it took another hour or so for Mr. Ravenwing to wake up. And, like the previous morning, he snuggled closer before waking, the arm over Conrad's chest wrapping around his shoulder and Mr. Ravenwing's face nuzzling against his cheek. Then the gentleman froze and tensed. This time, however, he didn't immediately move to the other side of the bed. He huffed against Conrad's cheek.

"You could shove me away, you know."

"That seems rather rude."

Mr. Ravenwing tilted his face a little and his breath was hot against Conrad's ear as he murmured, "Does that mean you like waking up with me plastered against you?"

"As I said yesterday," Conrad said, turning to face him with a smile. "I find it quite companionable."

Their faces were close and Mr. Ravenwing seemed to search Conrad's expression. Then at last he pulled away with another scoff. "You are the strangest creature I've ever met."

Conrad chuckled as he swung his now-free legs off the bed. "I've certainly heard that before."

"Going down to breakfast at a ridiculous hour again, are you?"

"Yes. Care to join?"

"Certainly not."

Conrad got dressed and then pulled the rest of his clothes out of the sack. He stared at each item and started mentally calculating how many times he'd need to do his cleaning spells, and how many ingredients to ask for.

Mr. Ravenwing shifted on the bed to watch him. "What are you doing?"

"Trying to determine how many ingredients I'll need to clean these."

"Clean—you do realize there are servants here who can do that for you, yes?"

Conrad met the other man's gaze in surprise. "That didn't occur to me. I've never had servants before."

Mr. Ravenwing grumbled as he got out of bed. He scooped up Conrad's clothes and dumped them into a large basket in the opposite corner of the room. The gentleman turned to face him and pointed at the pile of fabric within. "The servants will collect these when we've vacated the room. There's no sense in you doing their job for them. It's what they're paid to do."

"Thank you," Conrad said as the other man climbed back into the bed. "Only, where will they put them when they're done? I don't want them to think my clothes should go with yours."

Mr. Ravenwing's gaze raked over Conrad's body. "No one in their right mind would mistake us for the same size, Mr. Moore. They'll probably place them in the wardrobe, but I have no doubt I'll be able to locate them. Our tastes are decidedly different."

Conrad laughed and stowed his bag back under the bed. "That's very kind of you. I appreciate it."

Mr. Ravenwing flopped back onto his pillow with a grunt.

Conrad paused with his hand on the door handle. "And, as it happens, I'm not sure I'd say our tastes are all that different. I think the way you dress is very fine. Although I'm sure I couldn't pull it off half as well as you do. I may be many things, but elegant isn't one of them."

He opened the door and was nearly out of the room when he heard Mr. Ravenwing mutter, so softly he almost missed it, "Nonsense. You would look very well in a pastel palette."

Conrad smiled to himself as he proceeded down to breakfast.

Chapter 7
Sage

Sage tilted his head back as he drained the last of his drink, effectively breaking the trance he'd fallen into as he stared at the healthy fire set in the hearth. A steady, cool rain had been falling all day, which resulted in the entire party being trapped inside.

His original plans of speaking with Roger after breakfast had been thwarted when he was informed that both Roger and Wyndham were occupied with Mr. Moore in the study. After checking in twice, only to be told they were still busy doing whatever it was they were doing behind closed doors, Sage had given up. He found it incredibly discourteous that his hosts would occupy themselves with only one guest and leave the rest of them to come up with their own forms of entertainment. He settled for wandering the halls to observe every piece of artwork he could find and taking a late tea alone, followed by a nap. He had to admit—only to himself—that he was grateful when dinner was called.

The party converged on the dining room a bit more subdued than they had the previous two nights. It seemed the weather left everyone feeling drowsy. However, none appeared to be in low spirits, and soon the conversation was flowing with laughter and smiles abound. Roger regaled the table with mental notes he'd made during another session of observing Mr. Moore's magic. Sage was unable to decide which was more difficult to see: the self-indulgent gazes of affection that Wyndham gave to his husband as he spoke, or the thoroughly unrestrained pride bursting from Mr. Moore as Roger spoke about his aptitude in very high regard. *Practical* and *clever* were the two words he used most.

Before the conclusion of the meal, Miss Thackeray was bouncing in her seat, encouraging everyone to join in a round or two of charades. Sage would have rather plucked out his eyelashes one by one than play such a ridiculous game, but the thought of returning to his empty room again almost felt worse. He'd settled for a strong drink and a seat by the fire a safe distance from where everyone else had gathered around Miss Thackeray and a book of riddles she'd apparently bought in London specifically for this trip.

"That was an easy one," Lady Anthea Fitzhugh said, her tone on the verge of a complaint. "Give us a challenge."

Sage turned his attention away from the hearth

and set his empty glass on the small table beside his chair. He took the opportunity to covertly observe the group. Miss Thackeray was between Mx. Hillcrest and Mr. Thompson on the sofa; the space separating them on the cushions had been at Miss Thackeray's demand so neither of them could read over her shoulder.

To their left, Roger sat in a wingback chair with a very worried look on his face. Wyndham was standing behind him with one hand on Roger's shoulder, the other cradling a glass of wine. On the right were the Ladies Fitzhugh, both leaning in with anticipation. Another chair had been brought forward for Emrys. His arms were draped loosely around Torquil's waist, who was seated comfortably on his lap. The Rook-Worths had already gone upstairs.

When he finally found Mr. Moore, it was with much surprise. The man was seated on the *floor*, of all places, legs stretched out in front of him with one ankle crossed over the other, supporting his weight on both hands behind him. His grin was gentle, but his eyes were still wide and bright, as though he could not possibly get enough of his present company.

Miss Thackeray abruptly stopped flipping the pages of her book, eyes narrowing at the Fitzhughs as a smirk stretched her mouth.

"These ought to give you pause. It's why I had to travel all the way to the seedy part of town to find a copy."

"Oh dear," Roger murmured.

Cleaning Spells Before Courtship

Miss Thackeray cleared her throat theatrically before she read the lines.

> "The first, one might wish upon a lovely
>   spring day,
> On no account the thoroughbred you've
>   bid your coin;
> The second, foremost but never proud,
> Crest the summit and revel in the beauty
>   below."

A thick silence came immediately after as everyone's minds began to work over the words. The Ladies Fitzhugh leaned in close to one another and began whispering. Miss Thackeray read the lines again, careful not to place any emphasis that might give hints to the answer. The frown on Roger's mouth deepened, and he turned his face up to Wyndham, who looked cautiously thoughtful after a slow sip of his wine.

"The second part must have something to do with position," he mused. "Summit, crest, below."

"Perhaps the best of something?" This was Mr. Moore's contribution.

Wyndham huffed a laugh. "I've never known anyone who was the best at anything who wasn't proud." He angled a flat look at Emrys, who winked in reply.

"Thoroughbred, that'll be the races," Mr. Thompson said in the polished way only a man from

London could. "What do we never want to see in a horse?"

"Lameness?" Mx. Hillcrest guessed with uncertainty. Miss Thackeray patted their leg and gave them a reassuring smile.

"A lovely spring day." Lady Anthea Fitzhugh closed her eyes as if to imagine it. "Sunshine. Flowers blooming. A glass of lemonade. Relaxation."

Her wife nodded with a dreamy hum. "A treat I would hope never ends."

Mr. Thompson continued with his line of thought. "The best racehorse is a fast one. Time is money."

"Time indeed," Wyndham said before he took another sip of wine. He bent down closer to Roger and worked a few small circles into his husband's shoulder with his fingers. "What's that I've been telling you about why I enjoy being away from the city?"

Roger winced at being put on the spot, but he gave it some thought.

"Time...away from your family?" he asked. Everyone else laughed gamely, even Emrys. Wyndham made a face that said *you're not wrong* and kissed the top of Roger's head.

"I enjoy it because each day can be as easy as we choose. Slow."

All at once, every person in the room including Sage looked at Miss Thackeray to see if Wyndham's guess was correct. She pressed her lips together to create unnecessary suspense before she nodded enthusiastically. Quick praise was offered to Wyndham by those who were playing along.

"Slow what?" Lady Anthea Fitzhugh wondered aloud, doubling everyone's focus as they approached the final answer.

"Slowcrest," Lady Imogen Fitzhugh tried. "No, that was in the riddle. Slowpeak? Slowhill? It sounds like a mountain or somewhere high."

"Slowridge!" Mr. Thompson called out, even though he clearly knew it was incorrect. "Slowtip!"

Suddenly, Mr. Moore sat forward and clapped his hands. "Slowtop!"

Miss Thackeray nearly dropped her book as she leapt from her seat and pointed at him. "Yes! Slowtop is the answer." The rest of the group clapped wildly for the man with a few cheers mixed in. Once the noise settled, Lady Imogen Fitzhugh gave a small pout.

"I daresay I haven't a clue what slowtop even means."

Mr. Moore chuckled. He had pulled one leg up and was resting his forearm on it, the other hand behind him on the floor again. "It gets tossed around the shipyard so casually. It's another way to call someone stupid, or foolish." Without warning, he turned and looked directly at Sage, their eyes locking across the room. "Half-witted," he added with a small shrug, his grin never faltering.

By the time Sage recognized the reference to his own words, Mr. Moore had already turned back to the impressed onlookers. Sage forced his full attention to the fireplace to hide the heat that had blazed across his chest and up his neck after such a personal affront. But, again, how was he supposed to be angry? It was the kindest slight he'd ever been given.

Companionable. That was the word Mr. Moore had used for the second time when Sage woke to find he'd wrapped himself around the man far too intimately over the course of the night. There was no aggravation in his voice about it, which was just as well, because Sage felt it within himself enough for the both of them. The problem was that he did not know how to handle the situation without it. Companionable? Men who took him to bed never wanted anything of the sort, unless they'd had other things before it. Even then, it usually did not last very long, and certainly not until Sage woke on his own.

Sage had shared a bed with more men than he could remember, but what he said held true. Mr. Moore was the strangest he had ever met.

As Miss Thackeray prepared to read out another puzzle for everyone to solve, Sage slipped quietly out of the sitting room and went upstairs. He felt a small sense of relief when he looked at the bed. Without bothering to carry out his nighttime routine, he undressed and put the clothes where he'd instructed Mr. Moore to place his that morning. The old ones had been collected. A glance at the wardrobe told him they had not yet been returned.

Entirely unbidden, his next thought was to check in Mr. Moore's bag under the bed just to make sure.

Sage scowled at nothing as he pushed the thought away. Why did it matter where his clothes ended up? They were not expensive, or even of decent quality, only made worse by the way they'd been treated. Not to mention how uncouth it would be for him to go searching through someone else's belongings without their knowledge.

Sage snatched the covers back on the bed and slid underneath them. There was no way to know how long Mr. Moore and the others would continue their silly game, but his plan was to be solidly asleep before he had to find out.

He'd been called many things in his life. Rakish. Spiteful. Covetous. To deny any of them would be a wasted effort on his part. But companionable? Perhaps Mr. Moore did not understand the meaning of the word. It was exactly what Torquil and Emrys had told him he needed to be more of: friendly, affectionate. *Nice.*

With a groan, Sage blew out his candle and reached for the extra pillow he had requested. He turned his back to the middle of the bed and wrapped both arms around the pillow, before he dragged his bent knee over it, as well. It was a comfort to know that the staff Wyndham and Roger kept could be trusted with quiet requests. The lavender soap was not quite as strong coming from the pillowcase as it was from the warmth of a person, but it would do. He pressed his face into the soft fabric and breathed it in until his lungs ached.

If being more friendly and sociable was what it

would take to earn a place in Wyndham's life again, then he would try. Admittedly, watching everyone else enjoying the game had been entertaining in its own way. But if he was going to change his behavior, then he wanted the others to see it for themselves, not by word of mouth from Mr. Moore.

An evening in the sitting room when he would've rather been somewhere else had been the first step. He supposed only time would tell if it'd been effective. He knew at least one person had noticed his presence.

Sage buried his face deeper into the lavender pillow.

The second step was to give Mr. Moore less to talk about at breakfast. He could offer all the smiles and pleasant indifference that he cared to, but Sage was determined to not wake up for a third morning pressed hard against the man's startlingly muscular thigh. He knew little about being friendly with someone, but he was certain that was not the best way to go about it.

Another round of laughter rolled its way up the stairs. Losing Wyndham had been the most difficult thing he had ever faced, but he was starting to wonder if getting him back might be even worse.

Chapter 8
Conrad

Conrad was surprised when he arrived in the bedroom to find Mr. Ravenwing already in bed and, presumably, asleep. He placed the small stack of borrowed books on his nightstand, quickly undressed, and climbed into bed.

He was, however, unsurprised to wake up the following morning with Mr. Ravenwing curled up next to him, with his head on Conrad's shoulder, one leg sprawled over Conrad's thighs, and one arm draped across his chest. He smiled to himself, reached for the book at the top of the stack, and began to read.

Mr. Ravenwing seemed equally unsurprised when he woke up, although he groaned irritably. "I have come to the conclusion," he said, his words sleepy and slightly slurred, "that there is something unique about human bodies that allows them to defy physics."

Conrad lifted his book a little to look down at the other man. "Pardon?"

Mr. Ravenwing huffed against his skin. "It should not be so comfortable to rest on such a physique as yours. I blame this situation on you entirely."

Conrad chuckled. He stuck a finger over the page to hold his place and closed the book around it. "I could say the same about you."

"Oh?"

"A body as slight as yours should not provide such comforting weight."

"Is that the reason you never shove me away?"

"One of several. I also find it..."

"Companionable," Mr. Ravenwing said in a dry tone. He shifted so he could meet Conrad's gaze. "Is that the other reason?"

Conrad hummed thoughtfully. "It reminds me of home, I suppose. I quite like that."

The other man frowned. "What do you mean?"

"My family is rather large, you see. And my parents have always been stretched a little too thin by it. Not quite enough food to satisfy everyone, not quite enough beds, not quite enough attention." He shrugged. "Up until I reached my majority, I was sharing a bed with at least one sibling most nights. I moved out when I turned thirty to give my parents one less mouth to feed. I can't deny it's been nice to have a little more space in my boarding house. I like the privacy. I like having a little less to worry about. But...I also can't deny I rather miss parts of my family's home, as well."

Mr. Ravenwing was silent for a long moment. Finally he pulled away. "I'm not quite sure what I was expecting, but being compared to one of your siblings was certainly not it." He fluffed the pillow under his head. "And I'm not sure it's a compliment."

Conrad laughed as he sat up and grabbed a piece of paper from the bedside to better mark his place in the book. "My apologies." He got out of bed and reached for his bag automatically. "If it helps, they're all quite nice. Well, most of them anyway. You know how children are."

"I do not, in fact. Thankfully."

"Well, they're—" He broke off when he realized his previous day's clothes were the only ones in the bag. He glanced at the corner of the room where Mr. Ravenwing had dumped his own clothes the night before.

Mr. Ravenwing turned. "What is it?"

"I forgot I'd left my clothes out to be cleaned. Do you suppose they put them in the wardrobe?"

"That is the most likely place," Mr. Ravenwing agreed slowly. "They might be a bit busy with so many people in the house. If so, I'm sure no one would notice if you wore yesterday's clothes."

Conrad opened the wardrobe door and was relieved to see his clothing crammed in amongst the other man's. They were easy to spot, being of much rougher fabric and significantly less colorful. He tugged one suit out and paused, his gaze landing on a waistcoat. Without thinking, he reached up to run a hand over the purple velvet. "This is beautiful," he murmured. "I've never seen clothing in this color before." He realized he was touching someone else's belongings and quickly pulled his hand away. "It's a very striking shade. I declare I've never seen anyone dress as finely as you do."

Mr. Ravenwing was staring at him with an unreadable expression, but he shifted and looked back at the ceiling. "Don't say that in front of Wyndham."

"Oh, he dresses very well, too. I'd wonder if that was another fae trait, but Keelan and Emrys don't seem to share it with so much pride. Fern does, I suppose."

"You've gotten very chummy with everyone all of a sudden, haven't you?"

Conrad began to dress. "They've all been so nice, it's impossible not to. I think I may have even started to win Wyndham over," he added with a grin.

Mr. Ravenwing turned on his side with his back to him. "Then I daresay you got what you came here for, didn't you?"

Conrad paused in the act of buttoning up his waistcoat. "I suppose."

The other man grumbled. Conrad finished dressing and went downstairs. He greeted Roger, Torquil, and Keelan and joined in the discussion about what they would all do if it rained again.

After lunch, Roger invited Conrad to join him in the study, this time with Torquil, so he could observe the fae-human's magic. It turned out to be a remarkable thing to see. Torquil began with a human spell and then, as Conrad watched, the spell grew seemingly out of nowhere.

"That's my fae magic," Torquil explained afterwards.

"Fascinating," Conrad murmured.

They gave a self-conscious shrug. "My magic is str—"

"Remarkable," Wyndham cut in. His tone suggested this was an oft-repeated topic.

"Right. Shall I show you another spell?"

"Please."

Conrad watched Torquil perform spells as the others explained the details of the magic Conrad couldn't feel. When Torquil's face began to look a little drawn, Roger abruptly halted their work.

"Should I call for tea?" he asked, concern evident in his expression.

"Perhaps just some fresh air," Torquil demurred. "Conrad, care to join me?"

Conrad didn't hesitate to accept the invitation. They strode out to the garden together and Torquil set an easy pace.

"Are you all right?" Conrad asked.

"Oh yes," they replied with a small smile. "I have a history of working myself ragged and everyone is very solicitous of my health now. But I brought us out here to talk about you. How are you getting on?"

Conrad felt a grin tugging on his lips at their question. "I'm doing well. I like everyone here and I'm enjoying working with magic."

"I'm glad to hear it. See to it they don't push you

too hard, mind. They get very enthusiastic when it comes to magic."

He chuckled. "I've noticed. It doesn't bother me."

"Yes, well, take care all the same. We can't have you collapsing from fatigue. Trust me when I say it's a great bother and that everyone will fuss at you forever."

Conrad did not need to read much between the lines to determine that Torquil was referring to their own experience. "I'll keep that in mind, thank you."

Torquil gave them a wink, led them both on a circuit through the garden, and then back into the house.

Chapter 9
Sage

The moment the door to the study opened, Sage was met with a deluge of spent magic. It was overpowering in the worst sort of way. All he could think to compare it to was indulging in a favorite food or drink until the inclination to vomit was unavoidable. It was not so bad if you were present when the magic was cast, but to happen upon it after the fact was an altogether miserable experience, particularly in an enclosed space like a study. The more people casting at once, the stronger it was.

"Ugh," Sage gagged out, perhaps more forcefully than was really necessary. "Open a window, would you!"

"Oh!" Roger hurried to where the curtain was already pulled back and propped the window open. "Apologies, we had it closed because of the rain." It had only grown heavier since the morning. Droplets began to collect on the sill almost immediately, but that was not Sage's problem to worry about. He sat in the same chair he'd been offered the last time and focused on what little fresh air he'd been able to pull into the room. By the time Roger sat across from him on the opposite side of the desk, he was able to manage what lingered around them.

"Not all of us are able to handle others' magic so well as you and Wyndham." Sage glanced at the papers scattered across Roger's workspace. Everything written on them was entirely senseless to him. "You would be wise to keep that in mind while hosting."

Roger looked as though he was about to apologize again, but something seemed to shift in his expression before he spoke. "I see," he said carefully. "A-and what does it feel like to you?" He was not subtle at all as he reached for a clean sheet of paper and quill pen. Sage instantly grew defensive. The last thing he needed was to become any part of what Roger was looking to study next.

"I am not here to talk about myself. I am here to talk about Wyndham. I have been waiting several days to do so, in fact, but each time I've attempted it, you have been too preoccupied to see me." He hoped every bit of his frustration was coming across.

Roger's shoulders fell with a small sigh as he abandoned the pen and paper. "I truly am sorry about that. You must be able to recognize the opportunity that has happened upon us with Mr. Moore's arrival. When I wrote to invite you, I hadn't the slightest idea that we would have such a shift in focus."

"Perhaps I should take my leave, then?"

The words came out impulsively. There was still a small part of him that did want to demand that his belongings be packed at once. The entire experience had been less than enjoyable thus far. But there was something else in him that deeply wished he'd not said it. What if Roger agreed? Would he ever get another chance like this?

"As I said before, you are free to go whenever you wish." Roger turned slowly to look over his shoulder at the rain. The sill was slick with water now. His expression was pained when their eyes met again. They both knew how awful it was to travel in poor weather. "But I would very much like to continue with my plans, if you are willing."

"I still do not even know what your plans are," Sage snapped. Even he felt the venom in the emphasis he'd put on that last word. His jaw worked as he stopped himself from saying more. Somehow, Roger did not seem particularly rattled by it. *Of course not,* Sage thought. *He's married to Wyndham Wrenwhistle. He has likely heard far worse.*

Roger's gaze flicked to the closed door of the study, just as it had the last time they spoke. He did not lower his voice nearly as much this time.

"As I am sure you already know, Wyn is turning thirty, and I want it to be very special. I've sent out invitations to the rest of his family and mine. They've all written back to confirm they will be attending." He gave an unsteady little laugh. "As such, it is too late to cancel now."

"You could," Sage reasoned. "There would simply be a lot of unhappy people to write apologies to."

Roger gave him a tight grin. "We really do not know each other well at all, do we, Mr. Ravenwing?"

Sage arched a brow in acknowledgement.

"He is too clever for his own good sometimes," Roger went on. "My thoughts on inviting friends to stay with us for several weeks prior were to distract him enough that I could handle the planning without him noticing. We, er...spend quite a lot of our time together, when it is just the two of us." The light flush of his cheeks said more than Sage wanted to know. He slanted a look at the chaise where it sat empty in front of the fireplace.

"Yes, I can imagine he makes himself quite comfortable while you work."

It looked exactly like the sort of place Wyndham would choose to perch himself with a glass of wine, a book, or simply that alluring smirk of his that was impossible to resist.

The man across from him had gone completely red. Roger adjusted and readjusted his spectacles and cleared his throat before he gave a sharp nod.

"As I was saying. Distractions. Er, friends, that is." He gestured in the air a little helplessly. "Wyn and I hosted at our townhouse during the winter holidays, but it did not go particularly well—and we planned everything together then. After I started getting the acceptance letters for this party, I arrived rather suddenly at the realization that I was mad to think I could do this on my own with any level of success."

"Why not ask one of them to help you?" Sage tilted his head in the direction of the door, indicating the rest of the house guests.

"Because I am a terrible liar," Roger admitted. "If I asked Torquil or anyone else, Wyn would want to know what we were doing, and..." he shrugged.

After a pause, Sage snorted a laugh. "So your best option was to ask the one person you knew that he does not care to know anything about?"

Roger shrunk into a rueful smile. "Precisely."

They stared at each other for a long moment.

"Will we be hosting it here, then?" The words felt uncomfortable as he said them, but Sage managed to keep a straight face. Roger, on the other hand, looked pleasantly surprised. It shifted swiftly into excitement.

"Yes," he said as he pushed his chair back from the desk, making room for him to open the drawers. After frowning into several of them, he finally found what he was searching for. The stack of papers looked exactly like the ones covering the entire desk, but they'd been carefully folded in half and tucked between the pages of a book. Roger smoothed the creases with his hand before he held them out for Sage to take. At least the markings on these papers were words he could somewhat recognize, rather than the lines and symbols of human magic scratched into the rest. "Here's what I've come up with so far."

Sage read what he could of Roger's terrible handwriting. It left him with more questions than answers, but there was a knock at the door before he had time to ask any of them. It was the call for dinner. Roger took the papers and hid them inside the book again before returning it to a different drawer than the one he'd taken it from.

"We will make time to discuss it in more detail before the week is out, I promise," Roger told him before he went to the window and shut it.

As they left the study together, Sage was entirely unsure how to feel. He had never been responsible for planning or hosting anything before. Why did Roger have so much trust in him to make this work?

· ·. ·. . ·

It was decided before the second course that another round of charades would be the entertainment for the evening. Emrys all but demanded that Keelan and Silas stay to participate after they missed out on the fun the night before. Neither of them seemed particularly upset to have left early.

"Need we remind you that we ended our honeymoon early to be here," Silas said. "You are lucky to be seeing us at all."

Emrys waved a dismissive hand in Silas' direction.

"Fuck him in this house, fuck him in another, it makes no difference."

"Emrys!" Keelan turned pink and hid his face against his husband's arm. Silas moved to wrap that arm around Keelan's shoulders and held him protectively close, though there was a hint of a smirk on his features as everyone shared a polite laugh at the newlyweds' expense.

"As I remember it," Lady Anthea Fitzhugh said to Emrys, "you did not make a single guess last night. Your participation in the game was equal to theirs, all things considered."

Emrys' eyes lit with mischief. "And yet I consider myself the most fortunate of all. I enjoyed the game exactly as I wished to, and then I took my spouse upstairs to make love to them."

Wyndham rolled his eyes so hard at the far end of the table that it was nearly audible. "Enough," he said to his brother, but the implication was there for the rest of them, as well.

When the meal concluded, Miss Thackeray pranced her way into the adjoining sitting room followed by her loyal subjects, new and old. Each member of the party returned to the place they'd been sitting the night before, with the addition of two chairs for Keelan and Silas. After a moment of hesitation, Sage called to one of the servants and requested that his chair be turned to face the rest of the group, though not any closer. He'd only just looked up from settling in his seat when he found a pair of large brown eyes on him.

Mr. Moore was on the floor again, wearing that confident smile of his. Sage did not know what he could've done to deserve it being pointed in his direction. Despite his efforts, he'd woken up thoroughly entwined with the man again. His extra pillow had evidently not lasted very long. Not only had he let go of it at some point during the night, but he'd cast it to the floor beside the bed. He might as well have never asked for it to begin with.

"Attention," Miss Thackeray called out haughtily over the low chattering. It was followed by two sharp claps from Mx. Hillcrest. Miss Thackeray placed a quick kiss on their cheek. "Is everyone ready?"

The room went silent as everyone waited. The only sounds were the gentle pops coming from the fire behind Sage and a swell of rain as the wind pushed it against the side of the house.

Miss Thackeray cleared her throat.

"Forthwith!" Her gaze swept over the captive audience around her. "*Delicate sensibilities beware.*"

Roger made an uncomfortable sound.

> "Bucolic delight, verdant and pristine;
> A more magnificent expanse you have
>   never seen.
> Silk and silhouette, pay a visit to the
>   modiste;
> Couturier, spare no expense and give me
>   your finest, I must insist."

A chuckle burst out of Keelan as soon as Miss Thackeray finished reading.

"They really had to stretch on that last bit," he said.

"Go on," Emrys encouraged him.

"Er, well," he began shyly, leaning back in his chair as he was suddenly aware of everyone looking at him. "*Modiste* and *insist* work well enough together in English. It's not quite as beautiful in French."

Lady Imogen Fitzhugh settled an inquisitive look on Keelan. "You speak French, Mr. Rook-Worth?"

"Only a little." Keelan grinned when Silas took his hand and kissed the back of it. "My husband has been encouraging me to strengthen the skill again." He pursed his lips. "Would you read the riddle a second time, Harriet? I believe there were several hints to that vernacular, in fact."

Everyone listened closely as she repeated herself, though most kept their eyes on Keelan. He nodded confidently when she was done.

"*Modiste* and *couturier*, of course. Both designers of fashionable clothes."

"A dress," Mx. Hillcrest and Lady Imogen Fitzhugh guessed in unison.

"A gown," Mr. Thompson put in. "It speaks of expense."

"The use of both designers leads me to believe otherwise," Wyndham said sedately, unbothered by the competitive edge that both Ladies Fitzhugh were determined to incorporate into the game. "If it were one or the other, we could assume it was something more specific, such as a gown. I think it is vague on purpose."

"An outfit, then?" Lady Anthea Fitzhugh's brows shot up in the direction of Miss Thackeray. "Is that correct?"

"You're moving in the right direction," Miss Thackeray confirmed.

Lady Anthea turned to her wife. "So the second part is some type of clothing."

"*Fine* clothing," Mr. Thompson added helpfully.

"Yes, all right, fine clothing," Lady Anthea repeated with a roll of her eyes that one could only get away with to someone who was a close friend. Mr. Thompson smiled in response. "What of the first part?"

Lady Imogen turned to Keelan. "Any other helpful clues?"

"Oh," Keelan said. "Well..."

"Certainly it is not referring to London," Wyndham muttered.

Roger angled his head to look up at where Wyndham was standing behind his chair. "We do have the Park. I find it rather beautiful."

Wyndham's answering grin was soft.

"Wyndham is correct," Torquil said easily from Emrys' lap. "*Bucolic* implies somewhere not in London, or any city."

"A pristine expanse." Lady Anthea tapped a finger against her lips. "The countryside, then. Pasture? Meadow? Grass?"

Miss Thackeray shook her head at all of the guesses.

"I cannot imagine who would be offended by life outside of London and fine clothes," Mr. Thompson said. "Delicate sensibilities beware?"

Sage worked over the puzzle in his mind as the group continued to do the same together. He closed his eyes and thought of his trip out to the

Wrenwhistle estate—hours upon hours of staring out the carriage window at nothing. Not a city, Torquil had said, not a town or a village. Just the endless stretch of rolling hills, the occasional stand of trees, and fields full of sheep, a blemish of white to mar such an abundance of green. *Verdant. Green.*

Green outfit. Green clothing. Green...

Sage's eyes opened and he snorted out a laugh.

"Miss Thackeray," he said. "Wherever did you find this book?"

Everyone stopped talking and whipped their heads to look at him.

Miss Thackeray chuckled. "Have you got an answer for us, Mr. Ravenwing?"

The room was staring with intense curiosity. He knew that the moment he gave his reply, any shred of respect these people had for him would be gone for such indecorous behavior in polite company. Not that there was much to be lost. Sage's name had appeared in the *Tribune* so many times he'd long since given up keeping track. They all knew how Sage spent his time. All but one.

Then again, the answer would be revealed at the end regardless. They all seemed eager to hear it. Why shouldn't he be the one to tell them? Perhaps some of them even knew it already, if not by action then by phrase. Wyndham did. Wyndham was the reason Sage did.

Sage lifted one hand from the arm of his chair and twirled his wrist with a flourish, as if to say the answer was painfully obvious.

"Green garment, of course."

Miss Thackeray tittered in her seat. "That is correct!" she cheered.

The room was suddenly divided. Half of the party was looking around, slightly bewildered. The other half was very purposefully not making eye contact with anyone at all. He overheard Mx. Hillcrest murmur "grass stains" in Mr. Thompson's ear. Miss Thackeray cackled as the gentleman's face pinked. Sage was careful to avoid whatever Wyndham's reaction was. Instead, he found that his focus had fallen to Mr. Moore. There was no culpability in the man's expression, nor confusion, or even curiosity. Sage could only see his bright smile as he stared right back.

"Well done, Mr. Ravenwing," he said earnestly. "After last night, I assumed you're not the type to enjoy playing along with party games."

"I am not," Sage answered flatly.

Mr. Moore's smile grew. "I think I'll have to sit with you next time so we can work together like everyone else. Nobody would be able to beat us then."

Sage's expression curdled. "You would have me sit on the floor?"

"Of course not," Mr. Moore said, his forehead wrinkling. "We can both sit however we like. Only closer." Suddenly, he was on his feet faster than a man half his age might've managed. "I'll see you upstairs."

Sage blinked at the space Mr. Moore had left behind, and then again at the newly empty sofa and chairs around the sitting room. Apparently the answer he'd given was so scandalous that it sent everyone to bed. Sage got up to follow. There was no use staying in the room alone.

"Conrad is rather spry, isn't he?"

It took a moment for Sage to realize it was Keelan speaking to him.

"He is," Sage agreed warily. Keelan chuckled.

"Everyone else is a bit surprised, but I think the two of you look well together." He leaned in far closer than Sage was expecting him to before he added with a whisper, "Do not let anyone try to convince you that a man from the country is not perfectly capable of making you happy." With a smile and a satisfied nod, Keelan scurried off to where Silas was waiting for him.

Sage stared after him until the room was empty of everyone except for the servants moving the furniture back into place, snuffing the candles, and quenching the fire for the night.

Chapter 10
Conrad

Conrad woke the next morning to the sound of rain pattering against the window and the weight of Mr. Ravenwing at his side. His own arm had wrapped around the other man's shoulders, which was a new development. Conrad smiled and relaxed. He was unaccustomed to leisure and feeling cozy. For once, he didn't have to spend hours on his feet in order to eat, nor did he have to wrangle little siblings or help out in the kitchen. He was free to sleep in, to enjoy late evenings solving riddles, and to while away afternoons discussing magic. He wasn't sure he'd ever have this opportunity again, even if he did earn the position. Perhaps it was past time he reveled in it.

He closed his eyes and tried to doze alongside his companion. His mind, however, had not yet caught on to the idea of relaxation. It buzzed with questions, lists, ideas, and plans. Finally he gave up on the notion of complete relaxation and reached for his book on the bedside table, picking up where he left off.

Mr. Ravenwing had apparently also decided on a slower morning, for it was nearly two hours before he stirred. He seemed to have finally accepted his fate in terms of waking up on top of Conrad, for he didn't grumble or pull away. He simply sighed against his skin.

"More bloody rain," he murmured. "I might actually go mad here if we have to spend our entire time cooped up together in the building."

Conrad marked his place and set the book aside. "Look on the bright side: we're the best at solving riddles. It'll be harder to go mad when everyone is lauding our genius."

Mr. Ravenwing huffed. "Genius? I'm quite sure I scandalized half of the household with my answer last night."

"You weren't the one who picked the riddle," Conrad pointed out.

"True." He yawned. "I suppose I ought to move so you can scurry away downstairs again."

"No hurry. I've concluded that I ought to relax a little. I believe I'll be watching Silas cast today, if he leaves Keelan's side long enough. But I don't expect that to happen for a few hours yet. I'm so accustomed to having to plan and strategize that it's...taking me some time to recognize I might actually not have to worry anymore about the position."

"You've been working individually with each

councilmember in residence. I don't understand why you were worrying in the first place. You probably earned that position you're so eager for the moment they invited you to extend your stay."

"You're probably right. I don't like to depend on that too much, of course, but it is nice to have a bit of hope at last."

Mr. Ravenwing grunted.

Conrad idly trailed his fingers back and forth over the other man's shoulder, considering his situation. "The only real downside to this whole scheme is that the longer I stay, the more apparent it will become that I don't entirely fit in. All the singing and piano playing, the card games, the talk of fashion...I like to think that my experience is a benefit to the possibility of being on the Council, as I'll add a new perspective. But I worry a little that the differences might be too stark."

Mr. Ravenwing was silent for a long moment. "That doesn't appear to have troubled Mr. Rook-Worth."

"True," Conrad agreed. "But, truth to tell, he's of a higher status than I am, as well. He's never...he's never had to worry about whether he'll have dinner each night."

Mr. Ravenwing seemed about to say something, but then he cleared his throat and pulled away. "If they turned you down for the position for that reason, I can't imagine you'd want to work with them anyway."

Conrad laughed. "Right again. Thank you. You

really are marvelously good at helping me sort out my thoughts."

"Besides," Mr. Ravenwing said quietly, "Roger may be many things, but he's not a snob. I have a hard time imagining he'd send you away for being of a different class. None of us were under any illusions when you arrived."

Conrad felt himself beaming at the man's back. "Thank you," he repeated softly. "It is kind of you to let me voice my worries."

Mr. Ravenwing huffed, but didn't otherwise respond.

Cheered, Conrad dressed and went downstairs. The breakfast room was a little more full, considering his later arrival. Everyone turned as he entered and he caught more than one amused expression.

"Sleep well?" Torquil asked.

"Yes," Conrad said, as he filled a plate at the sideboard. "I don't think I've ever slept so well as I have since coming here. I'm getting dreadfully spoiled."

Emrys laughed. "I'm sure Sage could be convinced to assist with that when you get to London."

Conrad paused in the act of adding potatoes to his plate. He realized that the gentleman was making the exact reference that Mr. Ravenwing had been so upset about before. He debated whether or not to correct him. Remembering Mr. Ravenwing's request that he not make things worse, he simply replied, "Let's take it one thing at a time, why don't we? I haven't even left the house yet."

Emrys smirked, but seemed satisfied with the answer. Conrad hoped Mr. Ravenwing would be, as well.

"You two seem to be getting along quite well," Keelan commented.

Conrad sat down at the table. "We are," he said truthfully. "He's very kind." He saw as, almost as one, the entire table paused and looked at him. He could tell from some of their expressions that they wanted him to continue, but it occurred to him that he was chatting about a man who wasn't present, so he said, "Another rainy day, I suppose. How will we fill the time?"

"I would like to have you observe Silas today," Roger said, grinning at him. "And then Wyn and I want to see you work with raw materials."

Conrad stared at him. "I forgot about that discovery of yours. But I'm game to try."

"Excellent. After that, Wyn and I would like to see you work with another fae, the way he and I did last year. You're the only human, other than my family, who has expressed interest in that experiment. It seems a shame not to take advantage of the opportunity, since we have so many fae in the house."

"I would be delighted."

"That should keep you both busy for a couple of weeks," Torquil observed.

Conrad tried to hide his thrill at the casual remark. He was being permitted to stay that long? "I'm looking forward to it," he managed.

Torquil winked at him and went on, "And then, of course, Roger will want to put you through your paces on the rubric, if he hasn't already—"

"I haven't."

"So by the time we all return to London in the autumn, you should be up to speed."

Conrad's eyes widened. "Do you mean—"

"We have to get my father's approval still," Roger chimed in. "But from everything I've observed, I can't imagine he'll decline your application. I'm hoping to introduce you to him myself."

"Thank you," Conrad said, feeling as if he might burst. "Do tell me whatever you need me to do to clear up any doubts you might have."

Roger smiled. "No doubts at all. Although since I've been selfishly keeping you locked up and working in the study, we haven't given you much opportunity to interact with the rest of the group. Not that I have any concerns about you getting along with others or anything. But I do want to make sure you have a chance to socialize with the fae in residence, in particular, and those who are not on the Council in order to get a good sense of what we can do for them."

"That sounds reasonable," Conrad said.

"Although if Roger continues with his plans," Torquil put in, "you may have to find time to socialize on your own." They chuckled. "I'm not sure you'll get much opportunity to otherwise."

"Well," Emrys said, drawing out the word, "I can think of one fae he's getting to know *very* well."

"And if you can get along with him, you can get along with anybody," Keelan added.

Conrad shrugged good-humoredly. "I'm not sure I understand everyone's impressions of the gentleman. From everything I've seen of Mr. Ravenwing, he's really quite—"

"Sweet?" Emrys offered with a smirk.

"Kind?" Keelan added.

Conrad looked around at the expectant faces and chuckled. "Decent."

Torquil's amused expression turned thoughtful. "I've always suspected as much, but...I daresay if anyone can verify that, it's you."

"Agreed," Roger said. "I'm glad I invited him, after all. I think it's going to turn out to be very nice to have him here."

"Why *did* you invite him?" Emrys asked.

Roger blushed. "I have my reasons," he said, lifting his chin.

Emrys snorted. "If I wasn't certain that you were keeping my brother very busy, I'd think you were offering Sage up on a silver platter."

Roger's blush deepened. "Nothing of the sort. And besides—" He broke off and sighed. "That's all in the past anyway. I think we would do well to move forward."

Torquil nodded their approval at this, although Emrys looked dubious. Conrad didn't inquire into the details—for one thing, he agreed with Roger that some things were best left in the past, and for another, he was well accustomed to such vague references to past events by now. The group had a lot of shared history and it would take him ages to untangle it all. While he liked everyone there, his priority was not to root out old gossip. So he took a sip of tea and joined in when Keelan politely pivoted the topic back to how they ought to spend the time of another rainy day.

Chapter 11
Sage

Sage made the decision to skip breakfast. After witnessing the reaction to his answer the night before, he thought it best to give everyone time to get their gossip out of the way uninterrupted.

Wyndham would never be the one to speak about their first *green garment* encounter, or any of the times that came after, he was certain. But Torquil might. Stars above, Roger had even seen them once. It happened at the beginning of the previous Season, at a ball held by Lady Anthea's family of all places. Sage could still recall the look on Roger's face when he stumbled upon them in the garden beneath Wyndham's fairy lights. Even more vivid was the memory of Wyndham pushing him away after.

How was it possible that not even a year had passed since then?

When Sage finally convinced himself that he could face the house, he dressed in dark blue trousers and a matching coat to accentuate the luster of his silken white waistcoat and the various shades of color swirled into the paisley pattern of his cravat. He would not allow another day of rain to prevent him from looking his best.

The sideboard was indeed empty of breakfast when he checked. Everything had been cleared away except for a single bowl mounded with oranges. Sage took one glance down at his waistcoat and left them for someone else.

He passed by the Ladies Fitzhugh taking a stroll in the main hall, their arms linked in a private promenade. Miss Thackeray's spirited laughter spilled from the room with the piano. As such, it was his best guess that Mr. Thompson or Mx. Hillcrest— probably both—were with her as she played a melody Sage did not recognize. Upstairs, the door to the study was closed and several voices could be heard coming from within. He wanted to pause, or at least slow down to listen, but the memory of the air so soupy with magic from the day before was enough to keep him moving. More laughter coming from an open door finally made him stop walking.

It was another bedroom, furnished similarly to the one he had been using, though the colors were a few shades darker with more patterns on the walls and bed. There was a sitting area near the fireplace, only two chairs and a small table between them, but it was something Sage's room lacked. He supposed the dressing table and ottoman had been more useful to him.

Torquil was in one of the chairs, turned sideways with one leg tucked under them and an arm draped across the back. Keelan was standing behind the other chair, bent at the waist and supporting his weight on one forearm. In his other hand was a large goose feather. As he waved it through the air rapidly from side to side, the occupant of the second chair attempted to catch it.

"I presume this is the creature Roger and Wyndham will not stop talking about," Sage said as he took a step closer, tilting his head curiously.

"Her name is Peony," Keelan told him without looking up. Another few flicks of the feather had the small animal rolling onto her back and swiping at the air with two paws instead of one.

"Have you ever met a cat before?" Torquil asked.

Sage's brow furrowed. "I have seen them in the street before, yes. Chasing after rodents. Peering ominously from high places. I cannot imagine why anyone would want one in their home."

"Look at her," Keelan said incredulously. "She is adorable."

Moments later, the cat claimed victory on her prey and pulled the feather from Keelan's fingers. For some reason he could not explain, the three of them watched intently as she chewed on it a few times, holding it between her front paws and kicking at it with the rear ones. Keelan reached for the feather and yelped when Peony turned her teeth and claws on his hand instead.

"Adorable," Sage echoed dryly.

"She's only playing," Keelan said, defending her even as he rubbed at the place she'd just attacked him. With a small chirping sound, Peony abandoned the feather and the chair and was trotting across the rug directly at Sage. She sniffed at his shoe and then threw herself against his shins, rubbing a streak of orange hair across both legs of his trousers. He stepped carefully out of her way before she could do it again.

Torquil chuckled. "She likes you."

"Go on," Keelan said cheerfully, "she wants you to pet her."

Sage's eyes went a little wide at both of them. "Pet her?"

"Stroke her fur with your hand," Torquil explained, acting out the gesture in the air like he was some sort of...slowtop.

"She just bit you!" Sage complained, eyeing Keelan's hand.

The man shrugged. "Not very hard."

Sage let out a heavy sigh that ended in a groan. "Very well." He leaned down and flattened his hand, reaching for the place on her back that seemed safest to touch. Before he got there, Peony bumped her head up into his palm and did all the work for him, rubbing against his hand all the way to her tail. She was surprisingly soft. Sage pet her one more time before he righted himself and brushed his hands together.

"There, now wasn't that lovely?" Coming from

anyone else, it would've sounded far more cutting, but he knew Keelan actually meant it.

"I suppose I'll finally have an interesting story to tell at dinner this evening," Sage told him. "Both of you be ready with your testimony."

Torquil gave him a smirk. "As I said, there is nothing wrong with showing a little affection. Even if it is directed toward those you least expect."

Peony was still busy covering him with as much of her hair as possible, from what he could tell. When she noticed him looking at her, she let out a cry.

"Perhaps not. Now she's screaming."

Torquil and Keelan both laughed.

When Peony hopped back up into the empty chair, Keelan wriggled his fingers underneath her chin. She leaned heavily into the touch. "Are you making an effort to be more affectionate, then?" He smiled down at the little cat. "I'm sure Conrad is pleased about that."

Sage met Torquil's steady gaze.

"Would someone care to explain the fascination between myself and Mr. Moore? I'm quite certain neither of us has done anything to justify it."

In a matter of days, bold assumptions had become something far more serious. Sage had fallen asleep with his arms around the lavender pillow and his thoughts around what Keelan said after the game had ended. How could they look well together? The only time they'd been *together* was out of view, and even then it was in proximity alone. Sage had no reason to be worrying over what would make Mr. Moore happy.

"You are a bachelor. He is a bachelor. In case you've missed it, you are the only unattached people in residence. Can you blame us for wondering?"

Sage narrowed his eyes at Torquil.

"Your curiosities feel strangely like assertions, Mx. Pimpernel-Smith."

Torquil's answer was a blithe shrug.

"You must admit," Keelan said wistfully, "it would be an awfully romantic way to meet someone. Each of you traveling across the country for entirely different reasons, finding one another in the same gorgeous country house, letting your unavoidable feelings free."

"Feelings?" Sage blurted. "What are you—"

"None of us are trying to pass judgment, Sage," Torquil cut in. "I'm afraid you've simply found yourself surrounded by a group of people who are thoroughly preoccupied by love at the moment."

The word twisted sharply in Sage's chest. None of them knew how fortunate they were to associate love with happiness rather than heartache.

"I can only speak for myself, but I would appreciate it very much if you would all leave me out of it."

After one more glance at Peony, Sage whirled around and stomped down the hallway, this time trying exceedingly hard not to hear what was happening inside the study as he passed by.

His efforts were for naught. Sage couldn't have shared his story about Peony at dinner even if he'd been serious about doing it. It was as though Roger and Mr. Moore were the only two in the room, going back and forth with their excitement over what a successful day it had been in the study. Wyndham had joined them to watch Silas perform his unique blend of fae and human magic, which was apparently different from what Torquil was able to do with theirs. Everyone had read reports about the results of the Council's project in the papers, but Sage had to admit that hearing it directly from the people who were involved was considerably less boring.

Eventually, Wyndham broke up the frenzied chattering to tell the story of how Silas had to be paired with every available fae involved with the project—himself included—to find a suitable match. Keelan appeared increasingly more bashful as the narrative went on, until Emrys finally spoke out and divulged the secret relationship that had formed between the gentlemen, all thanks to a chance encounter weeks before the project ever began.

After a round of nearly the entire table telling the Rook-Worths how sweet their story was, Lady Imogen Fitzhugh recounted her own experience in her search for a partner. It had been a far more proper affair as she courted Lady Anthea with calls for tea, filling dance cards, and eventually winning her heart.

"I assure you," Lady Anthea had said demurely,

"there was never any doubt on my part that Imogen was the one I was meant to be with."

Miss Thackeray barked out a laugh in her direction. "Save for the months of worrying yourself sick to the rest of us if she actually meant to court you at all!"

Lady Anthea gave her friend a very disapproving glare.

The evening stretched on with little delineation, further supporting what Torquil mentioned about love being at the forefront of everyone's minds. By the time Wyndham declared the meal was over, they all agreed it was too late for gathering in the drawing room and made a slow parade up the stairs.

As soon as the bedroom door was shut behind them, Mr. Moore gave a strong yet airy exhale, almost dreamy in nature.

"That was a most entertaining conversation, don't you think?" He went on before Sage could reply, dragging his bag from beneath the bed. "It's wonderful to be surrounded by so many contented people."

"I am not sure those are the words I would choose," Sage said, peering at the man in his peripheral as he undressed, working deftly at the buttons of his own waistcoat.

They settled into the routine that suited them best, Mr. Moore propped on a pillow with one arm behind his head, reading one of the books he'd borrowed from Roger, and Sage applying the rose and sweet almond oil at the dressing table. He took his time, working slow circles into his skin, watching the reflection of Mr. Moore. The man was entirely at ease. Sage found it highly disconcerting.

"Is there nothing that bothers you?" he asked, tossing his silk banyan across the ottoman as he stood.

Mr. Moore looked at him around the pages of his book.

"Should something be bothering me?"

Sage blew out his candle before he slipped beneath the sheets.

"That is not an answer to my question."

Mr. Moore saved his place in the book by resting it open against his chest.

"We just spoke this morning about my concerns regarding the Council."

"Yes, and somehow you were still smiling the entire time," Sage said. "Quite the contradiction."

Mr. Moore hummed. "I apologize. I will attempt to better match my expression to my emotions moving forward." Deep wrinkles appeared on his forehead as his bottom lip jutted out. "How's this?"

The reaction was so unexpected that a laugh burst out of Sage. He covered his mouth and nose with his hand and willed himself to stop. Only after he regained his composure did he move his hand to the base of his throat and gave a short nod.

"An improvement," he agreed.

Mr. Moore's smile was wide enough to crinkle the corners of his eyes. He moved the book from his chest and rolled to place it atop the others stacked on his table before he blew out his candle. Sage blinked into the darkened space. He waited for Mr. Moore to settle beneath the covers before he spoke again.

"I am bothered by many things," he said, almost proudly.

"That's most unfortunate," Mr. Moore replied beside him.

"However, I find that I am usually able to find solutions to the things that unsettle me. It can be quite rewarding. And while I am most often focused on working through my own frustrations, it has occurred to me, after what you said this morning, that perhaps I could come up with something that will satisfy the both of us."

Chapter 12
Conrad

Conrad turned to Mr. Ravenwing. "Indeed?"

Mr. Ravenwing paused for a long moment. "You said earlier that it was pleasant to be surrounded by so many contented people. Does it not bother you that we cannot count ourselves amongst them?"

Conrad frowned a little in the dark. "I do not consider myself discontented."

"We are the only people in this house who are unattached," Mr. Ravenwing clarified.

"Oh! Yes, I suppose you're right." He glanced to the side of the bed where his companion laid. "This bothers you?"

"Naturally. Moreover, I believe the solution may be simple."

"Go on," Conrad said, smiling at Mr. Ravenwing's tone.

"You are concerned by your status presenting obstacles to your ambitions. I am concerned by the disparity in our circumstances with the rest of the household. I propose that we...alter those circumstances for the duration of our stay."

Conrad considered this. "You are referring to our unattached state?"

"Yes."

Conrad sat up a little. "You mean, you wish to... form an attachment between the two of us?"

"Only temporarily. Just while we are here. Being with me will demonstrate that you can be amicable with fae and that your class would not be an issue for you. And being with you would...it would make us both less isolated from these blissful couples."

"And trios," Conrad added.

Mr. Ravenwing grunted. "What do you think?" Without the benefit of the lamps, Conrad had only the gentleman's voice to go by, and he caught a note of worry in the question.

He sat up fully. "I like it. I think it's a brilliant strategy. Although I rather think it's more for my own sake than yours. I don't wish you to—"

"It is decidedly of mutual benefit. I assure you."

Conrad grinned in the dark. He didn't know his companion very well, but he had wondered at the way the man held himself so aloof from the rest of the group. But there had been moments—his participation in the riddles, his conversation with Conrad in the mornings, and, frankly, his presence in the house—which suggested that this self-imposed isolation was resulting in some amount of loneliness. Conrad liked the idea of helping the gentleman, if only temporarily. And if it helped him out as well, so much the better. "So, what will our strategy be?"

"I'm not sure we need much of a strategy. I shall sit beside you when we're in a group and we shall make it clear that we are an *item*."

"Simple strategies are often the best ones," Conrad said. "And since most everyone is already convinced that we're an item, I don't think it'll take much effort."

"No, it won't."

"Well, in that case, you ought to call me Conrad. Even better, you should call me Con. My family does, you know, and it would only make sense if my beau did, as well."

"Conrad will do. I cannot abide nicknames. You may call me Sage."

Conrad chuckled. "Very good. And I suppose we can set aside your concerns about waking up next to me each morning?"

"Yes," Sage said slowly. "However, that does bring up a rather important point. Are you...attracted to men?"

Conrad was surprised by the question. "No, I'm not."

Sage muttered something under his breath. "Women, then?"

"No. Not any gender."

"Oh." Sage was quiet for another long moment. "Then I suppose you do not partake of...you don't fuck anyone, I suppose?"

Conrad huffed out a laugh and laid back down.

"That is entirely unrelated to my attraction to people. And yes, I do, upon occasion."

Sage turned on his side. Conrad could see in the dim light that he had leveraged himself up on his elbow. "You do?"

"Oh, yes. I find the activity quite enjoyable. I know that many people prefer it as a way to get to know each other. I personally find conversation to be a more suitable means of acquaintanceship."

"I see. So you enjoy it, but you don't prefer it?"

Conrad mirrored the other man's posture. "I enjoy the aspect of giving people pleasure. And, of course, I enjoy experiencing that pleasure myself. But it is never the first activity that comes to mind." He cocked his head inquiringly. "Is it something you would like to do?"

"I...yes."

"All right," Conrad said easily. "As long as you let me know when you'd like to engage in that, I'm amenable."

Sage gave a little huff of his own. "Amenable. It sounds as if you're doing me a favor."

Conrad grinned. "Oh, I'm sure I'll enjoy myself. But if we were to simply talk every evening, I'd be content. So it's not something I'd ever suggest on my own."

Sage was quiet as he turned over onto his back. "Understood."

Conrad did the same. "Anything else we should discuss?"

"You are not attracted to me, but you are open to

113

physical intimacy, as long as I'm the one to suggest it. Does that go for kissing, as well?"

"I quite enjoy kissing," Conrad replied. "And I've already told you I enjoy waking up with you next to me." He paused. "You could fall asleep that way too, if you'd like."

"That...sounds amenable."

He laughed. "You did say I was softer than my physique implied."

Sage scooted over, carefully laid his head against Conrad's shoulder, and lightly placed his hand over Conrad's chest. "Is this all right?"

Conrad draped his own arm around Sage's shoulders. "Quite companionable. What else?"

"If we are to be convincing, it would be advisable for us to display affection in front of the others."

"All right."

"Anything I shouldn't do?"

Conrad smiled and rubbed his thumb over Sage's arm. "Nothing comes to mind. I'll tell you if that changes."

Sage breathed out. "Good."

"Anything you don't like?"

"No," Sage answered softly.

Conrad had a feeling this was not entirely true but he didn't press. "Then I suppose we are an item." He kissed the top of Sage's head. "Goodnight, Sage."

"Goodnight...Conrad."

When Conrad woke the next morning, he thought over the previous night's conversation. He didn't think anything would be all that different from his side of things. He would be addressing Sage by his first name and the two of them would share a more open form of affection, and he assumed Sage would request a little more activity in bed. It was Sage who would be experiencing the bigger shift.

He had no idea what sort of public affection the other man preferred. And he was still unsure if simple loneliness was the reasoning behind the initial suggestion. Was he attempting to make Wyndham jealous? Did he feel as left out in the group dynamic as Conrad often did? It was possible, of course, for the proposal to be primarily for Conrad's benefit, considering all the other kindnesses Sage had shown in the past several days. But he rather hoped it wasn't. He liked the idea of easing some of Sage's loneliness, if only for a few weeks. He idly ran his fingers through the man's hair and tried to imagine how their new dynamic would change in the company of others.

Sage woke at his usual time, yawning against Conrad's chest. "One thing is certain," he said, "I will not be joining you in your early attendance at breakfast."

Conrad chuckled. "I don't mind. Another thing is certain: the teasing will most decidedly increase."

"Yes, well, at least it will be true. Or...half-true."

Conrad hummed his agreement. "And if I come down to breakfast a little late, like I did yesterday, they will all make a great deal of assumptions. Might be helpful to our scheme."

"Does that mean my pillow won't be moving anytime soon?"

Conrad laughed and reached for his book. "It does." Sage relaxed against him.

After another hour, Conrad finally got out of bed and dressed. When he strode into the breakfast room, the same group as before turned to look at him, amusement and curiosity plainly written in their expressions. Conrad chuckled as he went to the sideboard. "You really oughtn't be surprised. After all, we were roomed together."

"I knew it," Emrys said. "Sage has been coy, but it's so obvious."

Conrad smiled, his back to them, as he dished out his food.

"It was obvious to you because Torquil mentioned it," Keelan retorted.

"And I mentioned it to you," Emrys replied. "I'm very generous in my gossip."

"He learns from the best," Torquil said, smiling at Conrad as he sat down.

Emrys pulled Torquil close and kissed them. "That I do," he murmured against their lips before turning back to Conrad. "Well, I hope you have a cheering influence on Sage's temperament. Always had the worst personality, that man."

Conrad felt a twinge of irritation at the casual insult to the absent man's character. "I cannot imagine what gave you that impression. His personality is perfectly–"

Emrys waved a dismissive hand and said with a smirk, "Yes, yes, I'm sure he improves upon close acquaintance."

"I think he's already influenced him," Keelan said, returning to the original topic. "We saw him pet a kitten yesterday."

Roger straightened in his seat. "He pet Peony?"

"He did," Torquil confirmed. "And she liked him."

Roger seemed nonplussed by this information. "My goodness," he muttered. "I never would have guessed it. I'm glad though."

"I've heard of this kitten, but I've yet to see her," Conrad said. "Where are you hiding her?"

"More like you're hiding in the study all day," Keelan said.

Conrad laughed. "True."

"I'll see to it you get to meet her soon," Roger assured him. "She's the sweetest little thing."

Keelan and Torquil nodded their agreement, but Emrys looked dubious. Soon the topic changed to the fineness of the weather, and how they all ought to take advantage of clear skies.

Chapter 13
Sage

Sage descended the stairs into a great commotion happening in the main hall. Most of the party, it appeared, had donned attire for an outing. Staff were handing out gloves and hats; Mr. Thompson was looking especially dapper with his walking cane in hand. The front door, which was being held open for their impending departure, allowed a thick band of sunshine to spill across the floor of the entryway.

Roger gave a broad gesture when he noticed Sage had appeared.

"Ah, Mr. Ravenwing! It is a most beautiful morning. Won't you join everyone for a stroll across the grounds?"

"I am not dressed for such an activity," Sage told him. He was wearing a rather expensive pair of shoes.

"Nonsense," Mr. Thompson said. "You look smart, as always."

"That is the opposite of what I meant."

"Besides, this is no Hyde Park," Miss Thackeray was quick to add, ignoring him entirely. "We are not looking to impress anyone." The way she had fixed her hair was indication enough of that. Half of it spilled down her back in unruly tendrils. Somehow, it suited her.

Sage scoffed. "I never said—"

"Not that you need to." Torquil gave him a knowing grin as they passed by on their way to stand beside Emrys. "You've already done quite well at it."

He met Conrad's gaze where he stood beside Roger, hands on his hips and bouncing slightly on his toes, too eager to be standing in one place for so long. Conrad gave Sage an open smile. It appeared that their secret was out.

"Now remember," Roger began, cluck-clucking like a nervous parent over his freshly-hatched brood. "Stay on the path and you will be perfectly fine. Wyn and I have walked it numerous times and we've yet to get lost."

"Where is the fun in that?" Emrys asked, wrapping his arm around Torquil's shoulders as they started for the door. "You cannot tell me you spent your entire honeymoon here and did not get the urge to wander."

"Roger has always had a fear of wandering!" Miss Thackeray called over her shoulder. She stepped through the doorway after the Ladies Fitzhugh, her arm linked with Mx. Hillcrest's. Mr. Thompson was close behind, followed by Emrys and Torquil. Keelan

119

and Silas were last. They looked like they would've rather still been in bed.

Sage paused.

"Are you not joining us?" The question was meant for Roger, but he looked at Conrad as he asked it. "You said everyone was going."

"Oh no, we're going to continue our work in the study," Roger explained. "It will be nice to have some time to focus without the constant distractions." He chuckled. "Though, I suppose it is our own fault for filling our home with people and then expecting them to entertain themselves without us."

"I would imagine it takes some time learning how to host," Conrad said. "It seems like an enormous responsibility. I think you've done a wonderful job of it so far."

"Too kind of you to say!" Roger held an open hand toward the door. "You'd better hurry along if you want to stay with the party, Mr. Ravenwing."

Sage wanted to tell him he had absolutely no interest in doing so. Days of rain only meant whichever path they were meant to follow would be a muddy disaster. And if Conrad was not going either, why should he even bother? It was yet another opportunity for him to be alone in a crowd.

He lifted his chin sharply. *Be amenable,* he told himself.

"Best of luck with your drudgery," he muttered before he left them to it.

The pace set by the Ladies Fitzhugh was surprisingly quick. What started as an opportunity to chat and comment on their pleasant surroundings had become an effort in keeping up and not panting audibly.

"Anthea! This was not meant to be a race," Miss Thackeray complained, though she did not appear to be struggling as much as some of the others.

"After so many days trapped inside, it would do us all well to get a little light exercise," Lady Anthea retorted.

"*Light* being the vital word," Keelan huffed out. He and Silas were still at the rear with Sage. "I was not prepared to exert myself with both arms pumping during this activity." This was exactly how their leaders were charging ahead, elbows bent and shoulders working.

Emrys gave a sly grin at the man. "Yes, Keelan, we all know you've perfected the one-armed approach."

Keelan gasped with great offense to the comment as everyone else laughed gamely. Sage found the reaction perturbing. Why were they able to find humor in such witticism when his answer to the riddle had been entirely unsettling?

The more thought he gave it, the more he had a sneaking suspicion that the answer had much to do with who said it. Emrys Wrenwhistle had always been able to command a room without even trying. He was charming and just ridiculous enough to put people at ease, all while being incredibly powerful. Sage was none of those things.

He decided it was further proof that this arrangement between Conrad and himself was a smart idea. Both had their concerns about blending with the present company, but Conrad was fortunate in ways that Sage could never be. He was new and peculiar. Nobody knew his story, beyond what he was willing to tell. His name had never shown up in the *Tribune* linked to questionable, salacious behaviors.

It was likely why everyone had been teasing them so. Sharing a bed with Sage Ravenwing meant something, and everyone wanted the gossip on how their new friend felt about that. To Sage's bewilderment, Conrad seemed...pleased by it. Unbothered, of course, but also willing to luxuriate in their shared moments like none had ever done before.

He thought of the way Conrad had offered for him to fall asleep in the position he'd found himself in every morning since they'd arrived, the weight of the man's arm wrapped around his shoulders, the—

"Careful!"

Another strong forearm was pressed against his chest, and Sage was brought back into the moment only to realize that he was being saved from his greatest fear. Keelan had shouted for him to stop just as Silas prevented him from stepping into a puddle that spanned the entire width of their path.

Sage swallowed and searched both of their faces

briefly as Silas moved to place his hand on Sage's shoulder instead, giving it a squeeze.

"Thank you," Sage said tightly.

Keelan gave him a soft laugh and nodded. "Not to worry, I've done far worse while I was busy daydreaming."

Sage's lip curled. "I was not *daydreaming*." He managed to successfully step over the mud without getting any of it on himself. The path was only wide enough for two; he gave Keelan a wary look as the man took up walking beside him. A strong urge to riot welled in his chest when Keelan linked his arm with Sage's like they were old friends, but he managed to contain it.

"Nobody could blame you," Keelan said with a shrug. "Conrad is very handsome. I've lost entire days thinking about Silas' forearms."

Suddenly, the speed at which they were walking became far less upsetting. The sooner this little outing ended, the better.

Chapter 14
Conrad

Conrad's work with Roger and Wyndham had shifted slightly in his time at the house. He had gone from simply showing his most frequently used spells, to observing each councilmember in turn, and now he was moving on to more advanced spellwork.

"I should warn you," he said, as the other two prepared the space for work, "I am proficient in the spells I need to do, but I wouldn't consider myself any great talent at magic. My interest in this position has more to do with the planning and problem-solving part of it."

Roger gave him a kind smile. "Magical prowess is certainly beneficial to working on the Council, but it is not a requirement."

"This isn't a test," Wyndham went on, picking up a long willow leaf from the table and running his thumb across the length of it. "It is more about acquainting you with our projects."

Conrad took off his jacket and rolled up the sleeves of his shirt. "That is good to hear. And I suppose if this project were to be expanded to the general populace, we would do well to know how it interacts with plainer magic."

Wyndham frowned a little. "I wouldn't describe your magic as plain."

"Not at all," Roger said. "The spell you showed us for keeping shoes warm was remarkable."

Conrad chuckled. "I'm glad you think so." Then he watched as Roger and Wyndham performed a breeze spell with the willow leaf, and listened as Roger talked through his notes on the subject. He got a little lost when Wyndham described how the magic felt. But when they were done showing him, he gamely stepped forward to give the experiment a try.

"Now, since you cannot feel magic," Wyndham said, "just focus on your spell. I'll tell you if anything needs to be adjusted."

Conrad took the fresh piece of spellpaper that Roger handed him, arranged the leaf according to his instructions, and copied over the sigils and calculations. He paused at one. "Would the Bokemann Modulation work for this one?" he asked. "I've never used this sigil before, so I'm not sure what adjustments would be needed."

Roger's expression turned thoughtful as he plucked a book off his shelf and leafed through it. "I believe so," he said at last. "It has most of the same directives. I'm a little worried about this bit about temperature though."

"That shouldn't be an issue," Conrad assured him. "I can use a sigil to cancel it out."

"Oh! Excellent! Do you need the book for reference?"

Conrad shook his head and wrote down the sigils. He cocked his head to look over his work. "That should do the trick. Yes?"

Roger pushed his spectacles up his nose and leaned forward to peer over the paper. "Very good. I think that will do nicely."

Conrad glanced at Wyndham, who nodded, and then cast his spell. The handkerchief that was being used as a focus fluttered around the room. Wyndham's expression turned inward and focused. "It's strong," he muttered. "But not overly chaotic. Try reducing the power a bit."

Conrad hastily wrote in an adjustment. The handkerchief slowed its pace.

Wyndham made an approving noise. "Efficient. Can you change the direction?"

"Not without looking it up first," Conrad admitted.

"No matter," Wyndham said as he caught the handkerchief before it fell. "That was quite good."

Conrad bounced on the balls of his feet, pleased by the praise.

Wyndham carefully moved the leaf and picked up the paper. "What was that new sigil you were discussing?"

Conrad pointed at it.

"What is the difference between this one and the one Roger uses?"

Conrad shrugged. "It's a sort of multi-purpose modulation sigil. It can adjust power, temperature, and speed of a spell. It's less...nuanced, I suppose, than the ones Roger was using. It does everything all at once. That's why I needed to add that temperature bit, so the kerchief didn't catch on fire or something."

"Fascinating," Wyndham murmured.

Conrad felt a little uneasy by the interest. The Bokemann Modulation was a common spell for his line of work, something people threw together when they needed to boost a spell quickly. He rubbed at the back of his neck. "It might be a little too...I don't know...rough for this type of thing."

Wyndham visibly appraised the spellpaper in his hand. "I wouldn't say that. The spell felt different than how it has in the past. Part of that is because your magic feels different than Roger's, Torquil's, and Silas'. But the...flavor of the spell changed slightly. Not in a bad way. But I would like to see it some more. Perhaps with a different spell, something you don't need to adjust the temperature for."

Conrad smiled, relieved. "All right."

They worked steadily through the afternoon. Neither Roger nor Wyndham seemed remotely perturbed by the spells Conrad cast to demonstrate his preferred modulation sigil, even though the spells were rather basic. Quite frankly, the modulation was basic.

When they finally began cleaning up from their work, Roger commented on it. "It's funny, I'm so accustomed to the way my family uses magic. They all approach it in a decidedly academic way, as do I, so we tend to use complicated and fiddly spells. You know, ones that are newer or..."

"Advanced?" Conrad supplied.

Roger made a face. "Yes? But I don't wish to suggest that your magic is not advanced."

"It isn't, really."

"But I rather like that about it," Roger went on. "It's...straightforward, the way you approach magic. Fewer frills."

"As I like to say," Wyndham added, "nature likes it when you keep things simple. I had a feeling the raw materials would work particularly well with your style of magic."

A knock came at the door and Torquil poked their head in. "I'm stealing Conrad again."

"Back from your walk already?" Roger asked. "Goodness, what time is it?"

"It's time for you all to stop working," Torquil said.

Wyndham looked at the clock. "We'd better change for dinner."

"Come along, Conrad," Torquil said, beckoning him over.

Conrad chuckled and followed them down the stairs and out into the garden.

"I thought I warned you not to overwork," they said with a grin.

"My apologies," Conrad replied with mock contrition. "We all got carried away."

"Mm. And you are determined to make a good impression."

He shrugged, not arguing the point.

"I spied some raw materials on the desk. Have you already progressed to Wyndham and Roger's advanced lessons?"

"I suppose so," Conrad said with a light laugh. "Although—" He broke off, unsure of how to voice his thoughts.

Torquil turned to look at him, their curiosity evident. "Yes?"

"I don't know. I think my magic is rather common. Roger and Wyndham have assured me it isn't, or that it isn't a problem, at least. But it feels out of place a bit with the grand magic the rest of you do."

Torquil shook their head. "My magic isn't grand. It's cobbled together and strange. I didn't use it for years because I felt too self conscious about it. When I was younger, people were cruel—I spent too long taking their judgments to heart. It wasn't until sharing my magic with Roger and Wyndham...and Emrys," they added with a smile, "that I started to feel comfortable with my particular style."

"I'm sorry people were cruel to you," Conrad said softly.

They shrugged. "Fae-humans are not typically treated kindly by society. Silas will tell you the same. His magic might be considered common as well, by many. He uses his magic for masonry and other types of manual labor."

"That's true," Conrad murmured. "I do remember him explaining that."

He thought back to when he'd observed the other man performing magic. He'd worn a belt filled with pockets and vials, which he'd reached into for ingredients without even looking. It had been seamless, like some sort of well-memorized dance. Wyndham later explained that Silas' magic essentially began before he'd even cast the spell. That had felt very grand to Conrad.

"I suppose I tend to think of fae magic being rather elegant," he admitted.

"Were there no fae working on the docks?"

"Very few. Most of the fae I encountered before were merchants."

They hummed in response. "I'd hardly consider my own magic elegant."

Conrad laughed. "You are impossibly elegant, Torquil."

They grinned and gave a mock bow. "Thank you. But Silas would certainly argue with you if you called him or his magic elegant. We have another fae-human on the Council, Miss Gloucester-Stone. She's lovely, but I doubt she'd describe herself as elegant." They paused. "What I'm trying to say is that elegance does not determine whether magic is good or valuable or worthwhile. And I suspect that you have a great deal to contribute, common magic or no."

Conrad couldn't help from beaming. "Thank you."

They quirked another smile at him. "Your history may be different from the rest of us, but that doesn't make you ill-fitting. If you understand me."

"I do."

"Good. Now let's go see if everyone has finished changing for dinner, shall we?"

Conrad's heart felt light as he followed them back inside the house and into a sitting room. His heart felt even lighter when he spotted Sage talking to Keelan and Silas. He approached the group and brushed a hand through Sage's hair. "How was your walk?"

Sage stood and bent down to kiss him. It was their first kiss and, frankly, unremarkable: a swift peck on the lips. Conrad knew it to be a public announcement of sorts. And he found himself pleased by how easily Sage had settled into his role. Sage pulled back and gave Conrad's plain cravat a tweak. "It was dreadful. I nearly ruined my shoes in a puddle. If Keelan and Silas hadn't saved me, I'm quite sure the one little walk would have ruined the entire trip."

Conrad chuckled and nudged Sage back to his seat. "Thank goodness for your rescuers," he said, leaning his forearm on Sage's shoulder and grinning at the other two.

Keelan was looking between them with a happy expression. "Silas is very good in a crisis."

Silas shook his head, amused. "And how was your afternoon?"

"It was good. Long. I worked on spells with raw

131

materials. Wyndham said raw materials work well with my magic, although I'm not sure how he knows."

"He's good at sensing," Silas explained. "Probably the best on the Council, if I'm honest."

They went into dinner, where the group described their walk. There were a number of complaints about the pace the Ladies Fitzhugh had set. Cyril was as put out about the state of the path as Sage had been. But Harriet had strong opinions about her hosts staying inside while their guests had ventured out.

"I've barely seen either of you since I stepped foot in this house," she proclaimed.

"You're sitting right next to me," Roger muttered.

She lifted her nose haughtily. "I shall require your attendance tomorrow."

"What are we doing tomorrow?" Roger asked warily.

"You're the hosts!" she said, exasperated. "You tell us what we're doing tomorrow. But, it must be outside and it must be everybody." She turned a beady eye around the table, as if daring anyone to refuse.

"If the weather permits," Wyndham said, "perhaps we can dine al fresco during the day. I can send word to the kitchen to prepare us something suitable."

Harriet beamed. "Excellent."

"But I must request that we have chairs or blankets or something," Cyril said. "I'm sure I couldn't bear to get grass stains on my clothing. Don't you agree, Mr. Ravenwing?"

Sage looked startled to be addressed directly, but

he gave a prim nod. "Indeed. I would very much like to depart here with my clothes intact."

Emrys snorted. "Is that the same thing you've asked Conrad? The poor fellow will have his work cut out for him in that case."

"My condolences to your spouse," Sage replied crisply, "if you cannot be trusted to discard their clothing in a careful manner."

"He can't," Torquil said, taking a sip of wine. "And it isn't just clothes either. You wouldn't believe the number of cravat pins and hair combs that get lost on the floor or in the bedclothes. The man has no patience whatsoever."

"Can you blame me?"

Wyndham groaned. "Must you discuss my brother's proclivities while we're eating? Or at all, for that matter?"

"I rather think he deserves it," Keelan chuckled.

"I don't mind," Emrys said with a grin. "I'm quite proud of how satisfied I've been able to keep Torquil. Do you know that—"

"Enough!" Wyndham said. "Yes, Cyril, we will supply blankets for the party tomorrow. I have no desire to see my clothes ruined either." He glared at his brother and reached for his wine, taking a long pull.

"I'm sure you all must be exhausted from your walk," Roger said. "Perhaps we ought to skip the riddles for tonight."

Harriet gave a hearty laugh. "You won't get out of

it that easily. I have my next one ready to go. And it's even more scandalous than the last one."

Roger moaned uneasily. "Must you?"

But when they all settled into the sitting room once again, Roger made no further arguments, although he did pull Wyndham to sit beside him. Conrad waited for Sage to take a seat in his usual spot near the hearth and then promptly sat down on the floor in front of him. Sage tsked and passed him a pillow. Conrad grinned and moved to sit on top of it, which allowed him enough height to lean his arm across Sage's thighs. He took a sip of the wine he had brought in from dinner as everyone waited with anticipation for Harriet to find her next riddle.

"This is still under the bit about delicate sensibilities," she warned them— with a particular look at Roger—and then she cleared her throat.

> "All matters continental and Gallic I
>   respect,
> Be they culinary, sartorial, or aesthetic.
> But epistoles and missives I appreciate
>   the most,
> Although of pressing news this type is
>   unlikely to boast."

Keelan made an annoyed sound. "They really must work on their rhyming. 'Respect' and 'aesthetic' is a bit of a stretch."

Harriet lifted her chin. "I defy you to think of a better rhyme."

"Especially with aesthetic," Fern muttered.

Conrad took a sip of his wine and looked up at Sage. "Any ideas?"

Sage leaned forward, plucked the wine glass out of Conrad's hand, and took a sip. "Gallic..." he murmured. "That's to do with France, isn't it?"

"You would know better than I would, with your fancy education," Conrad replied with a smirk.

The rest of the group was shouting out answers while Harriet shook her head, getting more and more pleased by the moment.

Conrad took the glass back to sip some more wine. "So let's assume it's France, or French," he said quietly. "I find these things often have a little more information than necessary, just to confuse people. The next bit has to do with epistles and missives." He handed the glass back to Sage. "Notes? Post? Letters?" He broke off and met Sage's gaze. Without another word, they both burst into laughter.

The rest of the room quieted and everyone turned to look at them expectantly.

"I take it you two have a guess?" Harriet said, looking giddy.

Conrad glanced at Sage. Sage gave a small smile as he looked down at the glass and swirled the remaining wine idly. "You say it this time."

Conrad turned back to the group. "French letters."

Emrys choked out a laugh.

"Really, Harriet," Roger said, his face red. "You are incorrigible."

"You're lucky your mother doesn't know about this book," Lady Anthea said.

"I think those two have an advantage in answers such as that," Lady Imogen added, waggling a finger in Conrad and Sage's direction.

Fern chuckled. "Oh, I don't know. You both knew what they were referring to."

Cyril laughed. "Mm. What would *your* mother think about that, Anthea?"

"Let's do another!" Harriet said, hopping in her seat.

"Let's do another on a different night," Wyndham said firmly. "I'm sure you're all quite tired from your walk. I know we are all quite tired from our work. And we shall all be in the sun tomorrow. Better to get our rest."

Conrad didn't move from his seat on the cushion. He grinned up at Sage, who was still looking at the wine as he swirled it, as if mesmerized. "I knew we'd make a good pair."

Sage hummed. "Yes, geniuses at salacious riddles." He tipped the glass towards Conrad. "Do you want the last of it?"

Conrad smiled, not bothering to point out that it had been his wine. "You can have it." He watched as Sage drained the glass and then stood and held out his hand. "Come on. Let's go upstairs."

Chapter 15
Sage

Sage fell asleep with his cheek against Conrad's chest and perplexing thoughts of pilfered wine. He woke with a start out of a dream that had come to haunt him. It was that dratted lavender pillow. The staff had freshened the pillowcase for him, and the scent was as strong as the first night he'd used it. With a groan, Sage swept his arm at the pillow in one easy motion and it fell off the bed onto the floor. He turned over to face his bedmate.

It had become so common to find Conrad reading in the early morning light that he was surprised to see the man's eyes closed, though a small, peaceful grin was settled at the corners of his mouth. Sage nearly rolled his eyes. Even unconscious, he still found something to smile about.

"Are you asleep?" Sage whispered at him.

The grin grew slightly. "No," Conrad whispered back.

"Gleaned all the information you were hoping for out of that stack of books, have you?"

"Wyndham told us to get plenty of rest for today," Conrad explained.

Sage snorted. "You can stop trying to win his favor now. If Roger likes you, that's all you really needed to accomplish."

"I am simply taking his advice. He's rather brilliant."

Sage's magic curled tightly in his chest, nearly to the point of pain. Whichever way Conrad meant for that word to be taken—intelligent, exceptional, marvelous—it was the truth.

"Indeed," Sage said, still in a whisper, though this time he knew he couldn't have managed more. Conrad seemed to notice. He opened his eyes and turned his head against the pillow to give Sage a curious look.

"You're very fond of him." It was an observation, not a question. Under normal circumstances, it would've set Sage on the defensive immediately. He had enough people speculating about his private affairs. But there was something in the way Conrad said it, perhaps the sincerity in his voice, that kept him from reacting so strongly. Combined with his lingering dream and his thoughts still being foggy with sleep, he found himself being far too honest.

"I am in love with him," Sage admitted into the quiet space between them. "Or well, I was. For a very long time."

He braced himself for Conrad to laugh at his

misfortune, or make a quip about how obvious it was. *Pathetic* was the word he used most often against himself when he had this recurring dream—the one that had woken him—of the night he finally confessed his feelings to Wyndham at Vauxhall. With how much drink he'd consumed that night, it was astonishing he remembered any of it at all. But there were parts that stood out: shouting in an alcove, a smashed wine glass, Sage being on the verge of tears, and Wyndham being infuriatingly logical about the whole thing.

Sage was entirely unprepared for the reaction he actually got.

Conrad rolled onto his side to face him and lifted his hand to Sage's hair, running his fingers through it in the most comforting sort of way.

"I am sorry," he said softly. "That must be so difficult."

Sage found that he could not look Conrad in the eye. Instead, he kept his gaze fixed on Conrad's bare chest as he continued to stroke his hair.

"I do not know how much everyone else has told you about me," Sage went on, for at this point there was no use in keeping it to himself.

"Very little," Conrad said plainly. "I have never cared much for gossip. I prefer to learn about people directly from the source."

"How refreshing." Conrad's hand moved from his hair to his shoulder, thumb sliding idly against the skin there as Sage continued. "I have a bit of a reputation in London. I will admit it has been well-earned, but in conjunction with my name constantly appearing in the *Tribune*, I believe most everyone has forgotten I am more than a few lines of scandalous entertainment to talk about amongst friends."

Conrad gave a slow hum of what sounded like understanding, probably making connections with the things he had been told. Not for the first time, but for the first time in a long while, a rivulet of shame streaked through Sage. What must Conrad have thought of him that night when he'd brought the oil to bed? It had become so normal to assume that any man with an inclination toward him would want to use him that way.

"Do you enjoy it?"

Sage's gaze flicked to Conrad's at the question.

"Do I enjoy being talked about? Absolutely not."

"I mean, do you enjoy the activities that have earned you a reputation?"

Sage bit back on the yes he wanted to say. It was the answer he would give anyone else if they asked. It was the answer he had convinced himself to believe. In his youth, of course, there was no greater thrill than a handsome gentleman taking him to his bed, or an empty room at a ball, or a darkened alleyway in a questionable part of town. But he discovered that as his feelings for Wyndham grew, his interest in anyone else became less about the excitement and more about filling the emptiness in his chest that the man he loved would not. And the men he'd been with since Wyndham and Roger's wedding? They were nothing more than attempts at distraction. Salve for his wounds.

"At one time, I did," he said finally. "That is, I still take pleasure in the act. Finding a pleasurable partner has been the challenge."

"I would imagine so, after falling for a man like Wyndham." Conrad slid his hand from Sage's shoulder to the sway of his lower back. Thoughts of shared wine came rushing at him once again.

Sage was aware that he really ought to stop talking.

"Stealing Wyndham's wine glass was my specialty," he said. "In the beginning, I thought it was great fun to see his reaction, because he would get so flustered about it. Eventually, he did not seem to care at all." Sage was quiet for a moment. "I wondered if he would notice last night."

"And did he?"

"I cannot say." Sage wet his lips before lifting his eyes to meet Conrad's again, holding the connection this time. "When you took the glass back from me, I forgot I was meant to be watching him. I was... surprised. He never wanted it back."

Conrad gave a gentle laugh. "I apologize. But you know, perhaps it is not the best idea to do things only to see if Wyndham notices. That's no way to heal. So tell me, is sharing a glass of wine something you like?"

Sage gave the question careful consideration. With Wyndham, it was a challenge, an attempt to capture his attention. The experience with Conrad had been entirely different. It felt easy. *Companionable.*

"It is," he finally decided.

"Excellent," Conrad said with a smile. "We are of the same mind, then." The man's fingers drummed against Sage's lower back. "Thank you for telling me all of that. I could tell it was not easy for you."

Suddenly, the touch was gone, and Conrad was out of bed, reaching for his clothes. Sage propped himself up on one elbow.

"Has it drastically changed your opinion of me?"

Conrad hauled his trousers up to his waist, but left them loose as he gestured wide with both arms, grinning.

"Your reputation is in London. We are not." He reached for his shirt and pulled it over his head, stepping closer to the window to peer out behind the curtains as he began tucking his shirttails in. "Now, why don't you come down for breakfast? You'll need the energy to get us wherever it is we will be dining outside. I can carry our blanket for us though, if you'd like."

Sage laughed and fell back against his pillow, wrist draped over his eyes.

"You expect us to carry our own blanket?" he asked incredulously. "The staff will do that, of course. You truly are the most puzzling creature. Go have your breakfast. I will arrive downstairs no earlier than necessary."

As Conrad closed the door behind him, Sage took a deep breath and let it out slowly. His magic stirred the air just enough to pull the sheer, feathery presence the man had left behind across the bed. It was not nearly as comforting as Conrad's touch, or his calm words, but he did not want to waste it.

Trust did not come easily to Sage. After so many years of being whispered about, he had become guarded and peevish. It was far easier to ignore such behavior if he kept himself at a distance. But he was beginning to realize that, with Conrad, it might be impossible to maintain that distance—not only because they were sharing a bed, but because Sage felt he might be willing to trust Conrad in a way he had never been able to trust anyone else before. The notion was terrifying.

. ˙.ˌ.ˌ.·

Sage, along with several other members of the party, were pleased to discover that Roger and Wyndham had a preferred location for their al fresco meal that was within view of the main house. As such, the kitchen was able to provide a spread nearly as impressive as what they normally managed indoors. The only difference was that, rather than using a knife and fork, their hosts encouraged them to eat with their fingers.

Bowls of sliced fruit, raisins, and nuts were passed between the layers of blankets spread out beneath the shade of the trees. Servants made their rounds with trays of thinly-sliced meats and cheeses, small sandwiches, and a wide variety of cakes and sweetmeats. Lemonade was the drink of choice.

It came as no surprise that Emrys insisted on making a show of feeding Torquil like royalty, refusing to allow them even the opportunity to place a slice of pear or walnut into their own mouth. Despite the audience, they were tangled like lovers atop their blanket. The Ladies Fitzhugh only shared contact through an occasional affectionate glance and the plate they had filled with each of their favorite foods, passing it back and forth between themselves as they chatted about the weather and which birds they recognized singing in the branches overhead.

Miss Thackeray, Mx. Hillcrest, and Mr. Thompson might've done well to select a larger blanket to better accommodate the space needed for three people sitting together, but somehow they managed. The only casualty was Mx. Hillcrest's glass of lemonade when Miss Thackeray moved her foot without looking first. They'd laughed it off as Mx. Hillcrest kissed Miss Thackeray's cheek while Mr. Thompson patted her knee reassuringly.

Silas had grown restless and invited Keelan to walk with him. One of the servants stepped up to collect their blanket soon after, noticing the way it was ruffling at one corner thanks to the steady yet refreshing breeze passing over the slight rise they were resting on.

It had also started to tease at the pages of the book Wyndham was reading. He was on his back, one knee bent with his head resting in the cradle of Roger's lap. Roger was a likeness of joy as he picked at sweets on the plate by his hip and tilted his face up into the sunshine peeking through the leaves.

"Shall I hold a strawberry for you to nibble on while I whisper sweet nothings into your ear?"

Conrad was entirely comfortable sitting on the ground, legs stretched out with his weight on his hands behind him, just as he'd sat for the first nights of charades. Sage gave him a dry look from where he was propped against a tree, knees bent and legs tucked to one side.

"You needn't bother," he told Conrad quietly. "Nobody is paying us any mind." Sage forced his focus down to their empty plates rather than staring at Wyndham and Roger again. "Besides, one more bite of anything and I might need to be carried back to the house."

Conrad laughed and patted his own stomach in apparent agreement.

"You might've been right about skipping breakfast this time."

Sage angled a quick, self-satisfied smirk at his companion.

"You are not the only one in residence with bright ideas."

With a soft grunt, Sage unbent his legs and stretched them out the same as Conrad's were. He adjusted so that his back was flat against the tree behind him. There was no question that he would be requesting a tonic to soothe his aches when they returned. Better yet, he would request the tonic and a hot bath. They'd been lazing about for several hours, and it did not appear that anyone was keen to move any time soon. Sage smoothed a hand over his hair where the breeze had blown a few dark strands across his forehead.

Keelan's words fluttered back into Sage's thoughts.

Conrad is rather spry, isn't he?

Sage allowed his attention to slide toward the man beside him. He was certain that when it was time to get up, Conrad would be on his feet in a matter of seconds. As was his inclination, Sage began to silently wonder more about the life Conrad led, and how he had managed to look like...well, that.

Then he realized that there was no need to wonder. He could simply ask.

"Why don't you tell me more about yourself?"

Chapter 16
Conrad

Conrad found himself smiling at the question. "What is it you would like to know?"

Sage shrugged, but Conrad didn't miss the way the other man's gaze stole over his body. "Whatever you'd like to tell. I barely know anything about you."

"I was born and raised in Bristol. I'm in the middle of a lot of siblings."

"How many?"

"Nine."

Sage made a face. "Stars above. I thought I had a large family."

"Now you can see why there was so much sharing of space."

"It's no wonder. What else?"

"My parents were quite adamant about us learning to read and write, and master basic spells. Schooling was...informal. But efficient. And a worthwhile endeavor. Having the little education I did provided me with better job opportunities."

"And how did you end up...at the shipyards?"

Conrad leaned back on his elbows. "My older brother worked there already and helped me get started. At first, it was just to help with some of the spell casting. But then they learned that I was nimble and could help with the heavy lifting by climbing and passing things down. And I took on additional tasks from there. The work in the shipyards is dependent on the merchant who owns the ship, how much material they have to load or unload, and how much they're willing to pay. But people are a little more inclined to hire you if you're willing and able to do more, and if you're punctual."

Sage was quiet for a moment, a small frown creasing his forehead. "Did you like it?"

"Well enough. The other people I worked with were quite friendly and nice, hard-working folks. We tended to help each other. I liked that. The sailors respected us if we were respectful of the boats and didn't make their jobs more difficult. The merchants...there were fewer of them that I liked, I'll admit."

"Hard to imagine you disliking anyone."

Conrad chuckled. "That's because you've only seen me interacting with kind people."

Sage's lips pinched together slightly. "Even when some of them tease you about your private affairs?"

"Even then. I'm no stranger to teasing. And I think I have a...gentler history of such things than you do."

"Yes, you're probably right," Sage said quietly. A breeze ruffled past them, toying at the strands of Sage's hair.

Conrad sat up and tucked Sage's hair behind his ears. His fingers lingered a little on the pointed ends of them. Sage searched his face guardedly. Conrad stroked the back of his fingers along the other man's jaw. "What else would you like to know?"

"How long did you do that work? And what caused you to leave it?"

Conrad moved one hand to the other side of Sage's legs and leaned against his palm. "It all rather blurs together, to be honest. But I think I started when I was fifteen or so. About twenty years, then?"

Sage's eyes widened. "Twenty years?"

Conrad laughed and used his free hand to trace a fingertip over the mother-of-pearl buttons on Sage's waistcoat. "As to what caused me to leave, that's a bit of a longer explanation. I liked my work well enough, but I didn't want to do it forever. As you can probably imagine, it's hard on the body. And there's only so long a person can do it. Not to mention, there's some amount of danger involved, so it's always a risk that you'll hurt yourself and be unable to work. I knew I liked helping people, I knew I liked making plans and lists. I knew I liked magic, for all that I was hardly the best at it. But it's...challenging finding work that suits such things when your education is informal and your means are small."

"How did you decide on the Council position?"

"I started following the news a little more closely

when Roger and Wyndham were assigned their project last autumn. No one in my family had a particularly high Hastings score. So when we heard that the Hastings Exam might be replaced with something more nuanced, we subscribed to the only source that was discussing it."

"*Torquil's Tribune.*"

"Yes."

Sage turned his face away. "So you have read the gossip then?"

"Not really. I wasn't subscribing to the paper for the gossip, only for news about the Council. Besides, what did I care about the goings on of strangers in another city?"

Sage stared at him for a long moment. "Go on."

Conrad let his free hand drop down to Sage's thigh. "It wasn't until I read that a number of the councilmembers were stepping down that I formed any plans at all. And then when the Council invited fae-humans to come and work on the newest rubric, my plans began to take shape a little more. It seemed to me that the Council was changing. They were getting to know the people more, getting to understand everyday magic a little better.

"With such changes as the Barnes-Wrenwhistle rubric, and the research on fae-human magic, it felt like...I don't know...a new age, in a way. One that I could be a part of building. I thought about my family, full of informally educated people with moderate magical abilities, barely managing to scrape together enough to live. And I thought of how many other people were like us, all over the country. Whatever the new rubric was going to be, I wanted to make sure it was something that would help people like me. The surest way to ensure that was to be a part of the group making those decisions. So I sold off whatever I could, bought myself enough to travel post, and..." He shrugged. "I imagine you know the rest."

Sage was quiet in response. Conrad didn't mind. He didn't require any sort of commentary on his story. He rubbed his palm over Sage's thigh.

"Thank you for telling me," Sage said at last.

Conrad smiled. "I'll tell you anything you like."

Sage huffed a laugh and looked away again. "I wish I was so trusting."

Conrad cupped his cheek and leaned closer. "I don't blame you for being slow to trust, nor do I take whatever trust you give me lightly." He rubbed his thumb over Sage's cheekbone. "There are some things that are rare, but all the more precious because of it. Trust and friendship being amongst them."

Sage swallowed and met his gaze. "You seem to make friends wherever you go."

"I am friendly with most everyone I meet, because I happen to like most of the people I meet."

"Such a strange creature," Sage murmured.

Conrad grinned. "But I would be a fool indeed to handle a friendship such as yours as carelessly as others have."

Sage peered over Conrad's shoulder, to where

Wyndham and Roger were sitting. Conrad cupped his chin and redirected his face back towards him. He leaned a little closer and heard Sage's breath catch. "You need never give me anything more than what you are comfortable offering," he said, his voice soft enough to only be heard by his companion. "And I will never demand anything that isn't given freely. Everyone deserves that much. You especially."

Sage closed the distance between them with a kiss, one hand coming to the side of Conrad's waist. Conrad smiled against his lips, keeping his hold on his chin as he kissed Sage back lightly, allowing the other man to dictate the pace. The kiss started out with a gasp of breath and the heated press of lips, but swiftly turned leisurely and indulgent, Conrad's favorite kind.

After they broke apart, Sage leaned his forehead against Conrad's. "I'm not sure how much I have to give anymore," he whispered.

Conrad moved his hand back to Sage's cheek. "Whatever it is, it's enough." Someone behind them whistled and Sage stiffened. Conrad rubbed his thumb over Sage's cheek. "You tell me if you need us to stop."

"No," Sage said quietly, his breath ghosting over Conrad's lips. "I don't want us to stop."

Conrad pressed a kiss to the corner of Sage's mouth and turned to face their hecklers. Unsurprisingly, it was Emrys, gawking at them openly with a cheeky grin.

"Are we bothering you?" Conrad asked.

"Oh, not at all," Emrys responded blithely. "I'm all for having entertainment provided for me."

Torquil rolled their eyes. "Don't mind him. Everyone else he knows is married now."

Conrad chuckled. "Speaking of which, how were the strawberries?"

Torquil smiled. "Delectable, thank you. I keep telling Emrys I can feed myself, but he insists on spoiling me."

"Can you blame me?"

Torquil placed a hand on Emrys' chest. "I'm not really used to being looked after, you see," they explained to Conrad. "I spent several years decidedly on my own. I worked myself into collapse, trying to run the *Tribune* and work on the Council."

"Not to mention all of the social gatherings my grandmother was foisting on you," Wyndham added, not looking away from his book.

"And that," Torquil agreed. "Ever since, I've had to constantly remind myself that sometimes the best way to take care of someone you're fond of is to let them take care of you."

"I like that," Roger mused.

"They're always saying things like this. So wise," Emrys said, his tone smug, before he pulled Torquil in for a kiss.

"It is good advice," Conrad agreed. He glanced back at Sage and then turned around and settled his back against the other man's chest. Sage's arms immediately wound around his waist. "This seems like a good start."

Torquil grinned at him. "You're picking it up faster than I did."

Conrad winked. "I'm a quick learner."

"Oh, I'm sure Sage will take very good care of you," Emrys drawled.

Sage's arms tightened and Conrad placed a reassuring hand on his wrist. He liked Emrys, but he did not like the sneer in Emrys' tone, and he liked even less the way Sage seemed to tense under the banter. "Well, considering how generous he's been in letting me share the room, helping to ensure my clothes are cleaned regularly, and giving me some much needed advice, I'm inclined to agree with you."

Emrys looked baffled. "Not entirely what I meant."

"Indeed," Conrad said, his tone more clipped than usual, "I'm sure I know what you *meant*. But I'll thank you not to say such things about Sage in the future."

Roger looked worriedly between Conrad and Emrys while Torquil raised an eyebrow at their husband.

Emrys smirked and said, "Glad to see you do have feathers to ruffle after all."

Conrad shrugged. "Doesn't everyone?"

Emrys laughed in response and the tension eased.

Sage kissed Conrad's jaw. "Don't worry about it, Conrad," he said, his voice soft but still carrying. "It's no worse than what everyone else says about me."

Wyndham turned his gaze to them briefly before returning to his book.

Conrad squeezed Sage's wrist and resumed his usual easy tone. "Well, I must say this has been a lovely afternoon."

"Yes," Harriet said, leaning forward. "And long overdue. I came here to visit with Roger and Wyndham and I don't much care for being neglected."

Roger looked chagrined. "I apologize. We really haven't been very good hosts, have we? It's just so nice to practice magic with someone new. And to have him in the house makes it even more convenient."

Harriet gave an exasperated sigh and flopped against Fern. "Then have him stay with you in London, for heaven's sake."

Conrad felt his chest tighten a little at her words. What *would* he do after he left here? He'd been so focused on the first part of the journey, he kept pushing the rest of his concerns to the back of his mind. It occurred to him suddenly that he ought to be a little more concerned with what happened next.

"Or at least alternate days," Cyril added.

"That might be best," Roger agreed. "We have a nice stable full of horses. Perhaps we can go riding tomorrow or the day after if the weather continues to be fine."

"Capital!" Cyril said. "I can wear my new hat."

Conrad tried not to show his own disappointment. He didn't care for the idea of sitting at home while everyone else left. But he didn't particularly care to admit that he couldn't ride either.

Torquil leaned their head against Emrys' shoulder. "I'm afraid I'll have to bow out of that one. I can't ride."

Conrad brightened. "Oh, good. Me neither. I'll keep you company."

Torquil smiled. "Excellent."

Emrys gasped. "Nonsense. You can't pass up the opportunity to wear that delectable riding costume. You can share my horse."

Chapter 17
Sage

Conrad's admission was entirely unexpected. For a man who seemed so capable of a great many things, especially those requiring physical aptitude, Sage never would have guessed that he could not ride. He had a suspicion that it was only a matter of lacking the opportunity. There was no question in his mind that if Conrad sat astride a horse, he would pick up the skills necessary within no time at all. Half the battle was staying on. With strength like his, certainly it would not be an issue.

It was this thought that carried Sage into the following afternoon. All of the councilmembers spent varying amounts of time in and out of Roger's study. Sage hadn't the slightest notion of what they could be doing for so many hours, other than keeping Conrad busy. It left him alone to ponder.

He focused on the issue of riding as a diversion from all the other things trying to squeeze their way

157

in, such as the tender way Conrad had spoken to him, or how he had practically thrown himself at the man as a result. And then, the way Conrad handled Emrys' teasing with such ease, all while comforting Sage with reassuring touches that had done strange things to the magic in his chest. He'd been so surprised when Conrad settled between his legs, but looping his arms around his middle had come almost innately. It was alarming how well they fit together.

But Sage was not ruminating on such frivolities. He was standing outside the study at a distance that kept the footman from appearing too unsettled. He'd been asked several times if he wished to speak with someone inside, but insisted that he did not want to interrupt. When the door finally opened, he stepped forward and followed with his eyes as Torquil exited, then Conrad, Roger, and finally Wyndham. Roger paused mid-sentence when he noticed Sage's presence in the hallway.

"Oh, Mr. Ravenwing." Roger glanced up at Wyndham, who was standing quietly beside him, expression neutral, though his eyes were hard on Sage. "Did you need something?"

Sage offered a small, polite dip of his head. "I hoped to have some time with Conrad before dinner."

There was an irritatingly smug look exchanged between Roger and Torquil over Conrad's head, whose ever-present smile had grown considerably at the request. Sage had never formally called on anyone before, but he imagined this was what it would feel like. He did not care for the way his magic swirled with uncertainty in his chest as he waited for an answer.

"I suppose we've all worked hard enough for one day," Roger agreed.

The notion that any of them could refuse was absurd. Conrad was older than all of them by several years at least, but the claim Roger had placed on him still felt like that of a protective parent. Sage let out a silent exhale of relief as Conrad stepped away from the group to stand beside him instead. They followed the others downstairs, and Sage placed a gentle touch on Conrad's elbow with his fingertips to guide him down the main hall toward the front door.

"Where are you taking me?" Conrad asked excitedly over the sound of the gravel crunching underneath their feet as they walked along one of the paths leading away from the house. Sage eyed the single pair of shoes Conrad owned. They were not ideal, and neither were his clothes, but they would have to do. "You must've known I was nearing my limit for one day. I believe Roger and Wyndham could do magic for a fortnight and never grow fatigued."

Sage decided not to mention that he had been waiting outside the study for nearly an hour.

"I wanted to return the kindness you showed me yesterday," he said.

Conrad's forehead wrinkled as his brows went up. "That's not necessary. I enjoyed our time together very much."

"Nevertheless," Sage went on, scarcely quelling the eruption of unfamiliar delight at the other man's words, "I feel this is the very least I can do. As fanciful and *romantic* as Emrys and Torquil will likely make it appear, two riders on one mount is something I am afraid my level of horsemanship will not allow. As such, I have arranged for a lesson so that you will feel more comfortable with our outing tomorrow."

With this information, Conrad's comparatively short stride faltered and he fell a couple of steps behind. "You're going to teach me to ride a horse?"

Sage scoffed. "Did you not hear what I just said? My skills are sufficient, but I am no instructor." In truth, he had never found much enjoyment in the activity. It was simply one out of a dozen or more talents he was expected to possess as a fae from a moderately wealthy family in London.

As they approached the stables, two horses came into view, already saddled and standing patiently with a groom holding their reins. From behind them, another endlessly smiling face emerged, dressed from top hat to boots like a man fresh off a fashion plate for the latest in stylish riding at the Park. Conrad laughed in delight and took a few long, skipping strides past Sage toward Keelan.

When they'd made the agreement earlier in the day, Sage hadn't known what to expect. All he knew was that Keelan thoroughly enjoyed his status as a skilled equestrian and had a far better temperament than Sage for giving a lesson. Everything started off smoothly, and after a short explanation of what each piece of tack was called and what purpose it served, Conrad fearlessly got himself into the saddle of his horse with the help of a mounting block.

Keelan turned to Sage with a grin. "Your turn."

"The lesson is not for me," Sage replied.

"I understand, but you cannot expect me to be shouting instructions from the back of my own horse as I demonstrate." Keelan gestured encouragingly to the other waiting horse. "We will watch you instead."

Resentfully, Sage helped himself into the other saddle, adjusting his seat as carefully as he could. He was not dressed for this any more than Conrad was.

"Start off at a walk, then," Keelan told him. "Nice and easy."

Sage did as he was asked, moving the horse into a walk, not entirely sure where he was meant to go. Fortunately, the horse seemed comfortable with its surroundings and needed little guidance to follow a path near the fence. As they circled back, Sage became conscious of how intently he was being watched. Keelan was standing to Conrad's left, stroking the other horse's face.

"Notice Sage's posture," Keelan said as he passed in front of them. "Shoulders back, elbows close to his sides. Absolutely no slouching." He chuckled. "I was always taught to sit on a horse the same way you'd sit for tea with someone very important."

On the second pass, Sage made the mistake of flittering his gaze to Conrad's. He'd become so used to the man always looking directly back at him. This time, however, Conrad's intense focus was aimed lower. A flash of warmth crawled its way up Sage's neck and he snapped his attention to where he was going again. In all the time they'd spent together, he realized, Conrad never looked at his body. So to feel his eyes on him so heavily now was rather staggering.

In all, Keelan had him make about two dozen circuits around the fenced area, talking all the while to build Conrad's confidence while still being very informative. He really would make a fine instructor. Sage eased his horse to a stop on Keelan's other side and dared another look at Conrad. This time, he was rewarded with the smile he'd been expecting before as their eyes met across the distance between them. It only lasted a couple seconds, but it was all Sage needed to know that he'd made the correct decision in arranging the lesson.

As he suspected, Conrad took to riding with little difficulty. Keelan held the reins at first, walking ahead of Conrad's horse on the same arc Sage had taken. Still under the guise of the lesson, Sage decided it was only fair that he should watch Conrad's body move in the saddle the same way Conrad had watched him.

"Do not use too much pressure in your legs," Keelan said after he'd observed Conrad take several laps on his own, slowly turning in the middle of the paddock, hands on his hips. "Focus your balance in your posture." He rested a hand on his stomach. "The muscles here."

Conrad nodded his understanding. Sage could see the moment he made the change and the resulting effect on his seat. A response such as that could only come from a lifetime of taking directions he had no choice but to follow.

Sage was captivated by the thought that he was getting a glimpse at the man Conrad used to be, putting every bit of himself into a task so that he could accomplish it to meet someone else's expectations. So that he could help feed his family. So that he could someday leave everything behind, with nothing but hope and three outfits to his name, all for the chance at being a part of something important to him.

Sage shook himself from his thoughts and dismounted his horse.

Chapter 18
Conrad

Conrad already felt the soreness in his muscles by the time Keelan left the horses with the stablemaster and strode back to the house. Conrad glanced at Sage, who was irritably brushing horse hair off of his trousers.

"That was really very kind of you," he said, his tone soft.

Sage waved a hand dismissively. "As I said, I wished to repay the kindness you had shown me."

Conrad smiled at him. "You might be surprised how rarely kindnesses are repaid. Besides, you've shown me a great deal of kindness since I entered the house. I'm not sure you were in my debt to begin with." Sage led them back to the house without a word. Conrad continued, "I take it from what you've told me of your reputation, you are unaccustomed to people appreciating you for anything other than what pleasure you can provide them—and not even then, from the sounds of it—so I can understand why you are reluctant to accept my thanks. But you have it. You're a good man, Sage Ravenwing."

Sage made a face. "I wouldn't go so far as to say that."

Conrad laughed and Sage gave a small smile in return.

At dinner, Keelan was full of praise regarding Conrad's lesson, and everyone else chimed in to compliment his speedy learning. Then the topic changed to where they would ride the following day and Roger and Wyndham both mused aloud the possible routes they could take.

They all retired early again, with the promise of a busy day ahead. As Conrad undressed in the bedroom, he stretched a little to ease some of the achiness. Sage paused in his nightly ritual of applying his fragrant oils to turn and look Conrad over.

"Are you all right?"

"Oh yes. A little sore."

"We could order a bath for you."

Conrad smiled. "That's very kind of you. I think I'll be fine. But it might not be a bad idea for me to take one tomorrow."

Sage nodded as he returned to his task. "We shall be sure to order one before we leave so it's ready for you upon our return."

Conrad got into bed. "Thank you." He heaved a sigh as he laid back against the pillow. "I must confess, I cannot decide which I like better—working on magic with Roger and Wyndham, or these little activities we've started doing as a group."

Sage slipped out of his robe and into the bed. "Can it not be both?"

Conrad chuckled and then blew out his candle. "Yes, I suppose it can. This place really is spoiling me."

The thought of what he would do after he left began to creep forward in his mind. He was always so busy now, he didn't know when he'd work those details out.

Sage leaned closer and traced a fingertip across Conrad's forehead. "It's not quite a frown, but it's the closest I've seen on your face since you arrived. You must be really upset about something."

Conrad chuckled. "Just thinking about what happens when I leave. Nothing too upsetting. But I do need to figure it out. And soon."

Sage hummed a little and then blew out his candle before curling up against Conrad's chest. Conrad wrapped his arm around Sage's shoulders. "Whatever it is, I'm sure you'll have a solution before you leave."

"I'll certainly have to."

He felt Sage shift to look at his face. "You really are worried."

Conrad shrugged. "Not yet. But the worries are beginning to sink inward."

"Hm. I can hear a smile in your voice now. You almost had *me* worried there for a moment."

He chuckled and rubbed a hand over Sage's shoulder. "Can't have that."

He felt Sage fall asleep against him, his weight getting heavier as he drifted off. But Conrad stayed awake for a while after, thinking about what his options might be when he left, and consistently getting pulled back to the memory of Sage arranging a riding lesson for him so he wouldn't be left behind. Perhaps he really did need to take Torquil's advice and let others take care of him for a change.

·˙·.·˙

The next morning dawned bright and clear. Sage groaned when he woke and nuzzled against Conrad's chest.

"I'm not sure why everyone is so bent on the idea of *doing* things here," he mumbled.

Conrad laughed. "I seem to recall you complaining about being cooped up in this house not too long ago."

"Well, if I'd known that I'd be victim to long and bracing walks, sitting on the ground and watching everyone in each other's laps, and then go riding for goodness knows how long, I'd never have said anything about the rain."

"When in the country..."

Sage made a disgusted sound. "I don't much care for the country. It's dull and it's quiet."

"You prefer London then?"

"Decidedly."

Conrad thought of the way Sage had talked about his reputation in London, the way he hadn't been able to meet Conrad's eyes as he spoke about the way people treated him and spoke of him. He found it strange that the man would prefer the place that was home to his misery. "Interesting."

Sage sat up a little to look at him. "What do you mean?"

"I just find it interesting how some people prefer London and others prefer the country. I've only ever experienced one place in my life and I can't say I have any particular preference for it, other than the fact that my family lives there."

Sage grunted and laid back down.

"So, what's the plan for today? In terms of our scheme? More of the same from the day before yesterday?"

"Yes, I think so. Although it will be different, of course, with us riding."

"Of course."

· ·. · . ·

As it turned out, it was very different when they were riding. Conrad found himself unable to contribute much to the chatter around him as he focused on his posture and staying on the horse. Thankfully, his new friends were encouraging. Keelan provided compliments and advice, and Sage seemed to keep a close eye on him to ensure he was all right. By the time they returned to the house, Conrad was desperately in need of the bath and was relieved to find it already being set up when he walked into the room.

He turned grateful eyes to Sage. "My savior."

Sage huffed a laugh. "Your standards are low."

"Nonsense. I have spent over half my life doing hard labor, and not once has anyone ever provided me with this sort of caretaking."

Sage bunched his lips in a way that Conrad suspected was an attempt to hide a smile. "I rather think that has more to do with lack of funds than lack of care."

"Perhaps," Conrad said as he turned his attention to the servants filling the bath with water and preparing a heating spell for the tub. "But I've seen my share of people who have plenty of resources to spare, yet don't use them to make others more comfortable. I don't take it lightly."

"You take everything I do with far more seriousness than it deserves."

"Perhaps you're the one with low standards, then."

Sage's lips pressed together more as he frowned.

The servants completed their task and closed the door as they left the room. Conrad made quick work of undressing. He couldn't have stopped the moan of pleasure that escaped him as he slid into the hot water if he'd tried.

Sage laughed as he sat down on his ottoman. "More sounds like that will definitely help our scheme."

Conrad grinned as he leaned back. "This is heaven."

Sage turned to his vanity and began puttering with the various oils and creams on the surface.

Conrad watched him in silence for a moment. "May I ask you something personal?"

"If you're wondering whether I really use all of these, the answer is yes. Perfection such as this takes work."

Conrad chuckled.

Sage met his steady gaze in the reflection. "Yes, I suppose you may."

"Why did you come to the house party when being around Roger and Wyndham is so painful for you?"

"Oh."

His voice was so soft that Conrad hastened to add, "You needn't answer. Forget I asked. It's just something I've been wondering."

"No, I can tell you. You probably deserve to know, considering the way we're—"

"You owe me no explanations, Sage, regardless of our arrangement."

"Nevertheless, I think I'd like to tell you." Sage sighed and slowly turned back around to face him. "Roger and Wyndham's engagement was sudden and...unexpected. One day I'm in Wyndham's bed, and the next I'm reading that he's to be married to someone else. Or at least that's how it felt at the time. There had been no warning, no indication that the relationship was..."

Conrad was deeply regretful of having asked the question. "I'm so sorry," he said softly.

"I was angry. And...hurt."

"Understandable."

Sage gave a humorless huff and looked away from him. "Less understandable, perhaps, were my actions. I knew Wyndham was working on a project with Roger. It was all over the *Tribune*. But the two of them had never gotten along. I always thought Wyndham despised the man. And I told him so."

Conrad slid the bar of soap between one hand and the other. "You told Roger that Wyndham despised him?"

"Yes. And when the engagement was announced, I was even less gracious to him."

"You were still in love with Wyndham. I don't know if graciousness was to be expected of you."

"Cruelty wasn't either. I was intentionally cutting."

Conrad thought of the way Roger always seemed a little jumpy when discussing Sage and felt some of the pieces clicking together in his mind. "What happened next?"

Sage drummed his fingers on the vanity surface. "Wyndham found out about it, of course. And he told me that he wouldn't speak to me again unless I apologized to Roger, and Roger accepted it."

"Oh," Conrad said, brightening. "That's good then."

Sage frowned at him. "I fail to see what's good about it."

"That's why you're here, isn't it?"

"I have yet to apologize."

"So you're here to apologize and make things right again?"

"I'm here because Roger is giving me a chance to make things right."

Conrad smiled warmly. "That *is* good."

"It is more than I deserve, I'm sure. But I do not know if I have it in me to apologize to the man who stole the heart of the only person I've ever loved."

Conrad hummed and slid the soap over his arms.

Sage looked up at him. "What?"

"I think if that were true, you wouldn't have come in the first place, and you certainly wouldn't still be here."

"I suppose," he said slowly.

"You want to be in Wyndham's life again, in whatever way he'll take you, because you still care for him, despite your hurt," Conrad guessed.

"Yes," Sage said on a sigh.

Conrad sat up and soaped his chest and neck. "And Roger has clearly indicated that he will accept whatever apology you have to offer. He wouldn't have invited you if he wasn't inclined to forgive you." Sage looked away and didn't respond, so Conrad continued, "And I expect that having a friendship with Roger, instead of a mixture of jealousy, hurt, and guilt, will go a long way toward healing your own heart."

"I'm not convinced that friendship with Roger is something I deeply want."

"Perhaps not. Then it's friendship with Wyndham that you truly want. What would that look like?"

Sage looked pensive. "We never talked much. But I always wished we would."

The sadness in Sage's tone made Conrad's chest constrict. "So you'd like more conversation with him?" Sage nodded. "What else?"

"I've always wanted to be the person that made him happy. I suppose if I could be a part of his happiness, that would be...something."

"Well then," Conrad said, returning his attention to his bath, "I guess you know what you need to do. I find it's always easier to do a difficult thing if I know what I'm doing it for."

"I suppose you're right," Sage murmured as he turned back to the vanity.

Conrad smiled at his back. If he could help soothe Sage's pain half as well as Sage had soothed his, he would be very pleased.

Chapter 19
Sage

Though he would never admit it to anyone who made the suggestion—a suggestion that had been made on more than one occasion—Sage did wonder if perhaps he was the sort of man who found gratification in his own misery.

Years of pining after Wyndham was certainly proof enough all on its own. Unfortunately, his proclivity for seeking out gentlemen who only desired him for certain reasons went far beyond that experience. It had taken him an embarrassingly long time to realize they never wanted *him*, they only wanted what he could provide. And yet he continued, willing to provide so he might earn the smallest satisfaction from the muttered words of appreciation he sometimes got after it was over.

If those utterances matched the strength of a flickering candle, Conrad's words of thanks burned brighter than the midday sun. Sage found that he could hardly endure the lack of restraint Conrad had on the praise and words of encouragement he offered, seemingly for no reason other than his desire to say them. It was entirely overwhelming and Sage was altogether helpless against it.

Every instinct told him to do what he had always done: offer himself in exchange, for what else did he have to give? But he'd already made a fool of himself trying to do exactly that. Conrad's rejection still stung, even if Sage now had a better understanding of why it happened.

In his effort to discover what else he might be able to extend of himself, however, he had done little more than add bricks to the walls of the chamber he was constructing for his own personal torture.

Riding lessons that forced Conrad's eyes to slide over his body? A brick there. Discovering that the lessons were painfully helpful, giving Conrad everything he could possibly need to sit astride his mount with perfect form and confidence? Another brick. Returning from the hours of sitting horseback while trying not to get caught staring, only to have Conrad rhapsodize over the bath Sage had organized for him? Brick. Realizing that he had set himself up to attempt to carry on a conversation while a man who looked like that bathed directly behind him? Brick. Trying to compose himself with some subtle deep breaths, only to be met with the intense burst of lavender from the soap he had forgotten to ask for an alternative for when he made the request?

Brick. Crawling between the sheets to settle against Conrad, his skin still hot and damp from the water, and fighting every urge to do more than close his eyes and fall asleep? Sun-baked, rock-hard, unyielding bloody brick.

Conrad had said he need only ask. It seemed like such a simple question. Better yet, he already knew what Conrad's answer would be, amenable man that he was. But the truth was that Sage had never actually asked before. He'd been open and willing, more often than he should've been no doubt, but the idea of requesting it was so outlandish that he hadn't the slightest bit of courage to do it.

It seemed courage was something he lacked in many aspects of his stay at the Wrenwhistle estate. Although, if Conrad was to be believed, he'd already shown a little courage just by accepting the invitation. With more time, and certainly with more encouragement from his companion, maybe he could accomplish the rest.

·˙·.·

The next afternoon, Sage was able to trade one form of torment for another. He could think of no better way to abate his desirous thoughts than to spend several hours locked away in the study with Roger while they planned this ridiculous party. The worst part was that Roger did not find any detail too small to discuss, which meant that they truly spent each moment of those hours working. Fortunately, Roger was the one doing all of the writing and most of the talking, and by the time he rang for tea, there were a few blissful moments of silence as he sipped from his cup, to which he'd added a double helping of honey.

Sage eyed him over the delicate, golden rim of his own cup.

"I'm surprised you did not add something a bit stronger than honey and lemon after yesterday's happenings."

Roger's expression pinched. While on their ride, movement of a hare or a bird in the grass had spooked his horse and sent her bucking several times. He'd almost managed to hold on, arms wrapped tightly around her neck and shrieking, until he slid from the saddle as slowly and ungracefully as one possibly could and ended up flat on his back on the trail. Naturally, it sent everyone into a panic, but other than a sore hip, Roger had declared he was fine and even got back in the saddle for the return trip. It was rather impressive.

"Oh, y-yes," Roger agreed unsteadily. "I probably would have, if Wyn hadn't already made certain that I was full of his preferred tonic for aches." He took another sip of tea and gave a small shrug. "I'm fine though, really. It was more startling than anything."

"I was thrown from a horse once, many years ago."

Roger hummed sympathetically around his mouthful of biscuit. "Were you hurt?"

"Only my pride."

"A fragile thing, indeed."

Their eyes met sharply across the desk. Roger's went wide with realization of what he'd said.

"Not yours specifically! I only meant as a general rule, that one's pride is damaged far easier than I think any of us care to remember."

"Pity there is no tonic for such an injury," Sage murmured into his tea.

Roger let out a breath, his shoulders relaxing. "Only time, I'm afraid. The reassurance of loved ones. Keeping in mind that we all make mistakes."

An apology, Sage thought.

As another stretch of quiet settled between them, he took the opportunity to really look at the man opposite him. Of course he knew what Roger looked like—aside from a significant upgrade to his wardrobe, he looked exactly the same as he always had: dark brown hair and eyes to match, light brown skin, a round face, and spectacles that never seemed to stay where they were supposed to be. It was one of countless things they'd all teased him about in school. Sage was personally responsible for one broken pair and had witnessed it happen at least two other times.

To look at someone and to truly see them are entirely different. Just as Roger had climbed back onto his horse after being forcibly removed, he had remained steady in the face of snide comments and cruel tricks for all those years. He had taken on the untamable force of a man like Wyndham Wrenwhistle and, with the help of a few strongly-worded letters to the *Tribune*, come out on the other side with a doting husband and his name glistening on the tongue of everyone in London—and beyond, according to Conrad.

There was nothing graceful about him. He was not charming like Emrys, or elegant like Torquil. None could ever match the wit of Wyndham. He was only a human, prudish and messy, stinking up the place with his complicated human magic. And yet, somehow, he was unbreakable, steadfast and hopeful no matter the circumstance.

All at once, an understanding hit Sage so hard that he had to set his tea on the desk for fear of dropping it. Was this what Wyndham meant when he'd said that falling in love had nothing to do with him and everything to do with Roger?

Sage rubbed a hand over his face, leaving it across his closed eyes as his mind worked clumsily over his thoughts. It was no wonder Roger had taken to Conrad so quickly. They were one in the same. Kind, humble, hardworking human men who wanted more for others than they did for themselves. Sage's hand came down to cover his mouth as he blinked at Roger, who was busy refilling the cup he'd set down. It was even less of a wonder how he'd managed to capture Wyndham's entire heart in such a short time.

"That was very nice of you to arrange a lesson for Conrad," Roger said as he set the teapot down. "He seemed to enjoy himself—"

"I'm sorry I misjudged you," Sage blurted. He fisted his hand and pressed it hard against his thigh, the other gripping the arm of the chair. He was certain he looked as uncomfortable as he sounded. Roger looked up at him in surprise, jaw slack. Neither of them said anything for a moment, and it only made Sage's heart beat faster. That was not the apology he was waiting to hear, but it had to be said before anything else. There was no going back now.

"Oh," Roger finally managed, with a tight yet encouraging nod.

"Wyndham never said those things about you. I did. I'm certain he's already told you as much, but it's only fair to hear it from me. I wish I could tell you I never meant them. Or that I only said them to hurt you, which I did." Sage dropped his gaze to his lap, swallowing hard before he looked up again. "I only knew you as the lad we all made fun of in school. And then, when I noticed how you'd taken so much of Wyndham's attention, I said whatever I could think of to try and come between the two of you." He huffed out a bitter laugh. "A lot of good that did."

"I see," Roger offered with far too much understanding.

Sage crossed his arms and hunched forward in his chair, unable to look at Roger for what he said next.

"You're not dull or stupid. You're not a waste of anything. I suppose after working so closely together, Wyndham was able to see in you what the rest of us had to wait until after your wedding to find out."

"And what is that?"

"You're intelligent, kind, and proper wonderful with your magic, and running a house, and everything else that you do." Sage winced. "And that you really were meant for Wyndham. You were meant for each other."

Sage pushed up out of his chair and kept his arms tight across his chest as he moved away from the desk, his back to Roger as he stared up at the shelves full of books without really looking at them.

"I do not expect you to actually forgive me for the things I've said," he admitted quietly. "But for what it's worth, I will always regret saying them."

A light touch on his arm brought his attention to where Roger had come to stand beside him.

"I think you'll find it's worth a great deal more than you realize."

Chapter 20
Conrad

Conrad had spent a marvelous afternoon with some of the other guests of the house. He found Wyndham in a sitting room, reading a book. Torquil and Emrys were sitting nearby, sharing a plate of biscuits.

Roger and Sage had disappeared into the study for an unexplained project. Conrad hoped Sage would say what needed to be said, and sent encouraging thoughts his way. He had a feeling Wyndham was hoping the same, as the gentleman seemed remarkably relaxed, considering his beloved husband and his former lover were spending hours together in private.

Emrys even commented on it at one point, making a teasing joke meant to get a rise out of Wyndham or Conrad, or both.

Wyndham arched an eyebrow at his brother over the book he was reading. "I trust Roger," he said simply.

Emrys glanced at Conrad, who shrugged. "Even if I didn't trust Sage, I don't have any sort of hold on him."

"You aren't jealous?" Emrys asked incredulously.

"Why should I be?"

Torquil stole a ginger biscuit from the plate. "Emrys has a tendency toward jealousy. You should have seen him the one time in my life I danced with anyone other than him."

"I do not! And that was one time!"

Wyndham snorted.

Before Emrys could say anything else, a small ginger kitten darted into the room and onto Torquil's lap. Emrys inched his chair away, looking wary.

"Is this the famous Peony?" Conrad asked, putting his own book down.

"More like infamous," Wyndham muttered.

Torquil murmured sweetly and scratched behind her ears, which was clearly what she had chosen their lap for.

"Emrys is afraid of her," Wyndham added.

"I am not!"

"Do you like cats, Conrad?" Torquil asked, ignoring him.

Conrad grinned and moved forward slowly. "I do." He reached a hand up for the kitten to sniff. She did so and then bumped his hand with her nose, an unmistakable command. He rubbed under her chin accommodatingly. "There were a number out by the docks that knew which of us would take pity and feed them part of our lunches."

She tucked her paws under her body and settled onto Torquil's lap, content to accept the offerings of chin strokes and head scritches.

"So what will we be doing tomorrow?" Torquil asked into the quiet. "I'm sure an activity will be expected."

Wyndham heaved a sigh and placed his open book onto his chest. "I'm sure I don't know."

"What would you do if we weren't here?" Conrad asked.

Wyndham gave a wicked grin.

"Do not answer that question," Emrys warned.

Wyndham laughed. "I often like to go to the lake, especially if Roger is focused on a project."

"Do you swim or simply enjoy the view?" Conrad asked.

"Both, depending on the day."

"A swim might be nice," Torquil said.

"I'm sure I'd love to see you swimming," Emrys added with a smirk.

Wyndham rolled his eyes. "Do you swim?" he asked Conrad.

"Living in Bristol, we could hardly help it."

"That's decided then." Wyndham picked up his book. "We'll go to the lake."

⁘⁛⁘

Conrad didn't see Sage until dinnertime. His face was drawn and he was even more quiet than usual. Conrad would have worried, except that Roger

184

looked positively glowing. He cheerfully dismissed all queries about what had kept him and Sage so busy all day, merely explaining that Sage had been kind enough to assist with a personal project. Emrys snorted at the word choice and Roger blushed. But Conrad had noted the way Roger was no longer referring to Sage with formal terms. It seemed Sage had done what he'd needed to do after all.

Wyndham explained to the group that a visit to the lake had been decided as the next day's activity. "So I expect that we will have to skip another round of riddles tonight, Harriet. I don't want anyone to be too tired for our outing."

Harriet pouted. "It's too bad. I've picked out some deliciously wicked ones."

Wyndham chuckled. "Well, we all know Conrad and Sage will be the ones to win those rounds anyway. You both are clearly the best at riddles."

Sage jolted as if he'd been shocked at the mention of his name. He stared across the table at Wyndham for a long moment. Wyndham didn't seem to notice, but he had a decided air of satisfaction as he sipped his wine.

Roger beamed. "Indeed, they really are quite a force to be reckoned with."

"At least when it comes to naughty ones," Emrys added with a laugh.

"Conrad knew slowtop," Torquil put in, with a smile at both of them. "I rather think they have the mind for riddles."

"More than I do, that's certain," Keelan muttered.

"Don't worry about it, Cricket," Silas said, patting his hand consolingly. "You have the best seat out of everyone here."

Emrys let out an exaggerated groan. "There's no need to discuss Keelan's seat, thank you very much."

The whole table laughed as Keelan blushed and Silas looked smug.

After dinner, Conrad listened to Cyril and Keelan chat about riding costumes until he could no longer pretend to be interested in the topic. He excused himself from the group and went up to his room. He was unsurprised to find Sage already there, dressed down to his robe, and methodically applying oil to his chest. Their eyes met in the reflection as Conrad closed the door.

"It sounds as if you and Roger had a good day together."

"I'm not sure I'd describe it like that," Sage returned.

Conrad smiled to himself and began getting undressed.

"I took your advice," Sage said quietly.

Conrad paused in the act of unbuttoning his waistcoat. "And?"

"He accepted my apology. Just as you said he would."

Conrad beamed. "I'm so glad. And how are you feeling about it?"

"Drained. But...relieved."

"I hope you're proud of yourself, too."

Sage gave a little huff and then poured more oil

onto his fingers. "I can't remember the last time I felt that."

Conrad continued undressing. "It is easy to make mistakes. Easy to act out of fear or hurt or jealousy. It is much more difficult to own up to those mistakes and to repair rifts made from such actions. I'm proud of you, even if you aren't."

"Thank you." The words were soft, and when Conrad glanced at his companion, he saw that Sage was looking downward.

Conrad stepped across the room and lightly kissed Sage's cheek. "You're a good man. I'll keep telling you that until you believe it."

Sage looked as startled by the kiss as he was by the words. He seemed to shake himself and returned to his task of applying the oil. "You'll have your work cut out for you, then. I'm not sure you'll manage that before this house party is over."

"Well, then I'll continue when we're both in London," Conrad said cheerfully, taking off his shirt.

Sage didn't respond, but his lips were pressed tightly as he stood and took off his robe. Conrad studied him as they both slipped into bed.

"Are you all right?" Conrad asked gently.

"Just tired." Sage blew out his candle and then moved over for his usual spot at Conrad's side.

Conrad lightly cupped Sage's chin and tilted his face to look at him. "It is troubling that you have an easier time talking about past problems than you do current victories."

Sage rolled his eyes. "I'm not sure I'd call admitting that I'd been beastly a victory."

"I would."

"Well, we've already established what a strange creature you are."

Conrad chuckled. "Undoubtedly so."

Sage sighed. "Thank you for the advice. It...was what I needed to hear."

Conrad stroked his cheek with his thumb. "Even the best advice cannot force a hand. You had the courage and the kindness to do what needed to be done. That's not insignificant."

Sage swallowed and gave a tight nod.

Conrad dropped his chin, blew out his candle, and then laid against the pillow. Sage wasted no time in settling in next to him.

"Wyndham spoke to me," Sage said quietly.

Conrad smiled into the dark and ran a hand through Sage's hair. "And how did it feel?"

"Startling. But good."

"The tentative start of a new friendship. A victory worth celebrating."

Sage snuggled closer. "I may have been wrong yesterday."

"Oh?"

There was a long pause. "I don't think I'd mind a friendship with Roger."

Conrad's smile widened and his heart felt light. "I'm glad to hear it."

"He reminds me of you a little, actually."

"That might be the best compliment I've ever

received." Sage gave a surprised sort of laugh. "I met Peony today. She's very sweet."

"She bit Keelan."

"Mm. Perhaps that's why Emrys isn't too fond of her."

"But you are. Of course. Shocking that you should find another being in the house that you like."

Conrad chuckled. "Yes, well I've always had a soft spot for prickly creatures who harbor gentle and sweet natures for those they trust."

Sage was still and silent for a long moment. Then he reared up a little and said in a thoroughly insulted tone, "Did you just compare me to a *kitten*?"

Conrad threw back his head and laughed.

Chapter 21
Sage

A light rain shower the next morning was not enough to deter the party from following through on their plans. After a hearty breakfast meant to last through to their evening meal, everyone gathered in the main hall just as they'd done before their last group walk and set out together. The only difference was that Roger, Wyndham, and Conrad joined them this time, as well as one servant carrying an armful of folded blankets and another with light refreshments.

When the path narrowed a short distance from the house, Sage and Conrad were shuffled to the middle with the Ladies Fitzhugh ahead of them and Keelan and Silas directly behind. Sage found no hardship in reaching for Conrad's arm, feeling Keelan's smile at the gesture without needing to see it. Their difference in height was enough that it was more comfortable for Sage to curl his fingers just above

Conrad's elbow. The strength he felt there under the man's thin shirt made it absurdly hard to keep his fingers still.

Upon further inspection, Sage realized that Conrad was not the only one dressed down for their outing. Silas was almost always dressed without a jacket, and Torquil often did as well, but even Keelan and Cyril had taken a similar approach with their wardrobes. Emrys and Wyndham had worn nothing but their shirts and trousers. Even those wearing dresses seemed to be lacking the usual frills and accessories one might expect.

"I did not realize this was to be such a casual affair," Sage said to Conrad without looking at him. The lush, rain-heavy grass was leaning in on both sides of the path, and he was focused on keeping the droplets that had collected on each blade away from his light-colored trousers.

"You should've come to breakfast," Conrad teased. "We discussed it at great length before we left."

"And you easily could've come to tell me at any point."

The words left Sage's mouth before he gave pause to consider them. Conrad had no reason to do such a thing. He was not responsible for looking after Sage's wellbeing. In all likelihood, Sage would not have wavered on his choice of outfit regardless. He'd worn light colors to help keep cool under the sun, and he was hardly interested in seeing his skin freckle, thus a hat was entirely necessary—at least until they reached their destination.

"You're right," Conrad said, sounding genuinely apologetic. "I should've gone up to tell you. Forgive me?"

Sage could see Conrad looking up at him out of the corner of his eye as he waited for a response. Heat built beneath his cravat and he cleared his throat before shaking his head.

"There's nothing to forgive."

It was for the best that Conrad had not come back to the room that morning. Before selecting the clothes he thought best for their jaunt to the lake, Sage had spent an inordinate length of time making use of the small jar of oil he'd left on the bedside table since the first night he put it there. Apologizing to Roger might've earned him more generous praise from Conrad—admittedly one of the reasons he made use of the oil—but until he found the fortitude to be more honest with Conrad than he'd already been, he was left to take care of himself in a way he hadn't needed to in a very long time.

With his hands in his pockets, Conrad shrugged. Sage's grip on his bicep tightened far more than he meant for it to when he felt the muscle flex against his palm. Stars above, he was hopeless.

"Either way, it will not matter once we reach the lake."

Sage's brow furrowed. "Why not?"

"Wyndham," Cyril called pointedly from somewhere behind them. His voice carried easily to where Roger and Wyndham were guiding from the front. It was quiet all around them, save for the gentle rustling of trees and bugs in the grass. "Is it truly a lake, or more of a pond? I daresay I could never tell the difference aside from size."

"Oh!" Roger said excitedly. "It has everything to do with sunlight, Cyril. If the water is shallow enough for plants to grow, it is a pond, and if it's too deep then it would be considered a lake."

Wyndham turned to look over his shoulder with a smirk and gestured to Roger with an upturned palm, as if to say, there is your answer.

"So which is it?" Harriet demanded.

"A lake, to be sure," Wyndham said as he turned back around. "Though the part we've gotten the most enjoyment out of is not so deep as to make you wonder what might be lurking beneath the surface."

Lady Imogen shuddered. "I have no interest in testing that theory, thank you very much." Her wife patted her arm supportively.

Before long, the stretch of water they'd all been anxiously awaiting to see came into view, and the entire party clamored to offer their thoughts on how gorgeous it was. Roger began to point out and name the various plants as they passed by, explaining why they grew so well in the damp soil there. As the birch trees and young willows became thicker, the grass gave way to spindly reeds and unruly ferns swaying gently enough as to make them appear mindfully curious about their visitors.

The dirt path ended at a wooden dock that stretched out over the water, where more plants reached from below the surface along the very edge. The rich color and condition of the wood indicated that it was something Wyndham and Roger had installed since taking ownership of the property. Sage was fairly certain he'd seen a watercolor painting of this exact scene hanging in the sitting room.

"Finally!" Emrys shouted, startling Sage out of his trance. With another whoop of excitement, the man went bursting by at a full sprint, his footfalls changing tone from solid to something more hollow when he reached the dock, and then took a flying leap off the end and into the water.

Sage stared in horror until Emrys resurfaced with a laugh.

"At least he removed his shoes," Torquil said breezily from where they were crouched to do the same. With a sweeping glance, Sage realized that everyone was removing their shoes, save for the Ladies Fitzhugh, who were helping each other into the small boat tied to one of the short posts of the dock instead.

"We're swimming?" Sage asked incredulously.

Conrad grinned up at him.

"It's the perfect day for it," he said, two fingers hooked into the heels of his discarded shoes as he stood upright. One of the servants was making quick work of collecting them to place in an orderly fashion at the edge of the path. Conrad's attention moved to the buttons of his waistcoat. "You'd better hurry. With all those clothes, you'll still be undressing by the time we're all ready to get out."

After a final mischievous smile, Conrad spun on his heel, darted toward the dock, and jumped, gripping his knees as he splashed into the water. Silas and Keelan were next, holding hands as they went, followed by a very enthusiastic Harriet and her much more reluctant admirers. Roger and Wyndham took a far more civilized approach to entering the water as they stepped in from the bank, Wyndham keeping a supportive hand on Roger's upper back the entire time. Emrys held his arms up for Torquil and did a terrible job of catching them when they finally hopped off the edge of the dock into the water.

Sage was left standing alone in the sea of abandoned waistcoats, stockings, and a couple pairs of trousers being collected and neatly folded. One of the servants offered him something to sit on—a towel, he now understood, not a blanket—and he allowed them to spread it out on the dock for him. Nobody seemed to notice that he had not joined in until Torquil swam over, pulled themself up out of the water, and plopped wetly onto the edge of the dock.

"You do not care for swimming?" they asked, dark curls dripping.

"I do not," Sage confirmed.

Torquil waved off the towel offered to them and settled with their back against one of the sturdy posts, one knee bent to their chest and the other leg hanging down into the water. The sopping white linen of their shirt and drawers left nothing to the imagination.

"It brings back fond memories of my childhood," Torquil mused. They both watched as Emrys emerged noisily onto the bank a short distance away, followed by Silas and Keelan, Conrad, and Harriet.

Emrys cupped his hand against his mouth and called out his brother's name, followed by, "Come and give your darling husband something to fantasize about!"

Wyndham rolled his eyes but placed a kiss on Roger's temple and began a lazy backstroke toward the shore. "Roger has no need for fantasizing," he called back. "He knows he can have anything he wants, if he hasn't had it already."

Roger's eyes went wide as he kicked his legs and arms to propel himself nearer to the dock. When he brought one hand up to hold onto the edge, water flung from his fingertips onto Sage's towel, nearly onto his trousers. Sage's lip curled slightly but he said nothing, as Roger hadn't even noticed it happen.

"I know he says such things only to rattle me," Roger muttered abashedly. He'd taken off his spectacles before getting into the water. It was odd to see him without them.

Torquil chuckled. "Yes, but we also know it's the truth."

Roger and Sage exchanged a passing glance at that. Blooming friendship or not, there was nothing to change the fact that they both knew Wyndham in a deeply intimate way—Sage formerly and Roger forever more. As badly as he did not want to think about it, there was a level of curiosity, of course. But Sage found it difficult to imagine an appropriate time or manner in which to inquire about any of it. What would he say? *I know you've only ever been with one man, but isn't he the most fabulous shag? Never set your eyes on a more winning prick, have you? Neither have I. Does he still—*

Suddenly, there was a scream. It came from the boat, which had only been paddled a short distance away from the dock. The Ladies Fitzhugh were nearly cowering on their wooden-slat seats, Imogen evidently shielding Anthea's eyes from something terrible. Collectively, everyone else looked to see what had frightened them so.

Emrys had climbed onto a thick branch of a tree overhanging the water. Hands on his hips, he stood as steadily as he could on his precarious perch, smiling widely. Every stitch of clothing had been peeled from his body.

"Oh, good heavens," Roger squeaked as he hid his face against his arm that was still holding the dock, but not before he went entirely red.

Emrys put one hand flat over his mouth and blew a kiss to Torquil before he bent his knees and pitched himself off the branch into the water below with a mighty splash. Fern, who seemed to be the only one entertained by his antics, clapped loudly. Cyril looked nearly as appalled as Roger, though he had not turned away.

"Ugh," Sage groaned. "Do you never grow tired of him?"

"Never," Torquil said affectionately. As Emrys broke the surface, Torquil gave him a wink, and his grin grew even wider.

Two new figures had appeared in the tree, also entirely free of their lake-soaked clothing. Silas wasted no time making his jump, but the resulting movement of the branch sent Keelan's arms flailing as he lost balance and practically fell into the water with a cry. He came up laughing, if not a little breathless. Silas collected him into his arms for a rescuing kiss.

"Harriet!" It was Cyril's turn to scream as they all looked up to find her as naked as the others, hair long and wild with a most gleeful expression as she carefully stepped her way out onto the branch and jumped in. Cyril was paddling his way over to her before she hit the water.

"Roger," Torquil said in a sing-song way a moment later. "Your turn."

"I already know what he looks like," Roger said miserably into the crook of his elbow. He was gripping the dock with both hands.

Torquil hummed appreciatively. "As do we all, now." A smirk curved the corner of their lips. "I can certainly see the family resemblance."

"Oh hush, you," Roger grumbled, but when he lifted his face, he was fighting hard to hide his grin.

Wyndham looked exactly as Sage remembered. He had always been slender, especially when he kept growing taller after the rest of the boys their age had stopped, but his fae blood kept him from ever looking anything less than willowy and irresistible. His wavy hair was sleek and tucked behind the points of his ears. Sage had just enough time to let his eyes linger in all the right places before, naturally, Wyndham made the most graceful dive into the water.

Emrys had stroked his way over to the dock in the meantime. After placing several scandalous kisses on the thigh Torquil still had dangling toward the water, he angled a pleading look up at them, a slight pout on his mouth.

"I might be half-fae," Torquil began, cupping Emrys' cheek, "but I am *wholly* certain that I will not take off my clothes no matter how much you beg."

"But even Harriet—"

"The answer is no," Torquil said softly, leaning down far enough that they were able to press a kiss to Emrys' lips. "You will just have to use your imagination until tonight." They tilted their head back theatrically, exposing the stretch of their throat as they splayed the leg bent up to their chest, wet fabric of their drawers keeping no secrets. "You can do that, can't you?"

With an impatient groan, Emrys pounced up out of the water and wrapped both arms tight around Torquil, hauling them off the dock and into the lake with a yelp. They resurfaced in the middle of a deep kiss.

Sage grimaced and brought his focus back to the

tree. There was still one member of the party who had yet to reappear. "Where is Conrad?"

Wyndham glanced over his shoulder as he glided through the water into Roger's waiting arms. "He was right behind me," he said, with only a hint of concern in his voice. Everyone's focus narrowed on the branch the rest of them had jumped from, but it was empty. Then there was a gasp from Keelan.

"Look!" he said, pointing up.

Conrad had climbed twice as high as anyone else. His stance on his chosen branch was sure and relaxed, as though he'd done this countless times before. The entire party watched—even the Ladies Fitzhugh—as Conrad turned around to give everyone a perfect view of his broad shoulders and firm backside before he tucked in on himself and pushed off the branch, somersaulting backwards into the water below.

Anthea and Imogen clapped from their boat like they'd just watched a gymnast perform at one of the great theaters in London. Harriet let out a whistle. When Sage was finally able to tear his attention away from where Conrad had landed, he felt the weight of eyes on him instantly. Roger and Torquil were both gaping up at him from the water. His face went warm and his magic swirled uneasily in his chest as he tried to think of how to respond.

In the end, all he could do was sigh defenselessly and say, "I know."

Chapter 22
Conrad

Conrad was having a marvelous time at the lake. It was freeing to have so much fun with his new friends; to be fully himself without worrying about the gap of education or polish. The only thing that dimmed his pleasure was that Sage was still sitting on the dock, fully clothed, and looking more isolated than ever. Conrad had hoped that after the conversation with Roger, Sage would be more comfortable with the rest of the group. The way he'd easily slid his hand around Conrad's arm had felt so relaxed, so simple. And yet, he hadn't moved since they'd all jumped into the lake, and he didn't appear to be changing that any time soon.

Conrad splashed Emrys as he teased him for the backflip and made his way to the dock. He hoisted himself up and sat next to Sage. "Not going in?"

Sage shook his head.

"You don't have to strip down if it makes you uncomfortable—"

Sage gave out a little huff. "It is not that."

"What then?"

"I am simply uninterested," he said crisply. But he didn't meet Conrad's eyes as he said it.

Conrad reached forward and cupped Sage's chin to direct his gaze to him. "Is that the truth?"

Sage pressed his lips together. "I do not want anything to happen to my clothes."

Conrad arched an eyebrow. "I'm sure the servants will look after them for you." Sage was silent, and Conrad leaned closer. "Sage?"

Sage sighed and said in a whisper, "I cannot swim. And I do not wish to make a spectacle of myself."

"I see." Conrad wiped one wet finger down Sage's cheek fondly. "I'm sorry you can't participate."

"It is nothing. I don't wish my clothes to be ruined anyway."

Conrad pulled away and leaned back against his palms, stretching his legs out. He felt Sage staring at him.

"You aren't going back in?"

"If my beau is not going to enjoy the lake, I'm certainly not going to let him sit by himself."

"You were enjoying yourself. Don't be silly."

"I will not enjoy myself if I know that you are sitting here alone. So we shan't say another word about it." He looked across the lake at the rest of the group frollicking. "Tell me something that surprised you today."

Sage made a small sound of uncertainty. "I've never seen Roger without his glasses."

Conrad smiled. "Mmm. Nor I."

"And what surprised you?"

"That the Ladies Fitzhugh didn't wish to swim, either."

"Humans are odd creatures. So prudish and fussy."

Conrad laughed. "Harriet isn't."

"An anomaly, to be sure." Sage paused. "You aren't, either. However, I've come to the conclusion that this has more to do with the fact that nothing seems to bother you. So why add nudity to the list?"

"A very kind assessment. Although not entirely accurate."

"You wish to pretend that you are bothered occasionally?"

"More than occasionally. I've snapped at a number of ship captains who demanded more speed than is safe. I've scolded fellow dock workers who were drunk while at work. I've even been known to raise my voice at sailors who made our work more difficult."

"My word. You *raised your voice?* How did you show your face again?" Sage asked, a smile teasing at the corner of his mouth.

"I'm only saying that I'm hardly a paragon of perfection. You'll recall that I was somewhat peevish to Emrys only days ago."

"I most certainly do not recall any sort of peevishness. Merely a slight deviation from your usual amiability. And it sounds to me like you only get agitated on behalf of others."

"That is the usual case for my anger, though not always." Sage rolled his eyes. Conrad nudged him. "Admit it. Admit that I'm bothered by things."

"An absurd admission by any standard. And no I won't." He nudged Conrad back. "I shall remain unconvinced until you lose your temper at the sort of things that irritate me—too much cheeriness, a potential mud splatter, or perhaps a prolonged evening of singing."

Conrad barked out a laugh at the very thought.

A few heads turned at the sound. Keelan gave a very unsubtle grin and Roger looked surprised. Torquil swam over to cross their arms on the edge of the dock, appearing quite pleased.

"We should do this more often," they said, resting their cheek against their arms. "Everyone is so relaxed today."

As if to prove this point, Emrys came up as well and wrapped his arms around Torquil's waist. "Am I dreaming or did I just hear someone laugh at a joke by Sage Ravenwing?"

Sage rolled his eyes.

"Sage is very witty," Conrad told him.

Emrys gave a look of incredulity.

"I believe it," Torquil said.

"You do?" Emrys asked them.

"Of course."

"He is one of the best at solving riddles," Conrad added with a sidelong grin at Sage.

Emrys glided away to tease Keelan. Torquil stayed where they were. "Cyril was suggesting we try a boating race sometime, but I don't think I'm up to that particular challenge," they said in a conversational tone.

"Nor I," Conrad said. "I've been around boats all my life, but I cannot be trusted to steer one."

"I will certainly not be participating in that," Sage agreed.

Torquil flashed a smile. "Well, I'm glad I'd be in good company then, if it happens. Apparently Roger is old hat at the game. And he's usually my co-conspirator in this sort of thing."

"Any race needs commenters and judges," Conrad said.

"Now that I would love to see," they said in a delighted tone before swimming away sedately.

"You really can join them, you know," Sage said quietly once they were alone again.

"I can't. I have to sit here and practice commentary with you. Who is the most graceful swimmer?"

Sage hummed. "That would be a tie between Wyndham and Torquil."

"The best jump?"

"You. Obviously."

"Very kind," Conrad said in a posh voice that made the corners of Sage's mouth quirk. "But I'm afraid I shall have to excuse myself from the running. Who else?"

"Silas."

They continued on amiably, exchanging observations of each member of the group. Conrad noted with relief how Sage's tone grew gradually more light. But the gentleman's stiff posture still left something to be desired. He glanced around his surroundings and began formulating a plan.

· ′ ·. ·. ·′

It didn't take much time for Conrad's plan to come to fruition. He wound up approaching one of the servants privately later that evening and asking for a couple of fresh towels, a small book of matches, and a lantern. Then he waited until he and Sage were in their bedroom. As Sage prepared to undress, Conrad stopped him.

"I'd like to return the kindness you showed me the other day."

Sage frowned. "What do you mean?"

"Do you trust me?"

Sage's expression went decidedly wary. "Yes?"

Conrad grinned and kissed his cheek. "Good." He draped the towels over his arm, tucked the matches into his pocket, and picked up the lantern by the handle. "Let's go."

"Now wait a moment. If you intend to get me into that blasted lake—"

"We'll hang your clothes on the tree. They'll be safe there. I won't let you drown."

Sage ran a hand over his face. "I can't see why you should bother."

Conrad cupped his cheek. "Because the next time you sit to the side and watch everyone, I'd prefer it was due to preference, rather than lack of knowledge. And I suspect that you would actually prefer to not be as isolated as you often are."

"What makes you think that?" Sage asked, his eyes averted.

Conrad rubbed his thumb over Sage's cheekbone. "A feeling. Do you trust me?"

Sage sighed. "Oh, very well."

The rest of the household had already retired, giving the building an air of quiet and secrecy. They crept down the stairs with more care than was truly necessary, and Sage shushed him when he laughed at how silly they must both look, sneaking around as they were. But Conrad's heart felt light as he grabbed Sage's hand with his free one and followed his lead in acting mysterious.

Once outside, Conrad struck a match and lit his lantern, guiding the way back to the lake. As before, Sage slid his hand around Conrad's arm, his body closer than it had been during the day. Conrad found he liked the closeness. He liked the halo of light from the lantern in the darkness, making them feel as though they were the only two people in the world. He liked the fact that Sage was allowing him to do this at all, and that he'd fallen silent beside him, his presence as comfortable as it was when they were in bed.

When they reached the lake, Conrad set the lantern down on the dock and pointed to a low hanging branch on the tree. "That should suit our purposes. It's high enough that nothing will get wet."

Sage looked skeptical and he made a disgusted sound as his shoes got too close to the mud. But he didn't argue as he stripped down and carefully set each item of clothing over the branch. He patted everything down when he was done, as if to assure himself of their safety. Conrad put his own clothes on the dock next to the lantern and the towels. Then he took Sage's hand and guided him to the bank and slowly into the water. He felt Sage tense as the water lapped at his waist. He turned and slid one hand to the small of Sage's back and the other to cup Sage's cheek again.

"I won't let you drown. I promise."

"This is ridiculous."

"Was it ridiculous of me to not know how to ride?"

"Of course not."

"Then relax. You can't help what you don't know any more than I can." He rubbed small circles on Sage's back. "We'll stay in the shallow part of the lake to start until you get the feel of things."

Sage gave a curt nod. Conrad stepped to his side and directed him onto his back, holding the man in his arms to keep him afloat. Sage was tense in every part of his body.

"The water will keep you up if you stay relaxed."

"Every drowning in history begs to differ."

Conrad chuckled. "I won't let you drown. Try to relax your neck a little. Good. Now your legs. Let your arms float beside you. Isn't that nice?"

Sage attempted to follow the directions, although it was clearly difficult for him to relax at all. His dark hair spilled out around him, making him look ethereal in the dark water. "It is novel to feel the effect of those muscles for once."

Conrad laughed again. "So you know I'd be perfectly capable of scooping you up if anything happened. Close your eyes. Breathe in. Breathe out." He pulled one arm away slightly, letting Sage's legs float on their own. "Again. In and out," he breathed noisily so Sage could follow suit, and then pulled his other arm away.

Sage floated for a moment and then seemed to register that his personal buoy had abandoned him and flailed. Conrad reached out and quickly scooped him back up again. "I've got you," he said gently.

Sage breathed hard. "No one else was floating on their backs like this."

"It's a start. And besides, I don't expect us to get to diving into the lake tonight. That's an advanced lesson." He waited for Sage to laugh, but he didn't. "All you need is enough to feel comfortable in the water. Just as all I needed was enough to stay in the saddle. Enough to feel safe."

Sage was silent as Conrad stood still and held him, the sound of water lapping against the bank the only sound. "I don't like feeling helpless," Sage admitted in a quiet voice.

Conrad dropped his arm from under Sage's legs and placed that hand on his chest. "You aren't helpless. You are brave, and you are clever, and you have everything you need to do this, I promise. And you have me. I would never let my friend get hurt."

Sage turned his head to look at him. "Very well," he said at last. "Let's try it again."

Chapter 23
Sage

There was water in both of his ears, the pads of his fingers were deeply wrinkled, and the night air had a considerable chill, but Sage was determined to force Conrad to be the one to end their lesson. He knew he could just as easily have Conrad's arms around him in the soft, *dry* comfort of the bed they'd been sharing. It would be nothing like what was happening at the lake, though, with Conrad's hands gliding over his skin in the water that had become too dark to see beneath.

The flickering glow of the lantern from the end of the dock helped only a little; mostly it was the stars that made it possible for them to see anything at all. And Sage wanted to see everything. He wanted to see the lines on Conrad's forehead as he focused hard on helping Sage stay afloat. He wanted to see when the scant light did catch in Conrad's brown eyes, and when he smiled over Sage's success in staying relaxed a few seconds longer than he had the time before.

Once it was decided that Sage had spent enough time on his back—not nearly enough time, Sage thought—Conrad encouraged him out into water that was a little deeper until only Sage's shoulders were above the surface and Conrad could no longer reach the bottom. He was all the more fortunate for it. Despite Wyndham's declaration that it was a lake, and Roger's explanation of the difference between them, Sage made a face at all the unknown plantlife his feet were tangled in.

"Whatever I am currently standing in is downright offensive," Sage muttered, shuffling uneasily from one foot to the other.

"Encouragement enough for you to tread water?"

Conrad made it look effortless. He moved his arms just enough to keep his chin above the water, and somehow even with all the motion he remained in one place. The gentle ripples he was making washed against Sage's shoulders and chest. Slowly, he put his arms out to match what Conrad was doing.

"Like this?"

His heart was beating so hard he was certain that Conrad could hear it.

"Keep your fingers close together so you can push at the water." Conrad lifted one hand out of the water to demonstrate. Sage showed one of his own to mirror the action. "Perfect. Have you ever seen a bird fly from the surface of a pond? A duck or goose?" Sage nodded. "Imagine you're trying to do the same. Not so quickly, of course, but think of the way they're lifting into the air. That's how you'll move your arms."

Sage scowled, his shoulders slumping. "You're having me on."

"I am not!" Conrad argued with a laugh. "You see I'm doing the same."

He was. With a groan, Sage relented and moved his arms at his sides, feeling every bit a fool as his companion watched. "Better?"

"Splendid," Conrad confirmed. "The only thing left to do is pick up your feet. Do you want to give it a try?"

"Not in the slightest," Sage whinged pitifully. "How are you supposed to catch me when you cannot even stand here?"

"I've got you, Sage."

The words made his magic flutter in his chest just as much the second time as they had the first. Even if there had ever been another man to tell him such a thing, he wouldn't have believed it. It would have been another empty promise whispered hotly against the back of his neck. He'd had his fair share of those.

This was not one of those promises.

"I trust you."

His admission ripped through him, turning his stomach. He swallowed hard and squeezed his eyes shut against how feeble it left him. Likely not the best state to be in whilst trying a new skill. Sage turned his focus back to Conrad and gave a small nod.

"Remember to relax, all right?" Conrad moved a little closer. "Keep moving your arms just as we practiced. Good. Now, let yourself sink as though you're getting down on your knees."

Sage snorted. "Oh, I'm rather good at that one, actually."

He expected some sort of sly response, the kind he was used to with such a suggestive remark, but he did not get one. Instead, it was perhaps the worst thing he could've said, because suddenly his focus was not on learning to swim but on something else entirely. As he wondered if Conrad had ever asked someone to get on their knees that way before, Sage's head slipped beneath the water.

There was hardly time to panic. He resurfaced with a gasp and threw his arms around Conrad's neck, who had kept his promise and grabbed him before Sage even realized what he'd done. One arm was wrapped tightly around his back as Conrad used the other to pull them through the water closer to the dock until he could reach the bottom and support Sage's weight.

"Sorry," Sage breathed into the space between his arm and Conrad's neck, chest heaving. His hair was plastered to his forehead and dripping into his eyes, but he didn't dare let go to brush it away.

"You forgot to move your arms," Conrad told him flatly, though there was still something playful in his tone.

"I never was a very good student."

"Oh, now you tell me."

214

Cleaning Spells Before Courtship

This was what finally pulled a laugh from Conrad, but it was nearly too much. With their chests flush, Sage could feel the way Conrad's entire body moved with it, which came as no surprise. The man was carved from nothing but muscle and joy.

Sage thought of the way he had demonstrated both so effortlessly when he'd jumped from the tree earlier, impressing everyone as he showed off more than just his daring feat. Torquil, Roger, and Keelan had continued to give him pointed looks all afternoon, waggling their eyebrows and nodding approvingly. It was all so peculiar, and not just because he'd never had...*friends* to tease him about such things, but also because he and Conrad had an arrangement. Granted, it seemed to be working incredibly well, but the fact remained that Sage could already no longer determine where the charade ended and his true feelings began.

These lessons were doing little to help the situation.

Sage knew there was no reason for him to still be wrapped around Conrad, clinging to his neck like a scared child. He knew, and yet he remained, nose pushed lightly against Conrad's clammy skin, breathing in the smell of him mixed with the earthy, slightly rotten scent he'd accidentally stirred up from the bottom of the lake.

Before the urge to press his lips against Conrad's neck overwhelmed him, he reluctantly found his footing again and tried to pull away.

"You know," Conrad said thoughtfully, "swimming

alone is never recommended." Sage was stunned to discover that the strong arms around him did not loosen. "Maybe it's best that we remain together."

The tips of Sage's ears burned as he cautiously slid his arms back around Conrad's shoulders and settled there.

"That seems wise," Sage agreed quietly, biting his bottom lip to suppress a grin. When one of Conrad's hands moved to the sway of his lower back, he finally let himself relax the way he'd been trying all night and brought his legs up around Conrad's hips, locking his ankles.

Entirely unprompted, Sage delved into an explanation about how he wasn't truly a poor student, only that he'd never cared enough to try very hard. Attractive boys and naughty tricks had been far more entertaining. Conrad lamented over how, even if he had wanted to find himself distracted by such things, he had no opportunity with his homeschooling. Sage was unable to imagine such a scenario and asked Conrad to tell him more about it.

Their conversation meandered through countless topics, each of them sharing pieces of their lives, until a shiver took Sage by surprise. He hadn't realized how cold he was. Tiny bumps lined both of his arms where his damp skin touched the night air.

"It seemed warmer when all of you were having your fun earlier," Sage offered as Conrad made a meager attempt to warm him by sliding both hands up and down his back. That would most certainly do the trick in another, drier situation.

"It was. Not much, but the sunshine helped." Conrad's hands stopped on his shoulder blades. "We should probably return to the house."

Sage sighed and leaned away from Conrad. The chill rushed in, stealing what little heat they'd managed to trap between themselves, and Sage fought another shiver. He focused on tangling his fingers together behind Conrad's neck instead.

"Hopefully one of the staff will be available to rekindle the fire in our room. The last thing I want to hear is anyone complaining about one or both of us falling ill and spoiling all the fun."

"If only I had some of my own ingredients," Conrad said, almost abashedly. "I would do it for us, if I could."

Sage's brows went up as his expression softened into a grin, tilting his head to one side. "Now who is the savior?"

"It's entirely selfish, really. You seem like the type of person to make recovering from an illness a rather tedious process. I would hate that for us."

Sage's gasp of offense quickly turned into a bubble of laughter.

"You cruel man," he scolded. They were both grinning like fools.

"Only a guess," Conrad said with a shrug. "Am I incorrect?"

Sage leaned forward to rest his forehead against Conrad's, his hands moving to either side of his neck.

"I believe I am a rather tedious person," he admitted. "Difficult. I have a propensity for moping."

Sage closed his eyes. He had long since accepted these things to be true. It was all he'd ever been told.

"Sage." His name was Conrad's exhale. "You are wonderful."

Sage's expression crumpled at the pang in his chest. With a small whimper, he angled his head and pressed their mouths together. Conrad's answer was immediate but gentle—almost heartachingly so. It was all the permission Sage needed to kiss him the way he wanted to, not the way he'd learned he was supposed to. He allowed himself to be slow and purposeful, trying desperately to tell Conrad all the things he did not yet have the words to say.

"Why are you so gracious with me?" Sage demanded when they broke apart, though there was little weight behind it. His entire body was waiting for the moment Conrad's hands started to wander; for when their kisses turned into requests for Sage to put his mouth here, touch him there. But it never came.

"I already told you." Conrad's voice was steady and sure. "Whatever you have to give, it's enough."

"Impossible creature," he whispered as he kissed Conrad again, his throat tight with emotion.

Sage Ravenwing found himself entirely lost in the moment. After sliding his arms around Conrad's shoulders again, he forgot he even had a body that was actively shivering. He forgot that he had thoughts, other than the ones about Conrad, and what a lovely night this had turned into. All he could feel was the way their lips moved together, the hot slide of their tongues, and the wild burst of magic in his chest.

With a breath and slow exhale, Sage leaned into Conrad, deepening their kiss enough to make himself moan. Nothing else mattered. Not Sage's reputation, not the teasing from the rest of the party, not his absolute failure during his swimming lesson, not the wind swirling around them, not—

A crash forced them apart.

Sage's first thought was that someone had come looking for them, but there was no light to signify such an intrusion.

His brow furrowed. There was no light at all.

"The lantern," Conrad said, noticing at the same time.

Sage untangled his arms and legs from his companion and stood up out of the water. His jaw began to quiver almost immediately. He wrapped his arms around himself to shield against the breeze that had settled to almost nothing again, but it certainly felt like something against his bare skin. By the time Sage emerged onto the grassy bank, Conrad was already leaving a trail of wet footprints on the dock.

"What's happened?" Sage asked helpfully. He looked for where Conrad had set the towels down next to his clothes, but they weren't there—the towels or the clothes. Frustration bloomed in him. "Is someone playing a trick on us?" He turned to the trees behind him, squinting into the darkness.

He spun back around when he heard Conrad curse under his breath. The man was on his hands and knees, reaching down toward the water. As he sat back, one of the towels came with him, soaked through and cascading water all over his thighs.

Sage might've focused on that a little longer than was necessary.

"I'm afraid the lantern met the same fate."

"And your clothes?" Sage lamented. "And the towels?!"

"The gust came out of nowhere," Conrad said as he hopped to his feet and made his way back down into the water. "I guess it was so strong that it knocked everything off the dock. I think I see one of my shoes."

Sage grimaced at the thought of wading into the shadows to help him find the rest of what had been lost. Conrad must've known, because he kindly did not ask for any assistance. When he emerged, he had the aforementioned shoe, the other towel, and what appeared to be his shirt in his hands.

Sage was still convinced that someone was hiding in the bushes and silently laughing at their misfortune.

"It seems awfully unlikely that a simple breeze could do such damage."

"I agree," Conrad said as he prepared to go back under. "I am no expert, but I have to say it almost felt like something I've seen Roger and Wyndham do in the study."

This earned Sage's full attention.

"What do you mean?"

"Well, I suppose you've seen it," Conrad went on easily. "They demonstrated their wedding spell. It was so impressive." There was the sound of splashing before Conrad produced another piece of his outfit.

"You mean...it felt like *magic*?"

"I cannot feel magic, sadly. Merely a human, remember?" He could hear the smile in Conrad's voice. "But it seemed strong like magic, yes."

Sage stepped away from the puddle he'd dripped onto the dock and glared into the trees. Someone must have been playing with them. It was the only answer. Emrys was the likely culprit, of course. Perhaps he'd even convinced Keelan to help, or simply join in for a good laugh. But there was no laughing. There were no sounds at all. Sage and Conrad were still alone, and if that was really true, then the magic could've only come from one person.

Him.

Slowly, he turned back to the dock.

"Impossible," he whispered to himself.

His magic could *never* have been so powerful as to move a single item that far, let alone dump everything they'd brought with them into the water. Sage pressed a hand over his mouth as he searched for some sort of explanation. He'd hardly even noticed what was happening until it was over. He was too focused on Conrad. On kissing Conrad. On becoming thoroughly *adrift* with Conrad. The magic in his chest lifted pleasantly at the memory.

Sage shoved it all aside. The faster they returned

to the house, the sooner he could stop shivering, and the sooner he could give this some proper thought. His skin was mostly dry, so he stalked toward the branch where he'd hung his clothes. At least one of them would not be naked for the walk back. He tried to think of something clever to say about that, hopeful for another bright laugh from Conrad, but instead he stopped dead in his tracks with a gasp.

Then, he screamed.

Chapter 24
Conrad

Conrad hurried over to where Sage was standing, his mind immediately going to a snake or a fox or some other wild animal. Instead, he found Sage standing over a pile of clothes. The man was shaking and Conrad was no longer sure if this was entirely due to the chilly night air. He felt a pang of remorse over his earlier assurances that the clothes would be fine. He bent down to scoop them up. The weight of them made it immediately clear that they had not made it through the event dry and unscathed. As he added each piece to the bundle in the crook of his arm, he realized that they were not only wet but muddy. The shoes were the only items that had remained where they'd been placed—thankfully on the grass.

Sage whimpered and Conrad hastened to put a hand on his back. "It's going to be all right," he said calmly. "We'll clean them up."

"They fell in the mud!" Sage all but shrieked. "They're ruined."

"Nonsense," Conrad said, taking care to sound neither amused, nor worried, nor callous. "I'll rinse them off in the lake and then we'll go straight to the study. I'm sure Roger has all the materials I need for a cleaning spell. I'll get them as good as new for you in no time."

Sage wrapped his arms around his chest. Conrad thought about all of the things the man had said about himself when they were in the lake. *Tedious. Difficult.* He would need to be careful of his handling of the situation, beyond the clothes.

"Why don't you grab the shoes?" he suggested as gently as he could. "They're still in good condition and you're mostly dry so you're the best one to carry them."

Sage nodded glumly and picked them up, his arms immediately wrapping back around his chest. Conrad waded back into the lake by the dock and dipped each piece of clothing into the water until most of the mud had sloughed off. Normally he would have wrung the fabric out for easier travel, but he didn't dare. He grabbed his own wet clothing, the sopping towels, and the lantern. Without another word, he led the way back to the house, with Sage close behind.

Reentering the dark and quiet house felt different than when they'd left it. Conrad had no idea what time it was, nor did he care. A few wall sconces dimly lit their way as they traipsed up the stairs. Conrad grimaced at how much he was surely dripping in his wake, but he suspected Wyndham and Roger would have less anxiety about their carpets than Sage had about his clothes.

The study was closed but unlocked, thankfully. Conrad placed the pile of wet items in front of the cold and dark fireplace. Then he stepped back out into the hall to grab a candle off a sconce and lit a few of the candles in the room. Sage stood next to the pile of clothes, naked and motionless, with his shoes still dangling from his fingertips. Conrad rubbed between his shoulder blades briefly.

"I'll fix it. Not to worry."

Sage didn't respond immediately, but then he gave the tiniest incremental nod. Conrad could tell in the dim light, in the way Sage was holding himself, that he was frightened. And he thought of the way Sage's voice had been soft as he'd told Conrad he trusted him. He wondered if Sage was as afraid of his own trust as he was for his clothes.

Conrad didn't waste any more time. He pulled out a large piece of spellpaper from Roger's roll on the table and placed it in the center of the room. Then he grabbed a pencil, along with some juniper root, lemon verbena, silver birch, and heather. He knelt on the ground and began hastily writing the sigils for drying and cleaning, adding as much power as he could reasonably do. Then he began sprinkling the ingredients in the right places. Sage hovered over him, silent and watching.

"Pity we don't have any cabbage."

That seemed to rouse Sage somewhat. "Did you just bemoan the lack of cabbage?"

"It is marvelously helpful when it comes to cleaning spells."

"I know human magic is strange, but you cannot convince me that you use such things for your spells."

"Asparagus will do in a pinch."

Sage sputtered.

Conrad allowed himself a small smile and then picked through the wet pile of fabric to extract Sage's clothing first, carefully placing each item in the center of the paper, and attempting to keep the dripping to a minimum. Then he cast.

Sage's anxiety must have affected him more than he realized because he let out a huge sigh of relief when the clothes dried instantly. Sage bent closer. "Fascinating," he murmured.

Conrad plucked out the waistcoat and held it up. "Could use another one or two castings," he said. "I got the bulk of it out, but I don't want it to stain."

He pushed the paper aside and pulled out a fresh sheet, smaller this time, and began the process over again. Sage perched on the edge of the chaise lounge. "You need to do everything all over again?" he asked. Conrad was pleased to note that his tone held more curiosity than fear or anger now.

"Usually," he answered as he finished the sigils. "Roger discovered that using raw materials allows for recastability, but I have not mastered those yet." He glanced up at Sage. "And I wouldn't feel comfortable using them without Wyndham here to ensure it was safe. They can be rather volatile."

Sage frowned, but in a thoughtful sort of way. "I see."

Conrad added the next batch of ingredients and cast again. He held up the waistcoat and gave it a thorough look over before handing it to Sage. "You will have a better knowledge of what it looked like before. Do you think it needs another casting?"

Sage met his gaze as he took the garment, swallowing thickly before he turned his attention to the waistcoat and inspected it carefully. "It looks a bit dirty here still," he said, handing it back.

Conrad gave him each item in turn. They were able to declare the cravat, the stockings, and the shirt properly clean, but the trousers, the waistcoat, and the jacket needed one more casting.

Just as Conrad was preparing to get a third piece of spellpaper out, the door to the study swung open and he and Sage blinked in the sudden brightness.

"What on earth is going on?" Wyndham asked in a rough voice.

"Oh," Roger said behind him. "I think it's just Conrad...oh, and Sage, too." He sounded relieved. "We thought there might be burglars."

Conrad wanted to laugh at how ridiculous it must look—Sage and him being caught in the study in the middle of the night, completely naked, with several piles of fabric between them, all in various stages of cleanliness and dryness. But Sage's eyes were wide and he remembered that the whole intent behind the late night jaunt had been to teach Sage how to swim in the privacy of darkness.

"I do apologize for alarming you," he said as smoothly as he was able. "And for making myself at home in your study. I promise I would never have been so presumptuous if it hadn't been an emergency."

Roger bustled past Wyndham into the room, and Conrad realized that the bright light had been a cluster of lights over their heads, not from a spectacularly strong lamp as he'd previously thought.

"Of course you're welcome to use whatever you need," Roger said warmly. Then he seemed to register that Conrad was naked for he blushed, gave a little squeak, and averted his eyes. Then he noticed that Sage was naked as well, glanced back at his husband, and then pushed up his glasses distractedly. "Oh my," he muttered. He rallied a little and focused on Conrad's face. "But what was the emergency? Is everyone all right?"

"Oh yes," he said, smiling. "Sage and I had such a nice time at the lake today that we decided it would be fun to revisit. Then we ran into a spot of trouble and our clothes did not come out as dry and clean as we'd hoped."

Wyndham made a low sound of acknowledgement. "Roger and I have visited the lake for many an evening swim."

"Indeed," Roger said, beaming at them. "It's very romantic."

Sage cleared his throat and then picked up the clothes that had passed muster. "Yes, well, Conrad was kind enough to offer his assistance in cleaning my clothes. I was quite alarmed by the state of them."

"I can imagine," Wyndham said.

Sage looked up and the two men exchanged a small look of—understanding? Camaraderie? Conrad couldn't entirely decipher it, but he couldn't help the warm feeling of pride that grew in his chest at the sight.

Roger didn't seem to notice. He looked from the wet clothes to Conrad, wringing his hands. "Did you say you had a spot of trouble at the lake? What happened? I hope none of the wildlife did anything."

Conrad chuckled. "No, nothing like that. There was an unexpected gust of wind. It blew everything off the dock and Sage's clothes off the tree. It was very strange."

Wyndham's expression seemed to sharpen. He stepped farther into the room and waved his hand in a lazy fashion, causing all of the candles Conrad had lit to blaze a little brighter. The lights around his head disappeared. "Very interesting," he said, shutting the door behind him. "You've certainly piqued my curiosity."

Conrad shrugged. "I'm afraid I can't offer much more than that. It felt strong like magic. But I can't feel magic, you know. So I can't tell you anything else. It was powerful. I know that much."

Wyndham looked pensive. "What were you doing when it happened?"

Conrad glanced at Sage for permission.

Sage heaved a sigh. "We were kissing."

Wyndham's mouth quirked. "I see."

Roger clasped his hands together at his chest. "That's very romantic."

Conrad smiled. "It was quite lovely. Unfortunately, the gust, or wind, or whatever it was, cut the evening rather short." He gestured to the collection of completed spells and the piles of fabric. "As you can see."

"Our staff can take care of all of this," Roger said. "You needn't do it. Especially after such an exciting night."

"Nevertheless, I promised Sage his clothes would be safe. I'd like to make good on my word, if you don't mind my using your study for the project."

Roger's smile was full of understanding. "Of course I don't mind. Please use whatever you need."

Wyndham was watching Sage with a thoughtful expression. Sage hadn't moved from his seat on the chaise lounge, although he'd gone back to having his arms wrapped tightly around his chest, and he was carefully avoiding making eye contact with anyone.

"Perhaps," Roger said after a long pause, "it might be advisable to finish cleaning everything up in the morning? I imagine you'll be much sharper then, and it'll certainly be easier to see your work."

Conrad glanced at Sage again. Sage seemed to

feel it because he turned his head to look up at him, and gave a small nod.

"Thank you," Conrad said to Roger. "We'll take your suggestion. It's very kind of you."

"You can leave everything here," Roger continued. "The servants know not to do anything in this room unless we specifically request it."

"Wonderful. I'll finish everything after breakfast so you can have your study back as quickly as possible."

Wyndham hummed. "Perhaps, if you're not opposed, Roger and I could join you both and watch?"

Sage's head jerked around to stare at Wyndham. Conrad shrugged again. "I'm not opposed. It's nothing particularly fancy or interesting, though. Just a standard cleaning spell. Although I did add some silver birch for an added boost." He grinned. "Sage was quite scandalized at the idea of my using cabbage or asparagus for the spell."

Roger chuckled. "Yes, human magic can be tragically lacking in glamor sometimes, can't it? Fae magic is so...majestic."

Wyndham snorted. "All right. That's all sorted. Off to bed now."

Conrad wanted to laugh at his bossy tone, but he took Sage's hand as they exited the study and returned to their room. Sage set his shoes and clean clothes by the vanity and they both crawled into bed, blew out their candles, and settled close without a word.

"Are you all right?" Conrad said, pulling an arm around Sage's shoulders.

"Yes."

"I'm so sorry about your clothes."

"It wasn't your fault."

"Well—"

"It wasn't your fault, Conrad." He sighed and nestled closer. "Thank you for cleaning them for me."

"I'll finish the rest tomorrow."

"I know." Sage slid his hand up to Conrad's chest. "I trust you," he whispered.

Chapter 25
Sage

Sage woke to the sound of hushed voices passing by
their door. He'd slept fitfully, waking several times
throughout the night but never long enough to force
him away from Conrad's side. Despite their closeness
under the layers of blankets and the other man's
warmth, Sage found that his toes and fingers were
still cold. In all the madness, nobody had lit a fire in
Roger's study or in the bedroom. The chill had well
and truly sunk in all the way to his bones.

To his surprise, it appeared that the murmuring in
the hallway was what woke his companion, as well.
Conrad drew in a sharp breath and stretched his
entire body at once, producing a satisfied little grunt
as he let it out and settled back into his pillow. Sage
shifted his cheek against Conrad's shoulder to gaze
up at him.

"Good morning," Conrad said, his voice a bit raspy.
He was rubbing at one eye with the hand not resting

easily over Sage's back. He opened the other and squinted at the window, where the curtains had been drawn. "Is it still morning?"

"I'm not sure." Reluctantly, Sage turned onto his back with his head on his own pillow, freeing the man. "What time do the Ladies Fitzhugh usually arrive for breakfast? I think I heard them just now."

"Difficult to say. Sometimes they've already gone out for a brisk walk or something of the like before any of us have sat down."

Conrad was out of the bed already. Sage carefully did not allow himself to imagine rolling over into the warm spot he left behind before it was gone.

"That sounds like a dreadful start to the day," he grumbled.

"Yes, I am learning it's one of the largest differences between humans and fae. Keelan seems to be the only one of you who cares to be seen before noon."

"Keelan has far too much energy for his own good."

"A fair assessment," Conrad said as he tugged his shirt over his head.

"Besides, you cannot give off an air of refinement with dark circles under your eyes. Beauty sleep is extremely important."

Conrad chuckled. "I suppose so. Is it the same in London?"

"We do our best. Social obligations sometimes require that we wake early, but any fae event is quite the opposite. It remains a point of contention between both sides of society."

"Something for everyone, then," Conrad said brightly. "That's what I always imagined it to be like in the city. Excitement at any time of the day, as long as you're willing to look for it. Back home, we were lucky to attend one dance a month."

Sage's brows went up slightly. "Do you enjoy dancing?"

"Oh, er...I only know one or two country dances well, to be honest," Conrad hedged. "Nothing like what you're accustomed to. I'm sure you dance beautifully."

For the first time since submerging himself in the lake, Sage felt a trickle of warmth in his chest that spread out in slow, gossamer curls. Conrad had finished dressing and sat on the edge of the bed as they talked, supporting his weight on one outstretched arm with one knee bent across the mussed blanket. On any other morning, he would've already been out the door.

"Country dances are often requested in London, as well. One can only dance the cotillion so many times over the course of an evening."

Conrad's smile grew as he slid his palm over the blanket until he was propped on his side across the bed. He gave Sage's ankle a playful, almost affectionate squeeze through the sheets before he sat up again and started for the door. "I'll meet you in the study after breakfast."

"Wait."

Sage pressed his lips together as Conrad turned back around.

"Yes?"

Unspoken words burned on his tongue.

"I...thought I might join you. If you do not mind."

Conrad's answering grin was achingly sweet. "For breakfast?"

Sage pushed himself up so he was propped against his pillow.

"I am still rather chilled from last night, I'm afraid." His toes were curled tightly under the sheets.

Conrad hummed. "A nice, hot cup of tea is exactly what you need, then." Without hesitation, he trotted over to the wardrobe and opened the doors wide, staring up at Sage's rainbow of clothes. "What are you going to wear?"

Sage pushed back the covers, placing his feet flat on the rug. "I had not given it any thought yet."

"What about this one?" Conrad asked, lifting his burgundy waistcoat with two rows of proud gold buttons down the front into the air. Not exactly a summer choice, but it would not matter if they were to spend the afternoon in the study.

"Do you prefer it?" Sage asked, coming to stand beside him.

"I've no idea," Conrad said with a little laugh. "I own three waistcoats and one jacket. Do you really think I have an opinion on fashion?"

Sage grinned and took the waistcoat from him. "Very well. What else am I wearing today?"

Cleaning Spells Before Courtship

As they entered the breakfast room together, Conrad leading the way, it was an effort for Sage to train his expression into something more neutral. He'd never had such fun getting dressed before. After rejecting three of the cravats Conrad found—mossy green, pale blue, and bold coral stripes—they'd settled on white. It was enough that he was going to be seen at the morning meal, he did not care to draw more attention to himself than necessary.

Whatever quiet conversation had been happening around the table stopped entirely as Conrad handed Sage a plate at the sideboard before he began filling his own. The air grew progressively thicker with curiosity until Torquil spoke.

"You two look well this morning."

"Roger told us what happened!" Keelan added excitedly.

"Keelan," Roger scolded under his breath.

Sage took a steadying breath as he added a pastry to his plate. Conrad had taken two of them, so he decided they must be good. He lifted his chin as he turned to face the table, but nearly dropped his plate when he discovered that Conrad had set his own breakfast down and was waiting for Sage to take the chair next to his, which he'd pulled out for him. He sat lithely in the proffered chair and glanced at Conrad as he settled beside him.

"We decided it was time to provide some fodder for the morning gossip," Conrad told them all with a smile. This earned him a round of mild laughter from the rest of the table. "Respectfully, I do not think I could've sat through one more story of what Emrys prefers in bed—or out of it."

"Hear, hear," Roger said into his cup of tea before taking a sip. Sage reached for his own cup the moment it was finished being poured. After a single, soft blow against the steam rising from the surface, he took a long pull and closed his eyes blissfully as he felt the heat of it traveling all the way to his belly.

"Well, someone has to provide a little entertainment," Torquil challenged with a smirk as they leaned into their chair, hooking their arm over the back of it. "What is a house party for, aside from giving in to our greatest indulgences?"

Roger huffed, affronted. "I did not invite all of you here to facilitate any such thing."

"Yes, Roger, we know why you invited us," Torquil said reassuringly. They exchanged a knowing look with Keelan. Sage arched a brow. "Unfortunately, when your estate is as idyllic as this, a little cavaulting can only be expected." Their attention shifted to Conrad and Sage. "To varying degrees of success, I suppose."

"Emrys is a poor influence on you." Roger shook his head disapprovingly.

There was laughter from the hallway.

"What've I done now?" Emrys asked as he strolled into the room.

"It seems everyone in residence is eager to splash

a bucket of cold water on us," Torquil told him. "Our host is scandalized."

Emrys clicked his tongue in disapproval. "When is he not?" After setting his plate on the table, he lifted Torquil's chin with a curled finger and kissed them. "Am I to be blamed for seeking a young, virile spouse?"

Keelan laughed. "Is that how you tell people you met?" He turned pointedly to Conrad. "Now that's a *real* story worth hearing."

Keelan and Emrys proceeded to take turns telling Conrad how the other met their partner—surprisingly similar in that both narratives began with a drunken night together, though Emrys and Torquil's romance spanned half a decade longer. By the time they were done, even Wyndham had joined the room, and the Ladies Fitzhugh had returned from their walk. Harriet, Fern, and Cyril were rather active listeners, but added little to the conversation. It seemed their dynamic would continue on as a mystery.

"But I daresay there is no greater modern romance than that of our hosts," Keelan said finally with a wistful sigh. There were various nods and sounds of agreement around the table. "The bookish yet reserved visionary swept up by his charming, handsome prince."

Roger blushed as he and Wyndham shared a soft grin.

"Charming," Emrys echoed. "I beg to differ."

"But I am handsome," Wyndham offered coquettishly.

Emrys rolled his eyes and took a bite of toast.

"Sage and Conrad make a handsome couple, as well, do they not?" This was Harriet's contribution. "Two very winsome gentlemen, indeed! Such luck that they have found one another by chance here at your home, Roger."

Sage had finally warmed up after his second cup of tea, but that did not keep him from feeling his ears go pink when Conrad placed a hand on his arm.

Cyril appeared to reflect on her observation, stroking his chin.

"It seems most everyone at this table can offer some level of appreciation to our hosts for our romantic successes."

They all sat in silence as they worked through the various connections.

After a pause, Harriet raised her teacup as though it were a wine glass.

"To Roger and Wyndham," she said proudly.

The rest of the party scrambled to lift their own cups. Knowing he would be the only one left out if he did not participate, Sage lifted his cup, as well.

"To Roger and Wyndham," they chorused.

Roger covered his cheeks with his hands, grinning widely and quite obviously embarrassed by the attention, as Wyndham put an arm around his shoulders and pressed a kiss to his temple. Sage could read his lips well enough to watch him murmur an 'I love you' into Roger's ear. To his surprise, Sage felt a faint grin tug at one corner of his lips at the tenderness of it.

"Perhaps we can claim a small amount of recognition for it," Roger said. "But we are no great matchmakers. There is much to be said for compatibility, as you all know."

Wyndham and Sage locked eyes across the table.

Unknowingly, Conrad had revealed far more than what he understood in the study the night before. Sage could hardly attest to understanding it himself, but if anyone could, it was the man staring at him.

Was the incident at the lake a result of his magic responding to his compatibility with Conrad? It would explain the fierceness of it that he had never felt before.

As their meal ended, Sage supposed he was going to find out.

Chapter 26
Conrad

Conrad couldn't put his finger on how his friendship with Sage was shifting, but he felt sure that it was. Holding Sage in his arms in the lake, with the other man wrapped around him, trusting him, was barely different than curling together in the bed. And yet, it had felt profound in a way Conrad couldn't explain. The way their voices had been mere whispers in the dark as they exchanged bits of themselves had felt more vulnerable than any of their previous confessions. And now, with Sage sitting beside him at breakfast, Conrad found his fondness for the man growing even more. It made him oddly wistful in a way that he had never before experienced.

He was worried about what lay before him when he eventually left the safety of the house party—details and questions that he felt sure he ought to have worked out prior to leaving Bristol. How was he going to get to London? Where was he going to live? What would he do before the Council convened in the autumn? He had settled on a vague plan of seeking out the docks in London and finding work until the rest of the Council returned.

Conrad now found himself adding Sage to his questions about the future. Would they see each other in London? Would Sage want to continue the closeness of this friendship back in the city that housed his scandalous reputation when they were no longer pretending to be an item? And come to think of that, Conrad had to admit to himself that there was very little pretense on his part. He had never lied to Sage, or anyone else, beyond some hints at activity that wasn't actually happening. His affection for the other man was genuine. He had a feeling that Sage was no more pretending than he was, but he was unsure of how far that extended. What would their friendship look like when they were in London?

He sipped his tea and glanced at his companion. The wistfulness was a new feeling for him—not one that brought an excess of melancholy, as Conrad rarely tended towards such moodiness. But he couldn't shake the feeling that sleeping alone would be much lonelier than it ever had been before. He would miss the weight of Sage pressed up against him when they were no longer sharing a bed. He would miss the smell of rose and almond as he undressed for the evening. He would miss whispered secrets, the way Sage's laughter always seemed to take him by surprise, and the taste of Sage's lips on his own.

He'd had a number of friends with whom he'd shared kisses and bedsport, but none whose trust felt as fragile and precious. As much as Conrad prided himself on his kindness and generosity, he wasn't sure there was anyone else he'd ever met for whom he'd have prioritized cleaning a cravat in the middle of the night over going to bed. And yet...he would do it all over again, and gladly. Although, he thought, as he smiled into his tea, perhaps with less catastrophic muddiness.

As if he'd read his mind, Roger stood and said that he was going to get the study prepared for more castings.

Harriet groaned. "See you in a few days," she said gloomily.

"We went to the lake together yesterday!" Roger protested.

Wyndham stood as well and put a hand to Roger's lower back. "This project might take us a couple of days. Perhaps we can offer you something in exchange."

Harriet's expression grew shrewd. "Such as?"

Wyndham grinned and his gaze flicked over to Sage and Conrad. "It's been a while since we had a riddle night. We can plan for one tomorrow."

Harriet clapped her hands together. "Capital! That will give me two whole days to find the perfect one." She looked positively wicked in a way that did not bode well for poor Roger's sensibilities.

Conrad chuckled and stood, reaching for Sage's hand when he stood, as well.

"You're taking Mr. Ravenwing with you, too!" Harriet pouted. "I call that too bad."

Sage looked taken aback to be included. Wyndham brushed past them, with Roger in tow. "You will be far too busy finding the most salacious riddle for us," he said. "And it wouldn't do for you to have our two riddle champions on the loose. They might get a hint."

"Mmm," she said. "True."

Fern laughed and kissed Harriet on the cheek.

Cyril shook his head. "You are incorrigible."

"Nonsense," she said primly. "You love it."

Conrad followed his hosts out of the room, up the stairs, and into the study. As Wyndham walked into the space, the lights blazed brighter and a wind pushed past the curtains, bringing in a wave of fresh air. Sage's soiled clothes were where they had left them. The towels and Conrad's clothes had been removed. Roger explained apologetically that he'd handed them over to the staff so they didn't get ruined by sitting overnight.

Conrad assured him it was perfectly fine. "These items are the ones of importance anyway." He held up the waistcoat and examined it, helped by the better lighting. "I can see what you meant about the staining here," he said to Sage.

Roger ripped off a piece of spellpaper and handed it over. The pencil from the previous night was still on the floor, along with the ingredients Conrad had used. He laughed when he saw that an additional one had been placed next to the rest. He scooped up the head of cabbage and tossed it up and caught it. "Now I can prove to you how useful it is."

Sage wrinkled his nose as he sat on the chaise lounge. "Such a strange creature."

Conrad grinned and looked down at the vegetable. "Although, I confess I've never used a fresh one. We usually boil them first. It works for dinner and casting."

Roger hummed and bent over his desk to make a note.

"It wouldn't be bad for you to use the raw materials too," Wyndham reasoned. "I can see to it that it isn't too powerful."

Conrad breathed out in relief. "That will do nicely, thank you. Shall we start with the spell I used last night then? And move on to the raw materials after?" With the rest of the group's agreement, he set the cabbage aside and began preparing. It felt strange to be casting the spell again, with less urgency and a great deal more eyes on him.

"Why don't we do one article of clothing at a time?" Wyndham suggested. "That way we can draw out the project for longer."

"And we can always get more items from the staff," Roger added.

Conrad placed the waistcoat on the paper and cast. As soon as he was done, he picked it up and checked over where he'd seen the slight stain before. He passed it to Sage for approval. Sage looked over it with painstaking care. Then he folded it onto his lap and nodded, a small smile at the corner of his lips.

Conrad beamed. "Glad it passed muster."

Sage's smile grew slightly. *I trust you.* The words were not spoken out loud, but Conrad felt them in the smile. Sage's trust felt all the more precious knowing that it was a secret between them. His chest warmed at the thought and he moved on to the next article of clothing.

Wyndham took a seat on the chaise lounge beside Sage, crossing one knee elegantly over the other and leaning his elbow against the arm rest. "One thing that never fails to fascinate me is the way that every person's magic has such a unique personality. I find that raw materials bring this out more when it comes to human magic. Why don't you try the cabbage on this next casting, Conrad? That way Sage can feel what your magic is like when you use it."

Conrad looked up to see Sage's startled expression. For all his work with the councilmembers, he and Sage had barely spoken about magic. He had no idea if Sage had felt it or, frankly, had any opinion on it—aside from a teasing snobbery about some ingredients. He also had no idea how to adjust the calculations when it came to fresh cabbage. He glanced at Roger. "I might need a bit of help with that, if you don't mind."

Roger grinned, ever happy to be of assistance, and bustled over, grabbing three books on his way. They both knelt on the floor together, and discussed the value of one sigil over the other, whether certain calculations might be better suited to such a plain item, and how much magic a cabbage could provide in the first place.

At length, they agreed upon a strategy and Conrad bent over a fresh spellpaper to prepare everything. Sage and Wyndham had remained silent throughout the exchange, but as Conrad wrote down the necessary pieces, Wyndham turned to Sage. "Remarkable, isn't it? Human magic is surprisingly complex."

Sage gave Wyndham a wary look and then shrugged. "I'm sure I wouldn't bother if I had to go through all that every time I needed to cast a spell."

Wyndham laughed. "You get used to it. Roger is quite brilliant when it comes to this sort of thing. The sheer knowledge he holds in his head is astounding."

Roger blushed, but looked undeniably pleased by the compliment.

Sage cleared his throat. "Indeed. Roger is probably one of the cleverest people I've ever met."

Conrad felt as though a sliver of tension in the room that he hadn't even been aware of fizzled out with Sage's words. Wyndham relaxed and bounced one foot idly. "Agreed. Although I'm pleased to note that there isn't a single person in this house who is foolish. It's nice to know we've surrounded ourselves with intelligent friends."

Sage swallowed and clasped his hands in his lap, on top of the folded waistcoat. "Yes," he said softly.

Conrad stole a look at Roger, who gave him a

small secret smile, and then he bent over the paper to hide his own grin. When he was satisfied with what he'd written and Roger had checked over his work, Conrad sat back on his heels. "Right," he said. "Ready?"

Chapter 27
Sage

Sage fretted at his jacket where it sat crumpled in the middle of Conrad's spellpaper, surrounded by the lines he had drawn, the dry ingredients he'd measured out, and the single leaf of cabbage sitting ominously in one corner. It was not his most favorite jacket, not even close, but he felt as though he was about to watch it burst into flames. No matter how much confidence any of them had in Conrad's ability to perform the spell, Sage could not forget the word he'd used to describe raw ingredients: volatile.

Conrad sat back with his hands on his knees. "Right. Ready?"

Sage made a strangled sort of sound and sat forward. "Are we certain nothing is going to happen to my coat?"

Wyndham arched a brow at him. "Aside from being cleaner than you found it? Unlikely. But perhaps you

would be more comfortable if Conrad practiced on
something else the first time?"

Sage nodded, offering an apologetic look to
Conrad. He did not seem to take any offense to the
suggestion.

Wyndham stood gracefully from the chaise lounge
and pulled an embroidered handkerchief from his
breast pocket, shaking it out by the corner. Sage
recognized it as the kind he had always used. After
perusing the top of Roger's desk, he found a pot of
ink and promptly dipped one corner of the
handkerchief into it, spoiling the fabric. After folding
it over twice in his palm, he gave the entire thing a
squeeze. By the time he handed it to Conrad, it had
the look of a terrier's coat, white with multiple large,
uneven black patches.

"That ought to do nicely," Wyndham said as he
resumed his position on the chaise beside Sage.
"Let's see it, then."

Conrad moved the jacket aside and replaced it
with the handkerchief.

"The smaller bulk of the fabric should matter
little in this case," Roger reassured him. "You'll need
the extra power with something as staining as ink."

"Spoken from experience," Wyndham added.

Roger flapped a hand in his direction. "Go on,
Conrad."

Conrad cast his spell. Sage watched intently,
hands pressed together and tucked between his
thighs as he leaned closer to watch. The blots of ink
faded from black to a light gray shade. He shifted his

attention to Conrad's face to determine if he was pleased with the outcome or not. It was difficult to tell, as he had been smiling from start to finish.

"Well done!" Roger patted Conrad's shoulder before looking up at his husband, pushing his spectacles up his nose. "How did it feel?"

"Solid." Wyndham angled his chin up at the paper. "You'll be able to cast at least once more." The cabbage leaf had shriveled some, looking wilted and slightly brown around the edges.

"Amazing," Conrad said, wasting no time. He repeated his spell and produced a crisp, white handkerchief, likely cleaner than it had been since before the first time it was used. Conrad let out a short laugh of delight and held it up for all of them to see. Sage couldn't help but grin at his excitement.

"I'm sorry I ever doubted you," he said.

Conrad was on his feet in a blink, already handing the handkerchief back to Wyndham. "I believe the mistrust was more on the cabbage than it was on me."

Sage hoped the way he pushed his fingers back through his hair disguised the way his shoulders shook with a silent laugh. The man's confidence was endless, even in front of two people as powerful as Wyndham and Roger. It was incredibly endearing.

"I'm sorry I ever doubted the cabbage, then."

"I am certain it forgives you," Conrad told him with a wink as he ripped another piece of paper to size. The warmth from earlier swirled in Sage's chest again. He all but forgot about the grin on his lips until he caught Wyndham staring at him with a smirk of his own. Sage straightened and tried to focus again as Conrad prepared to clean his jacket.

"Were you able to feel the difference in his magic?"

"I was not trying," Sage told him stubbornly.

Conrad made a sound of interest, though he did not look up from whatever he was busy writing. "So you can sense magic, as well?"

Sage shifted on his seat. "Modestly." What came so easily to someone like Wyndham required effort on his part.

"Try it this time," Wyndham said, leaving no room for argument. "I would be interested to see what you think. A new perspective." The intensity of what had remained unsaid about Sage's magic seemed to fade as Wyndham turned his focus back to the research he and Roger had been doing. The request was simple enough. Sage nodded his agreement.

With a slow exhale, he reached out with his magic as Conrad cast again. Those lazy, golden tendrils he'd felt in his chest before became a fountain of sunny warmth, filling every empty space within him until he gasped. Sage had the distinct feeling he'd experienced something similar once before, but that he'd been too distracted to take notice. The whole thing was over in a matter of seconds. It left Sage staggering.

His jacket was better than new—vibrant and soft, entirely free of mud, just as promised. Conrad was the only one looking at it, though. Roger and Wyndham spied Sage expectantly.

"Well?" Roger encouraged, eyes wide. "How did it feel?"

Sage's mouth had gone dry. "Powerful," he managed.

"Clearly!" Conrad was still admiring his work on the garment, holding it close to his face. "And that was in one go! I'm almost sorry I already cleaned the rest of your clothes last night, Sage. I wish to do all of them this way."

Wyndham chuckled. "There is plenty of time for the two of you to find more ways to befoul your clothes."

Sage considered challenging the notion of them seeking out more opportunities to potentially ruin his wardrobe, but he found he did not have the strength nor the heart to deny Conrad of something that thrilled him so. Instead, he accepted his jacket when it was handed to him and watched as the spell was performed on his muddy trousers to an equal effect.

Afterwards, Roger spent some time asking Conrad questions and taking detailed notes, each of them kindling the other's interest in the topic until they began repeating themselves with even bigger smiles. Wyndham had picked up a book off the side table and was reading with a satisfied grin. Sage felt terribly out of place, but he did not want to interrupt to tell them he was leaving. He held his clean clothes against his chest with one arm and wandered the study as he waited, inspecting the shelves and tamping his magic when it swirled each time Conrad laughed behind him.

When it finally sounded like their conversation was coming to an end, Wyndham snapped his book shut and set it aside, standing up off the chaise with that same smug grin.

"Roger," he began thoughtfully, gaining his husband's attention. "I do believe we should continue this experimentation tomorrow. As you said before, it is rare that we've had the opportunity to work with new subjects on this raw materials project thus far. If Conrad and Sage are open to it, I would like to see them cast together."

Roger was giddy at the idea.

Conrad and Sage exchanged a look. He had never seen a pair of soft brown eyes filled with such hope before. This was everything he wanted. It was what Sage had agreed to offer in their arrangement—to show the rest of the Council that Conrad could work closely with fae, and that he was more than capable of handling whatever they asked of him, despite his modest upbringing.

How could he refuse?

Sage relented with a nod, and Conrad closed the distance between them in a single leap, placing his hand on the back of Sage's neck so that he could pull him down for a chaste kiss on the cheek. Roger and Conrad exited the study together, leaving Sage and Wyndham alone.

He knew exactly what he was doing by asking Sage to use his magic with Conrad's again. It was obvious now that he had known from the moment Conrad explained what happened at the lake. His reaction to Conrad's cleaning spell only confirmed it. Was this retribution for what Sage had done to Roger? Another chance for Wyndham to prove how cold he could be?

Wyndham studied him for a moment and then smoothed a hand down the front of his waistcoat, before he gestured out the open door in the direction Roger and Conrad had gone. His explanation was simple, yet heavy.

"Now do you understand?"

Chapter 28
Conrad

Conrad's body was still buzzing with excitement from the spells he'd performed. He had gotten to know everyone well enough that he no longer believed he was experiencing good luck. Roger and Wyndham would not have suggested he and Sage perform magic together if they weren't truly interested, if they didn't believe it would be valuable or worth their time. He and Roger continued their conversation for hours, discussing different spells Conrad and Sage might try, what ingredients would be best to use, and how much time they could devote to the project now and how much ought to wait until London.

It was all Conrad could think about for the remainder of the day. When he and Sage were back in their room, getting ready for bed, Conrad continued to chatter excitedly about the possibilities. As he pulled back the coverlet, he realized that Sage had barely spoken.

"Are you all right?"

"Of course," Sage said crisply as he slipped out of his robe.

Conrad frowned, watching Sage slide under the sheets. "What's wrong?"

"Nothing." Sage met his concerned expression and sighed. "Nothing is wrong. I...I am not as strong with my magic as Wyndham, or Emrys, or even Keelan." The words were said quietly. Another whispered confession.

Conrad relaxed. "My magic is certainly not as strong as Roger's. And it is incomparable to Torquil's and Silas'. They don't want to watch us because our magic is powerful. I rather think it would be better for them to see a range of power anyway. We shall be a better indication of what they can expect of the general populace."

"I suppose." Sage hadn't moved from the other side of the bed, so Conrad turned on his side to look at him.

"How did the spell feel?" He'd been wondering about it for hours, but hadn't had a chance to ask the question. He felt himself holding his breath, waiting for the answer.

Sage licked his lips before responding. "As I said before, it was powerful."

Conrad laughed. "I cannot feel magic at all. I demand a better description than that. What does magic feel like to you?"

Sage turned on his side to face him, but kept his

eyes angled down. "I think I can better explain it in contrast to how my magic usually feels. It is normally a sensation in my chest, a light presence, tendrils reaching outward."

Conrad nodded, encouraging him to continue.

"When you cast your cleaning spell, I felt as though the warmth in my chest was filling my entire body. So when I say it was powerful, I mean that I could feel it everywhere. It was strong. Solid, as Wyndham said." He finally looked up. "I've never felt anything like it."

The words were said quietly and Conrad was familiar enough with his friend's moods to recognize that there was some unspoken emotion underneath the confession. But he couldn't place what the emotion was. He worried that it might be fear. He didn't want any part of him to frighten Sage. He also felt as though Sage was holding back more words and he didn't know what to do to encourage him to say the rest.

But then Sage reached out and stroked Conrad's cheek with the backs of his fingers. "You're remarkable, you know," he said softly.

Conrad smiled and caught Sage's hand in his own, placing a kiss on his knuckles. "Thank you," he whispered.

"Still strange, though," Sage added with a smirk.

Conrad laughed, slipped an arm around Sage's waist, and tugged him closer. "Thank you for telling me."

Sage closed the distance between them with a kiss. It was soft and sweet. Then he leaned his forehead against Conrad's. "Just rein in your expectations for tomorrow. I mean it when I say my magic is not strong. It will be nothing like Roger and Wyndham's breeze spell."

Conrad cupped his cheek. "Remember what I've told you? Whatever you have to offer, Sage, it's enough."

. ˙. . ˙

The next day, Sage joined Conrad for breakfast again. Conrad did his best to stifle a grin at having the man by his side at the table. He and Roger picked up the conversation where they had left off the previous day. Roger explained which ingredients he had prepared for their project, and they discussed which spell ought to be done first. Torquil joined in to give their opinion and express interest in the results. Sage was silent throughout the meal, but Conrad suspected it was due to nerves about his magic.

When Wyndham stood and said it was time to return to the study, Sage quietly accepted Conrad's hand and followed him up the stairs. Once the door clicked shut behind them, Roger clapped his hands together and launched straight into a little speech.

"Conrad and I have agreed that levitation will be a good start. It's something of a straightforward spell, more specific than a breeze spell. And Sage can help buoy the item with his own magic." He smiled at Sage as he said this.

"You can use wind currents to do that," Wyndham added.

Roger continued, "We'll use a handkerchief to start, which should keep anything extreme from happening, but Wyndham will be monitoring everything just in case. Any questions?" He glanced between them both.

Sage pressed his lips together for a moment. "Will Conrad be using raw ingredients again?"

Roger seemed delighted by the question. "Yes! We've found that raw ingredients work best for collaborative casting. The magic in the item is such that the fae participant can more easily access it. And as you've seen, it strengthens the power of the spell for the human, as well."

Sage nodded.

"And I thought it might be best for you to cast on the desk instead of the floor," Roger went on. "Easier for Sage to see your work, and then he can stand next to you. That sometimes helps."

Conrad cheerfully went to the desk and began writing out the sigils to the levitation spell. As he was using fresh clover instead of the powdered variety, he added the Bokemann Modulation to reduce everything in the spell. Then he glanced at Roger to look over his work.

Roger came forward eagerly. "I really appreciate how clean your work is. You don't add two sigils when one will do. You don't overcomplicate things. Your approach to magic is very concise."

Conrad tried not to puff out his chest at the praise. "Thank you."

"Perhaps you ought to feel out with your magic before Conrad casts, Sage," Wyndham said. "See if you can get a feel for the spell now. Familiarity with the setup will make it easier to integrate your own magic later."

Sage was tense beside Conrad, but he nodded his understanding. His focus seemed to go inward for a moment and his jaw tightened. He gave a slight nod.

Conrad took it as his cue and cast. The handkerchief flew to the ceiling. Conrad laughed. "Well, we know it was effective."

Wyndham studied it for a moment. "Indeed. It could probably do with further reduction next time. Sage, see if you can press the handkerchief downward with your magic."

A muscle in Sage's jaw ticked a little as he complied. The handkerchief bobbed a bit. Sage made a frustrated sound at the back of his throat and the handkerchief bobbed again.

Wyndham hummed. "Perhaps a different tactic. Working against Conrad's magic may not be the best choice, now that I think about it. Let's get your magics to work together. See if you can move it across the room, since Conrad's magic is keeping it afloat."

Sage took a deep breath and the handkerchief began to drift to the side. Conrad gasped in delight.

"Keep going," Wyndham murmured.

The handkerchief continued to move. Then it went from inching slowly across the top of the room to shooting across with as much speed as it had gone up. When Conrad's spell finally lost power and the handkerchief flopped down to the ground, Sage was breathing heavily.

"All right?" Conrad asked him with a hand on his arm.

Sage nodded, but his gaze was locked on Wyndham.

Wyndham smirked. "Interesting what happens to magic when it combines with another person's, isn't it?"

"I was having difficulty following along," Roger admitted. "What happened? Why did it start off so slowly?"

Wyndham didn't respond, waiting for Sage to answer. Sage swallowed. "At first, I tried to move the handkerchief independently of Conrad's spell. It's the only way I've ever used my magic. But then I felt out for Conrad's magic and was able to...weave the power he had put into the spell into what I was doing."

Roger grinned. "Delightful! Shall we try again with the same spell or something different?"

"You can decide," Sage said to Conrad without looking at him.

Conrad wanted to pull the other man into his arms and tell him he was doing marvelously. But Sage was keeping his emotions under guard.

Wyndham seemed to be studying the other fae with as much focus.

"Let's try this one again once more," Conrad said.

"Excellent," Roger said. "Since your spellpaper is so clean, you should be able to use it all again."

Wyndham plucked the handkerchief off the ground and handed it over. Conrad placed the handkerchief in the center of the paper again and glanced at Sage. "Ready?"

Chapter 29
Sage

Sage was not at all ready.

He'd barely managed to catch his breath when Conrad cast again, sending Wyndham's handkerchief soaring over their heads. He scrambled to reach out after it with his magic, finding it slightly easier to tangle it with the other man's this time as it swirled through the air. With their combined efforts, they pinned the square of embroidered silk flat against the ceiling and held it there.

"Less power, both of you," Wyndham instructed, his throat working attractively over his words as he stared up at their work.

Conrad bent over his paper and scribbled some adjustments. The handkerchief fluttered and sank in the air. Sage was able to settle his magic just enough to make it happen again, until the item of everyone's focus was levitating over the desk at chest height before it dropped lifelessly back to where it began in the middle of Conrad's paper.

Sage stared at the bundle of fabric. Not once in his entire life had he been told to use *less* power with his magic. In school, it had always been the opposite. *Try harder*, his instructors had always said, *you can do better than that.*

Suddenly, Conrad's hand was gripped tightly on his arm again, squeezing just above his elbow as he bounced on his toes.

"Sage, this is extraordinary! I've never done anything like this before. Even casting with Wyndham did not make my magic so strong. I cannot believe it!"

Those words cut through Sage like a knife through butter, melting him just the same. He had to brace himself with one hand on the edge of Roger's desk as he tried to breathe normally again. To his immense relief, Conrad was too preoccupied suggesting another spell he would like to try to notice his discomfiture. Roger told him they should go and have a look in the garden for a particular type of parsley to experiment with, and the duo were gone in a flurry.

As soon as their footsteps had quieted in the hallway, Sage collapsed against the desk where he stood, forehead against one arm as he smacked his fist against the workspace with the other, rattling some of the items around him. He let out a low moan of distress and squeezed his eyes shut.

Wyndham laughed like the villain he was.

Sage lifted his head just enough to glare at him.

"Think it's amusing, do you?"

Wyndham had his arms crossed loosely over his chest.

"A little, yes."

"Dratted imp," Sage cursed him.

He righted himself to mostly standing again, both hands on the lip of the desk this time. Thoughts of Conrad served as such a distraction that every issue he'd ever had with Wyndham seemed to disappear, leaving behind only the familiarity that had existed between them for so many years.

"This is what you feel with Roger," he guessed, staring out into the hallway.

"It is," Wyndham agreed sedately.

Sage shook his head before giving him a desperate look. "And he cannot even feel it. Can Roger feel it? Your magic?"

"To some degree, he can." Wyndham took a few steps closer to the desk. "Human magic is unique to each person, much like our own."

"You know my magic is not strong," Sage said in a hushed tone. "How could he possibly think that casting with me was better than with you?"

"Because it was." Wyndham's shoulders moved in a delicate shrug. "My magic might be more powerful than yours, but that says nothing about compatibility."

Sage groaned and stood fully, pushing a hand back through his hair in frustration. "Compatibility," he grumbled.

"I think you can hardly deny it," Wyndham said

smoothly, eyes dipping to the front of Sage's trousers with a smirk. Sage rolled his eyes and tugged at the fabric there, a weak attempt at adjusting himself. There was no use trying to hide it —Wyndham had seen him in such a state more than any other. "If you'd like, I can tell them you had a personal matter to attend to when they return."

Sage narrowed his eyes and offered him a tight grin.

"How thoughtful of you."

Wyndham sauntered to his throne and settled himself against the pillows on the chaise lounge, ankles crossed as he picked up his book from the day before. "You would not be the first man so overwhelmed by compatible magic that you had to excuse yourself for a time."

Sage's brows went up but then settled. He snorted at the confession, observing the elegant seat where Wyndham had placed himself. There was no question that the chaise in the study had been his idea, and likely for more than sitting comfortably to read or watch Roger work.

"I'll wager you do no such thing."

Wyndham peered at him over the pages of his book. Sage could practically feel how hard he was working to come up with a clever response. Unfortunately, being crass with his words was one area where Wyndham had always fallen short.

"You're right," he said finally, returning to his novel. "This is my house. I have no reason to excuse myself, if I do not wish to do so."

Before Sage could give any thought to that particular fancy, Conrad returned and the room lightened instantly, as did the magic in his chest. Somewhere along the way, Roger had found a small basket to help carry all of the leaves and herbs they'd collected in the garden.

"What do you not wish to do?" Roger set their spoils on his desk with little care, some dirt falling through the loose weave of the basket.

Conrad brushed at the mess with his hand as he came to stand beside Sage again. He offered a smile and Sage returned it, secretly pleased that it felt so natural for him to return to his side.

"I was only telling Sage that I do not wish to lose another round of charades this evening," Wyndham said casually as he turned a page. "So you'll have to excuse me if I reduce myself to our current champions' level of propriety in order to give the correct answer."

"Oh dear," Roger sighed.

"Not to worry." Conrad wrapped his arm around Sage's waist and pulled him close. Sage's heart tumbled. "Wyndham has no chance at winning when the two of us are working together."

Behind his book, Wyndham was smiling.

Chapter 30
Conrad

Conrad thought that working with Roger and Wyndham had been enjoyable before. But it turned out to be nowhere near as fun as when Sage joined. This was partly because Conrad's magic was so much more powerful when he cast along with Sage. He couldn't understand it, but he didn't entirely mind the mystery of it either. He knew it wasn't because Sage was fae; Wyndham was fae and Conrad's spells had not turned out like that with him. Conrad privately liked that Sage was the one who had such an effect. Considering his confession the night before, it felt right that Sage would get to be a part of something like this, to prove in a tangible way that he was more than how he thought of himself—even down to his magic.

Conrad found it all a good deal more fun too because he'd come to realize that he missed Sage when they were split up for a day. It was nice to have him by his side at the desk. It was nice to see him using magic, for all that Conrad couldn't feel it, he could see it. And he liked having Sage be a part of his Council work, even to a degree. A selfish part of him hoped that it would mean he'd get to see Sage more when they returned to London.

The levitation spell was not the only point of success. With Roger and Wyndham's help, Conrad and Sage performed a breeze spell, a cleaning spell, and even a fire spell. Conrad felt some slight disappointment at not being able to feel any of the magic happening before him, as the others could. But he could tell that the magic was sharper and more powerful. All of his spells seemed bolder than when he did them alone. It was a heady feeling.

They worked all day and by the time dinner was called, Conrad was torn between being ready for a break and wanting to work into the night. Roger chuckled at his expression as they filed out of the study. "I know the feeling," he said. "It is exhilarating working with another person."

Conrad grinned and glanced at Sage, reaching for his hand. "It is. I've never known anything like it. I could do this for days."

Sage wrinkled his nose. "Considering how much work you need to do for every spell, I cannot imagine you continuing longer. You'd collapse."

Conrad squeezed his hand. "You're right. It's probably just as well that we're pausing, isn't it?"

Sage nodded. "You missed lunch."

Conrad couldn't hide the smile that took over his

face. They had all missed lunch, but Sage was only thinking of him. "It wouldn't be the first time I missed a meal for work."

That set Sage's mouth into a grim line. "Yes, well, we've already established that you haven't been properly cared for in the past. There's no need to continue that pattern now."

Warmth blossomed in Conrad's chest at the words. He half wished they were alone so he could pull Sage close and discover the meaning behind the words. Did Sage intend to continue seeing him, looking after him, caring for him after the party was over? Since he couldn't ask, he tried for levity. "My hero."

Sage snorted and rolled his eyes. Roger and Wyndham exchanged a look that was undeniably smug.

Dinner was a lively affair. Roger and Conrad both answered a multitude of questions regarding what had kept them in the study for two days straight. Wyndham chimed in a fair amount, but Sage remained tight-lipped, only responding when he was directly asked a question. Conrad had no idea why he was still uncomfortable about the situation, but he took care to step in and answer for Sage whenever possible. He could feel Sage relax beside him when the attention was effectively deflected, but Conrad didn't let him off the hook entirely—he was eloquent in how impressed he was by Sage's magic and his impact on Conrad's magic. Thankfully, most of the people at the table seemed unsurprised by this, although there were more knowing looks exchanged that made Conrad certain he was missing some sort of valuable information.

The conversation flowed to how some of the other pairs had found their spells affected by working with their spouse. It made Conrad feel as if he was getting closer to the mystery, but just barely out of his grasp. He didn't dare ask though, for fear of making Sage go tense again. He was relaxed now that the focus had moved on to others.

When they gathered in the sitting room for the promised game, Sage took a seat on a settee, and pulled Conrad to his side. Conrad felt ready to burst with pride at seeing Sage sitting amongst the group. As soon as everyone settled down, Harriet arched an eyebrow and held her book up.

"I don't think I need to give the usual warning here," she said.

"No," Wyndham agreed. "We all know you've picked the most salacious option possible. We have all brought our figurative smelling salts." He wrapped an arm around Roger's shoulders as if to prove the point.

Harriet laughed, straightened, and then cleared her throat performatively.

> "We are feeling magnanimous indeed,
> For here are two hints for the first word
> of three:
> Think first of a point of a dagger or
> sword,

If that does not suit, imagine pouring
    something onto the floor.
But there is one item that you need not
    fear should fall,
It is of soft and heavy drape, be it used
    on rod, or dress, or curtain call."

"That rhyming should please you, Keelan," Emrys said, laughing.

Keelan tilted his chin up. "The rhyming was sufficient, but the rhythm was—" The other man cajoled him teasingly.

"Did I miss something?" Lady Imogen asked. "There are three words, but I only heard two hints. Well, two hints for one word, and one hint for another. What of the third word?"

"Perhaps the third word is simple enough that we don't need a hint," Fern offered.

"Or perhaps we'll know the third word when we get the first two," Cyril said.

Lady Imogen harrumphed a bit. "I think that's silly."

Lady Anthea patted her arm. "Let's take it in pieces anyway. Repeat the first hint, Harriet."

Harriet gave her a quelling look. "Repeat the first hint, Harriet, please."

Anthea rolled her eyes. "Oh, for goodness' sake. Please give us the first hint of this undoubtedly scandalous riddle again so you can watch us grapple together."

"That's better," Harriet said pertly. "Just because

you're a lady now, Anthea, doesn't mean you needn't abide by rules of politeness."

"Are you really chiding Anthea on politeness?" Roger asked. "Given what you're making us do right now?"

Harriet didn't respond to that, instead repeating the first part of the riddle.

"The point of a sword?" Keelan repeated. "Isn't that just...the point?"

"The blade perhaps?" Cyril offered.

"But you wouldn't call a blade something you pour on the floor," Sage argued.

"I don't think the second hint is the thing we're pouring onto the floor," Conrad said, bringing his hand to Sage's lap. "I think it's another word for pouring something."

"Yes, Sage," Emrys said.

Sage narrowed his eyes. "Don't pretend you knew that."

Torquil laughed and patted Emrys' knee. "Right, so we need to find a word that fits both, yes?"

"A blade and to pour?" Cyril asked, frowning. "There's no such word."

"Let's get away from blade," Wyndham said. "It clearly isn't that."

"A...prick?" Fern asked hopefully. Harriet threw back her head and laughed. "That would be a no then," they said cheerfully.

"Oh, but it was worth it to hear you say that," Harriet said, wiping fake tears from her eyes.

"To stab!" Cyril shouted.

"No, no," Roger said, "you don't stab something onto the floor."

"Well," Torquil drawled, "you do sometimes."

"I can stab you onto the floor tonight, if you'd like," Emrys said with a waggle of his eyebrows.

Wyndham groaned.

"Sounds messy," Cyril said with distaste.

Silas snorted into Keelan's shoulder.

"I think we should focus on the next part," Sage said.

"Agreed. The two hints are confusing us too much," Conrad said, smiling at him.

"Our champions have spoken," Wyndham intoned. "Please read the last hint again, Harriet."

"With pleasure, Wyndham."

"Right, so heavy fabric," Conrad muttered after she finished.

"And used for curtain calls?" Roger asked.

"The theater," Sage explained. "Velvet."

And then, as one, Conrad and Sage shouted, "Tip the velvet!"

Harriet cackled. "Yes!"

"You can't pretend you couldn't know that one," Emrys said to the Ladies Fitzhugh with a smirk.

"Tip!" Keelan said after a long moment. "The tip of the blade and to tip something onto the floor. I get it now."

"How is that salacious?" Cyril asked with a frown.

Fern chuckled. "I'll explain it to you later."

Harriet gave another hoot of laughter and Cyril

turned bright red when he seemed to realize what sort of an explanation that was bound to be.

"Right," Roger said loudly. "On that note, we really ought to go to bed now."

"Indeed," Emrys drawled. "What a good note to end on. Harriet, my congratulations. We ought to end every evening with suggestions for what to do after."

"Do not encourage her," Roger groaned.

Everyone began to get up and file out of the room. Conrad turned to Sage with a grin. "Still the reigning champions of salacious riddles," he said.

"Mm. It's nice to have something to one's name, I suppose."

Chapter 31
Sage

The sound of bedroom doors closing with varying amounts of enthusiasm echoed through the hall. Sage sighed in relief when Conrad shut theirs behind them, blocking out the rest of the world until morning. He was thoroughly exhausted from using his magic so much in one day. Not only was he physically spent, but his chest felt as though it had been trampled on after experiencing such wild emotions. As much as he wanted to crawl into bed and fall asleep, he knew he would be thankful in the early hours if he pampered himself with his familiar nighttime routine first.

Sage set the glass he'd brought along down on the vanity and began to undress. There were still a couple sips of wine left and he didn't want to waste them.

"Another rose and almond night, is it?" Conrad was sitting on the edge of the bed, removing his shoes. Usually he would kick them off with little care where they ended up. Perhaps he was feeling the effects of their day in the study, as well.

"It helps me relax," Sage explained. There were other far more vain reasons for it too, of course, but he had a feeling they would not matter very much to his companion. "Do you mind?"

"Not at all. I've come to enjoy it a great deal, actually." Conrad's grin bunched to one side, almost sheepishly. "I doubt I'll ever be able to catch a whiff of the combination again and not think of you."

Sage hummed softly, turning away to hide the curve of his own lips as he sat on the ottoman to pull his trousers the rest of the way off, leaving him in only his shirt and stockings. He turned back to study Conrad for a moment.

"Why don't you try it?" he asked.

Conrad's forehead wrinkled.

"I cannot have you waste your nice things on me."

"It would be no waste, I assure you." He stood and gestured to the ottoman. "Come and sit down." Conrad eyed him warily. "Please? It will make me happy."

"Oh, all right." He tucked everything but the trousers he was still wearing into his bag and pushed it under his side of the bed. The way he flumped onto the low seat told Sage he really needed no assistance in feeling relaxed enough to fall asleep within minutes, either, but the idea of applying the oil on Conrad's tired, handsome face was suddenly the only thing he wanted to do.

"Wine?" Sage held the glass out for him after taking a sip. They'd shared it during the game of charades as well, passing it back and forth like it was something they'd been doing for years.

"Thank you." Conrad accepted it and drained the last in one swallow.

"Excuse me," Sage protested. "I did not mean for you to finish it."

Conrad chuckled and leaned forward to set the empty glass down. "You already had most of it downstairs. Would you like me to go and ask for more?"

Sage grinned and shook his head as he reached for his jar of oil.

"That's quite all right," he said primly. "The last thing I need is to add a headache to what I'm already sure to feel in the morning after today's activities." With a small amount of the oil in one palm, he set the bottle down and rubbed his hands together a couple of times. "It might be easier if you close your eyes."

Conrad did as he was told.

"I am glad it's not just me," he confessed as Sage swept his fingers gently across his cheeks, first out and then back together at his nose.

"You seemed eager enough to continue."

Sage was standing behind Conrad, watching in the reflection of the mirror as his hands moved in delicate strokes, gliding his fingertips up Conrad's nose and over the creases of his forehead before finishing at his jaw and starting the methodical process all over again.

"Sometimes it is difficult to quit something you enjoy."

"Indeed," Sage murmured.

The glow of the candles sitting at the corner of the dressing table did a great kindness to Conrad's figure, and Sage found that he could not pass up the opportunity to admire him in the soft, golden light.

There was no denying he was attractive. But as he allowed his admiration to wander, Sage realized that those parts of Conrad had become captivating in entirely new ways. These were the brawny arms that held him at the lake; the ones he slept soundly in each night. His broad shoulders were where he rested his cheek in the silent hours of the morning when it was just the two of them. Those rough hands folded together on the vanity were the same ones that had been reaching for his own with increasing frequency over the last several days.

When his eyes dipped lower, Sage forced his attention back to Conrad's face, which had gone slack under his touch. Even though it was exactly what he'd expected to happen, it still pulled a gentle laugh from him.

"It appears you have found something else to enjoy."

Conrad let out a long, serene moan.

"I certainly do not want it to end," he mumbled. "Nothing could possibly feel better than this."

Sage's expression softened, despite the way his magic swirled in his chest. Had life treated him so harshly that a splash of oil and a little rubbing could bring him such pleasure? Sage's hands slowed as his lips curved into a frown. He supposed he was equally as easy to please, all things considered.

"I knew you would find it agreeable."

A short silence stretched between them until Conrad spoke again.

"It seems I am not privy to an entirely different sort of satisfaction, thanks to my inability to feel magic. Before our discussion at dinner this evening, I had no idea I was missing out on so much."

Sage had to close his eyes against the tone of Conrad's voice. So rarely did he sound disappointed. It was difficult to hear.

"Everyone's abilities are different," he said, trying his best to sound supportive, just as Conrad had done for him in so many of their private conversations. The party really had done a terrible job of being inclusive of those who were not as magically powerful, though. All they could talk about was how incredible it was to feel a connection with someone else on such a deep level. And of course Wyndham and Roger—plus the others when they eventually caught on—made pointed comments about it in Sage's direction. It had been obvious that Conrad did not understand, and he couldn't decide if that was better or worse.

Sage brought his hands up to Conrad's ears. As he worked small circles into them with the tips of his fingers and thumbs, he marveled at the smooth curve where he expected a point to be. If he was honest, they were rather darling.

If he was *entirely* honest, the man attached to them was darling, too.

Something squeezed in his chest at the thought. The trust that had cultivated between them made it so simple for him to talk to Conrad. Unnerving as it might be, he found that he liked being able to share things with someone so easily. Even things he would've otherwise found difficult to speak of came effortlessly when they were alone. It was this uncomplicated truth that had words burning on his tongue.

"I am afraid I've been less than forthcoming with you," Sage admitted quietly, still distracting himself with Conrad's ears. It had relaxed the man so much that his entire upper body was swaying a bit with the circular motions.

"Hmm?" was his drowsy reply.

"The incident at the lake was entirely my fault."

"Rubbish," Conrad said, a lazy grin tugging at his mouth. "It was a strong wind, that's all."

Sage let his hands rest on Conrad's shoulders. "And I was the one who caused it to happen." He watched as Conrad forced his heavy eyes open and they found one another in the mirror. "With my magic."

Conrad's confusion was evident. "Why did you do it?"

"I did not mean to," Sage said with a slight

whinge. "I did not even recognize that it was happening until I'd already ruined everything."

Conrad spun himself on the ottoman to face Sage, hands finding his wrists as he gave them a gentle squeeze. "It was an accident, then. No harm done. We were able to fix your clothes, and the lantern was not damaged." His smile returned. "And it allowed me to show you what a great tool cabbage can be."

Sage gave a pitiful little laugh, bottom lip poking out. He was doing a poor job of explaining what he truly wanted to say. After reclaiming one of his hands, he smoothed it over Conrad's short hair before he held the side of his face, sliding his thumb over his cheek as he considered his next words carefully.

"Do you recall the discussion at dinner? About magical compatibility?"

Conrad winced. "Hard to forget. Emrys was rather emphatic about it."

"Yes," Sage agreed, lip curling before he went on. "Fae consider magical compatibility to be highly important when it comes to matters of the heart. It signifies a strong connection between the two partners. It is the reason you find Wyndham and Roger's joint magic so compelling, beyond the fact that they are both apt on their own. They are highly compatible, as are Emrys and Torquil; Keelan and Silas. Traditionally, the first demonstration is performed at the end of the wedding ceremony, to prove that the marriage will be a successful one. However, as you heard earlier, this may very well be the first *public* demonstration of compatibility, but it is certainly not the first time the couple might have experimented with it."

"What does it mean? To be magically compatible."

The tips of Sage's ears went warm, and he had to look away from Conrad's intense focus for a moment before he could answer.

"One cannot explain it until they have experienced it for themself. There are rumors, of course. All young fae like to pretend they understand it to impress their peers."

Conrad chuckled. "Naturally."

"I will admit that I have given in to the temptation before. Even with Wyndham, on a couple of occasions, though it was never reciprocated."

"So you have felt it before."

Sage searched Conrad's dark eyes. "Not until very recently."

"And was it the way they all described?"

"I've never felt anything like it," he whispered, repeating his own words.

A muscle in Conrad's forehead worked as he seemed to recognize the line as familiar, before a wash of understanding coated his face. Sage's stomach roiled at the thought of what would happen next. Would he pull away? Had he been too bold in making such a confession? Conrad's eyes shifted back and forth rapidly as he seemed to search his thoughts, compiling this new information with what he'd already been told.

"Your magic makes my spells more powerful,"

Conrad finally mused. He locked eyes with Sage again. "And mine—"

"Inspires my magic to ruin my own clothes, apparently."

Conrad laughed as he stood up, reaching to hold both sides of Sage's face. Sage gripped Conrad's forearms in an effort to steady himself, brows still pinched as he waited to see what other conclusions the man would arrive at.

"My magic has grown fond of your magic, just as I have grown fond of you!" And suddenly Conrad was kissing him. Sage was so surprised that he did not even have a chance to close his eyes before it was over.

"What?" he managed on a shaky exhale after they broke apart.

"I hope you do not mind my saying so." Conrad kissed the corner of his lips. "It felt like an appropriate time to tell you."

"I..." Sage's jaw worked as he struggled to reply. "Yes. I mean no, I do not mind it." He was fairly certain his hands would've been shaking if they were not still wrapped around Conrad's forearms. He leaned in to rest their foreheads together. "I do not mind it," he repeated, softer this time, relief flooding him just as the warmth of his magic had as they worked together in Roger's study.

If this was to be a night for revelations, then Sage already knew what he needed to say next. Perhaps it was all too much at once, but if all the years he spent silently yearning for Wyndham had taught him one thing, it was that keeping his feelings a secret would only lead to more heartbreak in the end.

"You might have noticed that Emrys and the others were not so subtle in their hints at another sort of intimacy that often comes with magical compatibility," he ventured.

Conrad snorted. "I suppose that better explains why this entire house reeks of copulation." Sage couldn't help but laugh at that. Conrad pulled away to look up at him. "Are you trying to tell me you are equally as afflicted?"

He was not prepared to admit that he had been in a nearly constant state of arousal for three days. The look on his face must've been admission enough.

"Whatever are we just standing around for, then? You should've told me sooner. Come along."

Sage found himself being guided toward the bed. Conrad began removing his trousers as he did every other night, no fuss about it. Sage made quick work of pulling his stockings off and tossed them aside. By the time he had slipped his shirt off, Conrad was already under the blankets. Sage reached for the small jar of oil on his bedside table and crawled onto the bed on his knees.

Conrad gave a short gasp when he noticed the jar in his hand.

"Is this what that is for?"

Sage shut his eyes. "Please do not mention it."

Conrad's answering laughter was excessively cheerful. "I had no idea," he said. "That first night, I thought you were offering me some of what you'd used on your face and hands."

"I know," Sage said dryly, though he couldn't hide his embarrassed grin. "It was rather humiliating."

Conrad tutted and reached out for him. "It was nothing personal, you understand?" Sage shuffled closer, sitting back on his heels.

"Yes, I understand now." They shared a soft kiss. "Though I confess I am nervous about doing something that will make you uncomfortable."

"As I said before, I will let you know if that happens." Conrad's expression turned serious. "I am more concerned about you. I've no reservations about voicing what I like or dislike. Promise me that you will do the same?"

There was a weight to Conrad's question that Sage was not ready to work through. He had not earned his reputation by being a demanding sort of shag. He did what *other* men liked. It was the only reason they wanted him, along with the care he took in maintaining his appearance.

"I do not know the answer," he said, face warm.

Conrad kissed him again. "Then we shall find out together."

After a somewhat shy acknowledgement that he wanted Conrad to have him—and not the other way around—the other man accepted Sage's proffered oil in his waiting palm and pushed the covers away with his free hand.

"Will it bother you if I watch?" Sage asked.

"I won't mind it," Conrad told him. They shared a

kiss before Sage collected some oil and tucked his upper body against Conrad, cheek on his shoulder so he could easily go between kissing his neck and watching him work the oil onto himself. The moment was so easy between them that Sage almost wished they could stay that way. Several slick fingers later, he was ready in no time at all.

Rather than worrying too much about what would come next, Sage decided to do what felt right in the moment. He pressed his lips against Conrad's neck as he shifted one leg over to straddle his hips. Conrad's hands moved to the tops of his thighs and remained there as Sage returned to kissing his mouth, unhurried and indulgent.

"Is this how you want me?" Conrad asked when he got the opportunity.

Sage hummed his agreement against Conrad's lips and felt him smile.

When he could not take the anticipation any longer, Sage sat up and let his hands slide over Conrad's shoulders and chest to his stomach, just as he had been wanting to do. It was everything he'd imagined it to be. He lifted himself up slightly on his knees and reached behind to take Conrad in his hand, giving him a few strokes.

"Are you ready?"

Conrad nodded, his head moving against the pillow in a way that reminded Sage so much of their sweet mornings together that he nearly lost his breath. With his free hand on Conrad's shoulder, he set them into alignment and pushed back against his length, going as slowly as he had not always been allowed to do. His companion remained perfectly still while he became comfortable, giving Sage the lead. It meant more than he could possibly say.

Tentative movements melted into a rhythm as Sage began to rock his hips, one hand still behind him to help keep them together and also to explore delicately into what else Conrad might enjoy. Sage found that it was surprisingly easy to clear his mind of all the techniques he'd saved up for wanting to please the man beneath him.

"Where do you like to be touched?" he asked, silently cursing himself when he realized how far away on the bed he'd left the oil. Fortunately, his fingers were still able to glide smoothly over the base of Conrad's erection and bollocks.

"Sage," Conrad cautioned. He pulled his hand away immediately. "I want you to focus on yourself, not on me."

"But—"

"I am happy simply to be close to you," he went on. "Please trust me."

"I trust you."

Sage pushed his thoughts aside. This was what he wanted—what he'd been craving since their night at the lake when his magic found Conrad's and set his entire world out of balance. Although, it had likely started long before then. The memory of seeing Conrad for the first time, hair damp and skin flushed from his bath, bloomed in his chest. Had he known from that very moment that something was different about him? That this strange creature would warm his bed, his magic, his heart, with little more than his bright smile and endless encouragement? That he would no longer be able to imagine returning to the life he had before without him?

"I trust you," he promised again, leaning forward to kiss Conrad deeply, a moan escaping the back of his throat as he moved his hips with more purpose, taking what he needed from the man who was so willing to give it.

He felt when Conrad pulled his legs up, bending his knees to provide them both more support against the give of the mattress. His hands had not moved from Sage's thighs.

"Touch me," Sage breathed. "I want you to touch me."

"Where?" Conrad asked.

"Anywhere," Sage answered between kisses.

Conrad obliged, one hand cradling his neck as the other found the curve of his lower back. There was no pulling of his hair, no nails scratching across his skin, no roughness of any kind, other than the callouses on Conrad's hands from his years of working with them.

A small voice in the back of Sage's mind cried out at the thought of him ever being forced to return to such a life. He imagined them together in London instead, sharing a bedroom that really did belong to both of them, sitting up in bed and talking for hours about everything and nothing as Sage rubbed oil into

291

Conrad's hands every night until the rough patches were nothing but a memory.

On the next thrust of his hips, Sage caught himself at exactly the right angle and huffed out a mixture of surprise and pleasure. The sensation set off the beginning of something familiar within him. Rather than trying to forestall it, he went after it with abandon, setting his magic free.

Sage pressed his face against Conrad's neck as he slipped his hand between them, gripping himself tightly as he chased after what he now knew only Conrad could give him. One of the candles snuffed out as Sage's heart raced.

"Oh, Con," he whimpered, "I-I'm—"

His next words went nonsensical and shaky when he came, coating his hand and Conrad's stomach and chest as pleasure cleaved through him, filling him just the same as Conrad's compatible magic had.

Familiar fingers tucked sweat-dampened strands behind the tip of his ear. There was a kiss on his shoulder. Sage swallowed and opened his eyes.

"Give me just a moment," he said, still breathless. "I will help you."

"I do not require it," Conrad replied, his voice just above a whisper to match. "Let us get cleaned up so I can hold you. You're shivering."

Chapter 32
Conrad

Conrad made quick work of getting them both cleaned up with one of the hand towels by the wash basin. He wanted to spend some time thinking about everything Sage had said before, and then some time thinking about what it meant in terms of how their magic had interacted, and then some more time after that thinking about how glorious it had been to watch Sage take pleasure for himself for once. But for the moment, he put all of his focus on taking care of the man beside him. The rest could wait.

After they were both cleaned and the cloth had been discarded, Conrad returned to his side of the bed and pulled Sage close. Sage nestled against him as easily as ever, tangling their legs together, pressing his lips to Conrad's neck, and draping his arm over Conrad's chest. Conrad slid an arm around the other man's shoulders and kissed his hair.

They were silent for a few moments.

Then Conrad rubbed Sage's shoulder a little and said, "I wonder if this will change how our magic works together—now that I understand it better."

Sage shifted a little. "What do you mean?"

"I mean, now that it would be intentional, and now that I have a better idea of what to look for."

"I'm not sure," Sage said at last. "I have rather limited experience with this sort of thing."

Conrad chuckled. "To be sure. Perhaps we could ask about it the next time we cast."

"Perhaps." Sage sounded dubious.

"Or we can keep it to ourselves," he amended.

Sage sighed. "Wyndham already knows. He's known since you described the wind at the lake. And if he does, then Roger probably does, too."

"Oh." Conrad considered this for a moment. "Does it bother you, having Wyndham know?"

"It bothered me when I was still coming to terms with it, I think. But in regards to how I used to feel about him...no, it doesn't."

Conrad let out a relieved breath. "I'm glad to hear it."

"Are you always this chatty after a shag?" There was a smile in his voice as he asked.

Conrad grinned. "Sorry. Am I ruining the mood?"

Sage let out a sharp laugh. "No. I like it. But I'm not accustomed to it." As if to prove the point, he nestled a little closer. "It sounds as though you expect us to do more magic together tomorrow."

"If not tomorrow, then another day before we leave." Sage hummed against him in response. "And of course," Conrad continued, "I wouldn't be surprised if they asked us to continue the experiment when we return to London."

"I'd like that," Sage said quietly.

Conrad felt relief and joy fill his chest at Sage's words. A silent answer to an unspoken question between them: they would continue to see each other in London. He curled a finger under Sage's chin and tilted his face so he could kiss him. "Me too."

Sage's answering smile was soft.

They continued to talk idly about what they could expect from the rest of their stay in the country: what other riddles Harriet might have up her sleeve, what other spells Roger might want to see them try together, what other activities their hosts might come up with. As their words grew softer, a little more slurred with drowsiness, and punctuated with yawns, they gave in to the inevitable and fell asleep, holding each other with more intention than they had in their previous nights together.

.·.·.·.

The following morning, Conrad woke with Sage practically on top of him, and he smiled at how their friendship had grown and evolved in a matter of weeks. There was a feeling of contentment that he had never expected with another person. He liked the way they fit together, the way they never ran out of things to talk about, and how they kept finding new ways to take care of each other.

But underneath the contentment was a niggling worry that Conrad did not anticipate. He had formed a vague sort of plan about what he would do when he got to London, but he couldn't figure out how Sage might fit into it. He knew how to take care of himself, but he also knew that working at the docks would not provide him enough to take care of another person. He knew little about what the Council might pay if he got the position, but he also knew that everyone on the Council, other than Silas, had sufficient money from inherited wealth. Silas was the closest to him in terms of finances and class, but even his family owned a modest amount of land and a thriving business. Conrad had no idea if he would ever earn enough to support Sage. And Sage, with his gorgeous clothes, high quality oils, and a lifetime of having servants and grand houses, would need more support than he could ever hope to obtain.

Did Sage expect anything from him, in terms of their previous night's conversation? He remembered the talk about magical compatibility and wedding spells. Was magical compatibility a precursor to matrimony? He certainly didn't mind it if it was. He could think of nothing better than to have a friend like Sage at his side for the rest of his life. He remembered how Sage had called him Con right before he came. He felt sure they could build a life on that—the trust, the tenderness, the friendship, and the affection between them, as new as it all was.

But what happened when a pair was compatible magically but not...financially? It was yet another distinction between himself and his new friends. He was sure none of them had ever had to worry about such things, so he couldn't very well ask for advice on the matter.

Sage stirred beside him and he set aside his concerns for a later date. If nothing else, he could take advantage of the time they had together. The future would come whether he worried about it or not; he might as well enjoy the time he had left.

Sage stretched and then looked up at him and Conrad wasted no time in kissing him good morning. The kiss was languid and sleepy and utterly perfect. Sage rested his cheek on his shoulder and smiled drowsily.

"You smell like roses and almonds now. I like it."

"Mm. If that's enough incentive for you to spoil me with a massage before bed each night, I won't complain."

Sage chuckled. "Ridiculous man. You know you need only ask." He yawned. "Are you going down to breakfast?"

"Yes. I'd like to find out what the plan is for the day. Would you like to come with me?"

Sage grumbled a little and tucked in closer. "I'd like to stay in this warm bed with you all day, but I have a feeling I'll be outvoted."

Conrad laughed. "I don't think you're in danger of being outvoted when there's only two of us."

"But when Roger and Wyndham and Torquil and Keelan and Emrys all clamor at the door for you to go and rejoin the living, I shall certainly be outvoted."

"They'll be clamoring for you to join them too, you know. Harriet was most put out that you were disappearing into the study with us."

Sage wrinkled his nose. "It was very strange. I've barely spoken three words to her."

"Your friends like you," Conrad said as gently as he could.

Sage grunted. "It's taking some getting used to."

Conrad pressed a kiss to his forehead. "I know. Shall we put that into practice now with breakfast?"

Sage groaned, but got out of bed. They took their time getting dressed. Each item that was donned, it seemed, was punctuated with another kiss or a cheek caress, fingers gently tucking hair behind ears. Conrad felt as though they were both reluctant to break the spell of togetherness when they left the room. But he had never been one to daydream his problems away. If they joined the rest of the group, they could talk with more people, or practice more spells, which would increase the likelihood of Conrad getting the position, which would then increase the possibility of seeing Sage in the future. And perhaps then he'd find a way to keep Sage in his life more fully.

This time, Sage's entrance in the breakfast room caused little clamor. It seemed as though his presence was now anticipated. They filled their plates and sat together, and Conrad was immediately pulled into a conversation between Roger and

Torquil. When he noticed Keelan and Silas chatting amiably with Sage, Conrad relaxed, pleased and proud.

He had not been wrong in guessing that Roger wished to see more magic from the two of them. But he was relieved that the man wanted to go over the notes he had compiled before continuing.

"I'll admit this is only the second time we've had a full-blooded human work with a fae," he explained as they all sat together in the study.

"And I'm guessing I'm the first person who hasn't been able to feel magic," Conrad said.

Roger winced. "Yes. I wish we could do something about that. Although if it makes you feel better, I barely feel magic. It's more of a *something* just out of reach. And I certainly can't control it like Wyn or Sage."

It didn't really help, but Conrad appreciated the attempt.

"However," Wyndham said from his seat on the chaise, "I suspect that most humans we work with will not be able to feel magic either. So your participation is exceedingly valuable."

"Exactly," Roger said. "Perhaps before we continue, we ought to pause and go over any questions you might have. Anything we need to explain better?"

"Perhaps you could give a better explanation of magical compatibility," Sage said. They all turned to look at him. "I did my best, but I'm not sure my explanation was sufficient. And the conversation at dinner last night was full of the expectation that everyone present knew the subject matter intimately."

"We did get a bit carried away," Roger admitted. "That's a good suggestion, Sage. Thank you. Wyn, would you mind?"

Wyndham got up from the chaise and perched on the edge of the desk. "Tell me what you know so far."

"I know that the wedding ceremony is when the compatibility is first publicly demonstrated, but that a couple will likely have experimented in private beforehand. I know that it is the reason your magic together is so remarkable." He glanced at Sage for permission. He gave a nod and a small smile. "And I know it's the reason Sage inadvertently kicked up a wind when we were in the lake together. And it's the reason my magic is so much stronger when we cast together."

Wyndham smirked. "That's a good start. Let's take a step back for a moment. People often bandy about the expression of magical compatibility to mean something particular. But, in point of fact, everyone has a level of compatibility or incompatibility with every other person. This past spring, we invited a group of fae-humans to London to help develop our third rubric. And compatibility between them and our fae volunteers was a major component of the project. Silas' magic was incompatible with practically everybody. His magic was constrained, sometimes painful, and sometimes explosive in a negative way with others. When he and I cast together, it was better. His magic was sufficiently powerful. But when he cast with Keelan... it filled the entire room."

"I see," Conrad said slowly. "And that's the case with two humans casting together as well, is it?"

Wyndham nodded. "Although since most humans cannot sense magic, they probably don't know how their magic is interacting with each other."

"Not to mention most humans cast spells together differently," Conrad said.

"Something for us to explore further, I imagine," Wyndham said with a smile over his shoulder at his husband.

"Oh, trust me, I've already been thinking about it," Roger said, laughing.

"So, to get back to the main point, you and I have some amount of magical compatibility. We've cast together several times. Your magic gets along with mine well enough."

"But not as intensely as when Sage and I cast together," Conrad guessed.

"Definitely not," Wyndham said. He glanced between them. "I'm not going to pretend I understand your relationship or know of your plans. But I would recommend that, if nothing else, you two might form a partnership for casting together. Your magics are impressively complementary."

"I'd like that," Conrad said, smiling up at Sage. Sage didn't meet his eyes, but he nodded his agreement.

"Does that clear things up a little?" Wyndham asked.

"Yes, thank you."

"Good. Now that you're both aware of the situation, I imagine our experiments will be even more interesting."

He wasn't wrong. Their work began to turn into a combination of experimentation and lessons, as Wyndham taught Sage how to blend their magics together more seamlessly, and how to communicate what changes Conrad needed to do to the spells. In turn, Roger sat next to him and gave him advice on how to observe his fae companion, what to look for when he was reaching for magic or when he was struggling to control it.

Although Conrad couldn't feel magic, he could tell when he and Sage began to take their instructions to heart. His spells seemed smoother, while still powerful. Sage seemed less tense as he carried out Wyndham's directions. They spent hours churning out spell after spell. It was exhausting, but Conrad couldn't deny it was also thrilling. To see Sage sensing a part of him that he could not, joining their magics together with progressively more ease, felt like a language Conrad hadn't known existed. They didn't stop until dinner was called.

"Goodness," Roger said, organizing his pages of notes. "We really worked you two hard today."

"We'll have a good start for when we return to London," Wyndham said, looking over Roger's shoulder.

"My father is already pleased to know that you work well with everyone. He'll be delighted when I tell him that you're diligent when it comes to projects, as well."

Conrad froze. "You've told him about me?"

Roger laughed. "Of course! I wrote to him shortly after you arrived and I've been sending him reports ever since. If you ask me, he already likes you."

Conrad couldn't stop the grin that took over. "That's wonderful."

Sage chuckled beside him. "You were worried about it, weren't you?"

"I don't like to take anything for granted."

Sage leaned down and kissed him. Then he seemed to remember they had an audience for he pulled away and cleared his throat. "I'm quite sure everyone else here has known for weeks that you had the position secured."

Wyndham laughed as he brushed past him. "He's right. But I'm not sure why you're embarrassed, Sage. We also all know that you two have been in each other's pockets for a while now." He opened the door and turned back to look at them with a smirk. "The wind on the dock confirmed it."

Chapter 33
Sage

"All of this was so much easier when we held the event at our townhouse."

Roger was behind his desk with his head in his hands, staring down at the most disorganized stack of letters Sage had ever seen. The man had nearly spilled his tea on them, his cravat was crooked, and there was a smear of powdered sugar on his chin from the biscuit he'd been eating. It was all enough to make Sage grimace and wish to suggest that he call for his husband to settle his nerves, but it was still all meant to be a secret between the two of them.

"Mrs. Wrenwhistle somehow managed to get a large fraction of London out to their family estate for your wedding, Roger. I am sure you've done everything necessary to host a simple party here." Sage had even helped write out some of the final pieces of correspondence—it all seemed to be in place.

Roger groaned. "Wyn's mother is a force to be reckoned with. I am not."

Sage set his empty teacup down in hopes that refilling it would help distract Roger from his worrying. "She is not so frightening. I've always admired her strong personality, to be honest." Wyndham's mother had a bit of a reputation; she was a no-nonsense sort of lady who would not accept anything less than exactly what she wanted.

"Try being married to her son!"

Roger's mouth fell open in surprise at his own words. He began sputtering over what was likely supposed to be an apology, but Sage waved a hand at him.

"Listen. If we are to have any sort of relationship moving forward, we are going to have to accept this uncomfortable truth between us. We were in love with the same man and he picked you over me. It is that simple."

Roger finally straightened his cravat. "D-do you still love him?"

Sage gave a small shrug and looked out the open window over Roger's shoulder. "I suspect I always will, in some way. I am certain you of all people would understand that he is not someone your heart can easily let go of." He turned his attention back to Roger. "Does that bother you?"

Roger pressed his lips together and shook his head.

"No. I understand."

Sage gave a short nod and watched as Roger poured more tea in his cup.

"But if you're wondering whether or not I still have feelings for him, rest assured that I've no interest in trying to come between the two of you. In light of recent events, I...feel I have a far better understanding of how significant your connection is with him."

Roger's expression softened considerably.

"You and Conrad make a lovely pair," he cooed.

It had only been three days since they'd confessed their true feelings for one another, but they had been the best three days Sage could remember having in a very long time. He had never experienced such closeness with another person. It was more than the warm embraces and stolen kisses, it was feeling like a part of him had somehow been left behind when they were not in the room together. He and Roger had only been in the study for a couple of hours—he had lost count of how many times he checked the clock—and yet he found himself missing his companion as though they had been apart for months.

"I hope your father is serious about offering him a position."

Roger paused in sipping his tea. "You've nothing to worry about. It has all but been decided."

"He has put everything into this decision," Sage went on, feeling himself becoming a little desperate. "He deserves it more than anyone I could possibly imagine."

"You really do care for him, don't you?"

Sage felt himself go warm. Just as he was trying to collect his thoughts into some sort of explanation, there was a knock at the door. Roger called for the footman to open it. Sage turned in time to see Conrad stepping into the room, hands clasped behind his back, smile bright.

"Conrad," Roger said warmly. "We were just talking about you. Sage and I have been—er..." he was not at all subtle as he hastened to collect the papers spread out in front of him into a messy stack. "Talking," he finished weakly.

"I've come to ask if I can borrow something from your study."

"Of course you can," Roger said, still distracted. "Anything you need." He pushed his chair away from the desk and leaned down to shove some of the letters into a bottom drawer, disappearing from view. "Working on your day off, are you?"

"Something like that," Conrad said. He rushed forward and grabbed Sage's hand, giving him a mischievous grin as he tugged him up out of the chair. "I promise I'll return it when I'm done!"

Sage gave a final glance over his shoulder as he followed Conrad out of the room. They did not stop running until they were out of the house and alone in the garden. Conrad finally let go of his hand and wrapped his arms around Sage's waist instead, head on his chest.

"Are you mad?" Sage asked, laughing as he worked to catch his breath. His arms found their way around Conrad's shoulders as he relaxed into his embrace. The shorter man lifted his head to peer up at him.

"Perhaps," he said. "But if I am mad for wanting to see you, then I will wear the title with honor."

Sage hummed. "There are too many madmen in London as it is. We should probably pick a different designation for you, if you wish to have one so badly."

"Very well. Let me know what you decide." Conrad stepped away and took his hand again. "In the meantime, I thought it would be nice to walk through the garden together. I only got to see a little bit of it when Roger brought me to collect some materials for our spells."

"Roger would be able to identify what you are looking at far better than I ever could. He has dozens of those illustrated books about plant life on his shelves." For a fae, he knew shamefully little about such things.

Conrad chuckled. "That would be far less romantic, though."

Sage's magic shimmered in his chest.

Together, they ambled through the garden for hours, following each path several times as they talked. Whenever they found a bench, they sat for a while. Sage found that he liked it very much when Conrad allowed him to hold their hands in his lap, tracing his fingertips lightly over the bend of Conrad's knuckles. In the fading afternoon light, Sage discovered a scar on one of them, and he asked to hear the story of how he'd earned it. When Conrad was done telling him, Sage lifted his hand and placed a gentle kiss on the spot.

They enjoyed each other's company until dinner was called, when they reluctantly rejoined the party for what Sage knew was coming: a fresh wave of teasing remarks about their extended time in the garden. However, to his surprise, he found that he almost did not mind them as much as he had before. All he had to do was look at Conrad for a reassuring grin.

"Apologies if you found the bench near the willow at all unsound," Emrys said at last with a smirk. "There is a possibility that it was sat on a bit too roughly a couple of evenings ago."

Torquil rolled their eyes with a grin as everyone else around the table expressed various sounds of anguish.

"Oh good," Keelan said with a sigh of relief. "I thought we might've been the ones to—" he stopped suddenly, realizing what he was saying a bit too late. His blush was instant as he hid his face against Silas.

Wyndham appeared thoroughly rankled by their antics in his place at the head of the table. He took a slow sip of wine and reclined in his seat just far enough that his head met the high back of his chair.

"Someone is counting the days until we all go home," Sage commented. Wyndham shifted his gaze so their eyes met. He was silent for a moment before his focus returned to his wine.

"You have absolutely no idea," he agreed.

Chapter 34
Conrad

As dinner ended, everyone wandered into the sitting room and began discussing possible activities for the evening. Harriet was swiftly outvoted in the prospect of another game of charades. She pouted briefly but, characteristically, quickly rallied and suggested a card game. Roger grabbed several decks of cards and Wyndham directed a couple of footmen to have a large table cleared for their use.

"What shall we play?" Roger asked. "Cribbage?"

The entire group groaned.

"You *would* suggest something so tedious," Cyril said.

"Besides, that's only for two players," Emrys pointed out.

"We shall play Speculation," Harriet announced, taking a seat primly.

"We shall *not* play Speculation," Anthea said.

"What's wrong with that one?" Keelan asked.

Roger gave Harriet an apologetic look. "Harriet is..."

"A menace," Anthea supplied.

"Bloodthirsty," Cyril added.

Keelan gave her an assessing glance. "Yes, I suppose I can imagine she would be."

Harriet gave them all an arch look.

Conrad felt somewhat out of his depth. He didn't know any of the games they had mentioned so far and didn't quite dare suggest the ones he knew. He leaned towards Sage. "I might just watch tonight," he whispered.

Sage frowned. "You don't know those ones?" he whispered back.

Conrad shook his head.

"What about Pope Joan?" Torquil asked the group. "I've always enjoyed that one."

"My family loves that game," Silas said, smiling at them. "We play it every Christmas."

Sage gave Conrad a questioning look and he shook his head, regretfully.

"We don't have the board for that one," Wyndham said decisively. "How about Loo?"

This suggestion was met with enthusiasm, but Conrad shook his head again to Sage's inquisitive glance. Sage strode to the table, picked up a deck, and said, "If you don't mind, I'm going to borrow Conrad for the evening. I hope you'll excuse us tonight."

Roger chuckled. "That makes both of you owing me a borrowed friend."

Harriet and Cyril complained that the card game was meant to include everyone, but Torquil added their encouragement, "Let's give them some privacy. It must be difficult falling in love with everyone watching them all the time."

Wyndham gave Torquil a pointed look. "You're one to talk."

Their answering grin was sly. Roger laughed and cheerfully waved Sage off. Sage grabbed Conrad's hand and led him to the bedroom without a word.

As soon as the door was shut, Conrad pressed Sage against it and kissed him. "That was kind of you," he said softly.

"They ought to have been making sure everyone knew the games they were suggesting."

He shrugged. "They've been very good about that sort of thing for the most part. I can't blame them for forgetting occasionally."

"I can."

Conrad smiled and kissed him. "You're sweet. Did you steal me away just so I could save face?"

Sage held up a pack of cards. "We're going to have a lesson."

Conrad laughed. "Another one?"

"Yes. And the next time someone suggests a game of cards, you will be prepared," Sage said matter-of-factly. "We'll sit on the bed." He carefully took off his shoes and lifted a knee, thought better of it, and began taking off his jacket, followed by his waistcoat and trousers.

Conrad watched with amusement. "Exactly what sort of game are we playing?"

Sage gave him a mock glare. "I have no interest in mussing my clothes, thank you very much."

Conrad chuckled and stripped down to his shirt, as well, and joined Sage on the bed.

"Now, what games do you know, if any?"

"All-fours?"

Sage grimaced. "Not likely to be played in London sitting rooms, I'm afraid."

"Then I'm at your disposal. What game would you suggest?"

"I quite like the sound of that," Sage mused. Then he cleared his throat. "They were suggesting round games. But that might be difficult to teach with just the two of us."

"Cribbage?" Conrad offered with a grin.

Sage rolled his eyes. "That's the sort of game you'd play with your grandparents. Or if you're Roger, apparently. Besides, it takes hours." He considered for a moment. "We'll play Euchre."

He leafed through the deck and pulled out a number of cards and set them aside on the nightstand. Then he explained the rules of the game. Conrad tried to pay attention. He really did. But he kept getting distracted by how adorable Sage looked when he was focused and how endearing it was to see him attempt to be serious. When Sage ruminated aloud over what they should bet with, Conrad suggested kisses.

Sage sighed. "That will not be properly motivating—"

"I disagree."

"You're supposed to want to win. And if the winner gets to kiss the loser, then there's no motivation to win."

"Which means we both win."

"You're impossible."

"You love it."

Sage's mouth quirked. "Try to be serious about this, would you?"

Conrad schooled his features into an exaggerated expression of focus. "How's this?"

A laugh bubbled out of the other man. "Good enough, I suppose."

Conrad was not particularly good at Euchre, as it turned out. Though with kisses as the winnings, he didn't exactly mind. When Sage beat him roundly for a full rubber, Conrad climbed onto his lap to better offer the reward.

"See, this is exactly what I was afraid of. You weren't in the least bit motivated."

"Nonsense," Conrad murmured. "I owe you ten kisses and I'm very motivated to pay my debt."

Sage grumbled, but his hands slid up Conrad's back and a grin tugged at his lips. When Conrad closed the distance and kissed him, Sage gave up all pretense of minding his lack of motivation. The kisses started off playful and then turned lazy and decadent. The cards were quickly forgotten, scattered under their feet as they leaned against the pillows and lost count of kisses distributed.

"Apparently you are just as poor a student of card games as I am of swimming," Sage decided.

"If it means I get to hold you in my arms the next time we swim and then sit by and watch you play when the cards are brought out, I will happily accept those circumstances."

Sage chuckled, his fingers skimming over Conrad's skin. "I suppose I can accept it too, when you put it like that."

"You see? I did learn something from your lesson. You told me to be strategic."

Sage hummed against him and resumed the kisses. Conrad wrapped his arms around Sage's neck and tried to push away all the concerns that were pressing into his mind about how he never wanted their time together to end.

Chapter 35
Sage

There was no doubt that the house was of an appropriate size to host a party for the number of people Roger had invited.

Since the day after Sage had agreed to help, the two of them had been sneaking through the place like thieves so Roger could show him the various rooms he had in mind to use for the occasion. At first, Sage had only admired each space with little concern for how they might actually use it for their purposes. But as the date drew nearer, Sage had asked how Roger meant to ready any of the rooms and still keep it a surprise.

Now, they stood beside one another and stared out at what looked to be nothing more than an empty field.

"Well," Roger said, thrusting his arms out in front of him as though he was showing off a new prized racehorse or great sculpture. "What do you think?"

"I think I am looking at a lot of grass and trees," Sage said dryly.

"And the ideal place for the party!" Roger took a few steps out across the lawn, which looked to have been recently tended. "It is just hidden enough that you cannot see it from the house, but close enough that it will not require too much walking." Sage glanced over his shoulder to discover that it was a rather secluded location.

"Are we meant to stand the entire time?"

"Not at all." Roger spun to face him, gesturing to his right. "There will be tables and chairs here, with the dance floor opposite."

"A proper garden party, then."

"Yes! I think it will be perfect. Wyn dearly loves to be in nature."

"I do not recall seeing any receipts for flowers. I suppose you are not trying to impress your mother-in-law, after all?" The space had a rough beauty to it on its own, with a smattering of petite yellow and purple wildflowers blooming amongst the trees. It would take a great deal more than that to match the sort of garden parties they all attended in London, and especially the magnificent displays that Wyndham's mother was known for at her own events.

"Wyn has told me before that the sight of cut flowers upsets him, so I thought it best not to worry overmuch about the decorations."

Sage pursed his lips. "Perhaps he would not mind it as much if they were a careful selection from your own garden? Just some small bouquets for the tables. You cannot have a garden party without flowers."

Roger seemed cautiously pleased with the idea. "That might do nicely."

With a fortifying breath, Sage wandered a short distance from where he had been standing, peering up at the canopy of ash trees overhead.

"I suspect you'll want lanterns and fairy lights in the branches?"

"Oh, yes," Roger said on a dreamy exhale.

"You will have to ask at least one other fae for their assistance, then. I cannot call them as the others can."

Roger seemed taken aback by this information. "Really?"

Sage lifted a hand and snapped his fingers. Nothing happened.

"Afraid not."

Roger's hands curled into fists at his sides, fingers waggling and likely desperate for a quill and paper to make note of such a discovery. Just as fast as he'd seemed to imagine the fairy lights, he let the thought go and moved on to an alternative. "Lanterns will be fine. Plenty of candles will do the trick."

"You've the budget to light this entire space with candles?"

"Yes." Roger frowned. "Do you think it's too much?"

Sage snorted a laugh and shook his head. Of course they could afford it.

"I don't believe there is an alternative, unless you want us all to be dancing in the dark." A smirk curled at the corner of his lips. "You might even make the papers with that one when we all return to the city."

Roger let out an uncomfortable groan. "I'd rather not."

"Why will you not ask someone? I am certain Keelan or Emrys would be happy to help you with the lights."

"You know how they all are," Roger said with a full-body, helpless sort of shrug. "Everything turns into a laugh." He sighed. "Or worse, something indecent." Color crept across his cheeks as he adjusted his spectacles. "I mentioned my idea to Torquil before we all left London at the end of the Season, and they suggested that a *private* party would make Wyn happier."

"Is this not a private party?" Sage asked. "Forty people you are both well acquainted with is hardly a public affair."

"A different sort of party," Roger strained. "You know. *Alone.*"

Sage made a face. "What's so special about that?"

"That's what I said!" The man huffed and slapped his hands against the outside of his thighs in exasperation. "This is supposed to be an opportunity for everyone who loves Wyn to come together and celebrate."

"And you've nearly done it," Sage said, surprising

himself with how reassuring it had come out. Roger sounded like he could really use it, though. "We both know he's going to appreciate all the work you've put into this. Even if it is too dark to see."

Roger laughed and nodded his agreement. "I know you're right."

They both turned when Roger's man Notley appeared.

"Sir, there seems to be an issue in the kitchen."

"Oh dear." Roger hurried over to him. "What is it now?"

"It is in regard to the ice cream." Notley put a special emphasis on the last two words; Sage couldn't decide if it was because he was unaccustomed to saying them or if he was indicating yet another problem. Roger's groan of frustration was answer enough. Without a glance, he left with Notley. Sage shook his head after them with a faint grin and took the long way back to the house as to not let them be seen returning from the same direction.

Chapter 36
Conrad

When Sage disappeared into Roger's study for the second day in a row, Conrad grew restless. As much as he would have liked to steal Sage away again, he couldn't do that to Roger a second time. Considering how stressed Roger seemed at dinner the night before, it was reasonable to assume that whatever they were working on together was the cause of the stress. Conrad couldn't deny Roger of Sage's calming presence when it was needed most.

He found Wyndham, Keelan, Torquil, and Silas entertaining Peony in one of the sitting rooms and joined them. Wyndham was using his magic to whirl a piece of string in the air and the kitten was chasing after it. When the string spiraled in a small funnel of air, Peony flopped onto her back and batted at it with her paws.

"Is this how all fae play with their pets?" Conrad asked.

"To be honest, it hadn't occurred to me to do it this way," Keelan admitted. "My father has dogs. There are always a number of loose ribbons around my father's room so we never had a shortage of these sorts of games, but we didn't use magic for it."

"I've never had a pet," Torquil said.

"And I can't use fae magic like these three can," Silas said. He reached forward and tickled Peony's chest. She turned her attention to him instead, batting at his fingers playfully. He laughed and covered her body with his large hand, swishing her gently across the floor.

Wyndham snatched the string out of the air and curled it around his finger idly. "Do you have pets, Conrad?"

He shook his head. "We couldn't really afford it. But I do love animals."

"You? Enjoy adorable creatures? Shocking," Torquil said with a laugh.

"You sound like Sage," he replied.

"Where is Sage anyway?" Emrys asked as he strolled into the room.

Conrad leaned back against his palms. "He's working with Roger again."

Emrys sank into a plush armchair. "Oh, that's right. That secret party we're not supposed to know about."

Wyndham gave his brother a sharp look.

"What?" Emrys asked defensively. "You can't pretend you don't know about it."

"Of course I know about it," Wyndham snapped.

"I've known for months. And I intend to act very surprised and delighted when it happens." He glared. "And you would do well to do the same."

"There's going to be a party?" Conrad asked.

"For Wyndham's birthday," Emrys replied. "Roger is planning a huge surprise party in his honor."

"Should be fun," Keelan added. "Both Wyndham's and Roger's families will be there. There'll be cake and music and dancing."

"I have been working hard to discourage Emrys from following suit and surprising me for my birthday," Torquil said dryly. "I'm not fond of dancing, nor of being the center of attention."

"You'd be surprised how easy it is to be the center of attention when it's what your spouse wants," Wyndham remarked.

"Do you dance?" Keelan asked Conrad.

"A little. I know some country dances."

"Perhaps we should teach you," Emrys suggested.

"Excellent idea," Wyndham said, standing abruptly.

Emrys blinked at his brother. "It is?"

"You're bound to have one occasionally. But Conrad and I are both restless with Roger and Sage busy. It's the distraction we need."

"I'll bet Imogen will play the piano for us," Keelan suggested, getting up as well.

"And the others can add to our numbers," Wyndham said. "Come along."

So Conrad soon found himself paired with Wyndham, with Keelan and Emrys on one side, Fern and Cyril on the other, and Harriet and

Anthea completing the group. Imogen played the piano as requested, while Torquil and Silas watched.

Conrad might have worried that the lesson would go as poorly as the cards had. But he was not quite as distracted this time, and his friends were determined to see him successful. Also, as Keelan helpfully pointed out, Conrad was accustomed to activity, so learning something physical, like dancing, came rather naturally. He learned the quadrille and the waltz within hours.

Keelan was just about to suggest a third dance when Torquil intervened, looped their arm around Conrad's, and said, "Give the poor man some time to rest before you teach him another."

"But the party's tomorrow!" Keelan protested.

Torquil held up a hand. "Conrad knows enough to impress Sage already. Give him a quarter hour to catch his breath and then you can have him back until dinner."

"Where are you going?" Emrys asked.

"We're taking a turn about the garden," Torquil replied, leading Conrad out of the room. "And no, you're not invited. I'll return him shortly."

Conrad grinned as he allowed Torquil to set the pace out the door and down the garden path. He was taken back immediately to his afternoon of stealing Sage in much the same way. "Thank you."

"I've been on the receiving end of Wyndham's generosity before," they said with a smile. "Hours of dancing lessons and I thought I might collapse. You are far hardier than I am, but that doesn't mean you couldn't use a rest."

Conrad drew in a deep breath and let it out slowly. "I appreciate it. It's certainly exhausting, but I have to admit that I will miss all of this when I leave."

"Are you planning on leaving soon?"

"Well, I really do need to speak to Roger's father. So much depends on his decision."

"He's coming to the party, remember? You don't need to go find him. He's going to be delivered directly to you."

"But that's Wyndham's birthday party. Won't that be pulling attention from him?"

"I imagine Wyndham would be grateful for that," they replied. "And besides, you'll soon learn that Council business tends to leak into personal lives whether we like it or not. Roger, Wyndham, and I were all invited to be on the Council during Roger and Wyndham's wedding."

Conrad laughed. "I didn't know that." He paused. "You seem to be acting like I'm already part of it."

Torquil gave a little hum. "You very nearly are. You haven't met Roger's father yet, but his son takes after him a great deal. Roger likes you. His father will too. Wyndham, Silas, and I all like you. You have ideas, enthusiasm, and determination. You've been living in a house with a mixture of fae, humans, and fae-humans—something that would have been practically unthinkable a few years ago—and you've gotten along with all of us."

"You really think so?"

325

"I'm not one to give false hope."

Conrad smiled at them. "I suppose that's true. I'm still trying not to get carried away with my excitement until I've met Councilmember Barnes though."

"That's wise," they replied with a grin. "I can also add, confidentially, that we've been having a hard time filling that final position. It's been difficult finding someone who shares our vision for the future of the Council, who has fresh ideas, but is open to other suggestions. We had applications, but many of them were hoping to replace Williams or Gibbs in terms of their philosophies. A few even suggested we shouldn't be focused on blending our societies so much. Iris, Williams, and Gibbs stepped down from their positions on the Council over six months ago. We need to have that position filled before we reconvene in the autumn."

Conrad chuckled. "So what you're saying is, I'm your last resort."

"What I'm saying is that your timing is perfect and you are exactly the sort of person we've been looking for. We turned down any number of applications in the hopes of finding someone like you. And then you stepped into our lives in a way none of us could have expected."

Warmth spread through Conrad's chest. "That's very nice to hear."

"I understand why you're trying to rein in your expectations," they continued softly, "but I want you to know that when I, or any of the other councilmembers here say that you're practically part of the Council already, we mean it."

They walked in silence for a few minutes as Conrad let their words settle.

"What do you plan to do when you leave?" they asked, breaking the quiet.

"Go to London. I'll need to find a place to stay. And I'll probably need to find work in order to do that."

"What sort of work do you have in mind?"

"What I used to do, most likely. There are docks in London. If I can find work there, that should keep me busy and housed until the Council convenes."

Torquil seemed to consider this. "You know," they said slowly, "you might be the solution to a problem I've had for several months now."

"What problem is that?"

They grimaced. "Before I tell you, let me preface this with two things. First, I haven't always been this wealthy. It's a rather recent change. Just before Emrys proposed, I was living in a room above my press and barely earning enough to eat. So I understand what it's like to have wealthy friends who seem to be living in a separate world from you. And I understand how galling it can be to accept charity disguised as generosity. Second, with that in mind, I recognize how utterly preposterous this problem is going to sound."

Conrad laughed. "All right. Duly noted."

"I probably ought to give you some context first. When my parents fell in love, my grandfather was very upset about it. My mother was a member of a prominent fae family and my father was a human nobody. When they refused to be split apart, my grandfather disinherited my mother and sent her away."

"That's terrible."

"By all accounts, he was absolutely dreadful. My grandmother had no say in the matter and she was forced to keep her communication with her daughter a secret from her husband. I didn't even know my grandmother *didn't* hate me until after my grandfather died and she approached me to suggest a reconciliation. Part of that reconciliation was a change in inheritance. My grandmother was able to ensure I inherited everything."

"That's a clever bit of revenge," Conrad remarked.

Torquil laughed. "Indeed. The only challenge is that shortly after inheriting everything, I got married to Emrys, who's an heir in his own right. So now I have more property than I know what to do with."

"I can see what you mean about this problem sounding absurd."

"I did warn you. Now, my grandmother has graciously been taking care of the London townhouse for me. This has allowed me to keep all of the staff, and ensures everything of value is safe and that the house is being maintained properly. But I don't think she cares for the house."

Conrad considered this. "If she spent so much time living with a dreadful husband, I can imagine it would sour the location for her."

328

"Exactly. I'd like to free her from that obligation, but it's been challenging when Emrys and I don't really need it. And I could close it up, but that would mean letting some of the servants go and I hate to do that." Torquil turned to face him on the path. "If I could ask a friend to stay and take care of the house for me, it would mean a great deal."

Conrad stared at them. "You're asking *me*?"

They nodded, smiling. "I would take care of the expenses. It's my house, after all. So you wouldn't need to worry about the staff's salary, or the cost of firewood or candles, or anything like that. Frankly, even paying for the food would mean that I could ensure the entire kitchen staff had something to do."

"I can't let you pay for my food, Torquil."

They arched an eyebrow. "I wouldn't be doing it for free. In return, you'd be making use of a property for me so that I wouldn't have to worry about it. You would be helping me keep a number of good people employed. You'd allow me to give a *very* big signal of what I think of my grandfather's ideals." The glint in their eyes softened. "And you'd be giving me peace of mind that a friend of mine is safe."

"Torquil," Conrad breathed. "Do you have any idea—"

"Yes," they said cheerfully, tucking their hand around his arm again and leading him back down the path. "I know exactly what I'm offering. And, I'd like to add, this offer extends to anyone you'd care to invite over. So if, for example, you had a mind to propose to someone in the future..." their tone dripped with insinuation, "rest assured that this offer includes you and any spouse you might happen to have. If you'd like to invite some of your family to visit, you could do that. You can host parties there. Invite me over for dinner. Consider it yours in everything but name."

"I could hug you."

Torquil held their arms out. Conrad gave them a tight embrace, feeling as if he might cry from the complete change of fortune they had dropped into his lap. He pulled away with a sniff.

"You're very trusting very quickly," he said. "We met less than a month ago."

"I'm very good at reading people," they said, leading the way back to the house. "It was my idea to have you room with Sage. Remember?"

Conrad stared at them incredulously. "That was intentional?"

"Of course. It was a hunch, mind you. But I wasn't the writer of London's most popular gossip column for nothing."

"You nosy little matchmaker. I don't know how I shall thank you...for any of it."

"Just take good care of the house for me. And of Sage, too."

Conrad grinned. "With pleasure."

As they walked back to rejoin the others and continue the dance lessons, Conrad began formulating new plans. Now that he had a future to offer Sage, he only needed the right words to say.

Chapter 37
Conrad

The morning of the not-so-secret secret party, Conrad stayed in bed longer than usual, reluctant to lose the weight of Sage beside him. Sage seemed to notice.

"Aren't you going to breakfast?" he asked sleepily.

"In a minute," Conrad assured him.

Sage hummed and nuzzled against his neck. "I've finally won you over to the idea of morning leisure, have I?"

Conrad laughed and turned his head to kiss him. "If I understand correctly, tonight marks the official end of our house party. Which means this idyllic experience will soon be over."

Sage went still. "But we'll still see each other in London."

"Yes, of course. But we won't be able to wander

down to breakfast with the others like we do now. There won't be any more picnics or swimming in the lake. I'll miss it, that's all."

"I can't say I'll miss all of that," Sage muttered. "And there's still plenty of entertainment to be had in London. Arguably more entertainment to be had."

"Really?"

"Oh, yes. I quite hate the country."

"What do I have to look forward to in London, then?"

"I'll show you the opera, of course. And we can go riding in Hyde Park now that you know how to ride. And there will be garden parties and dinner parties. You now have a number of people to call on for tea whenever you feel like pestering people—or visiting them, depending on your point of view. I'd love to show you Vauxhall Gardens."

"I've heard about that one," Conrad said, excited. "Is it true they have fairy lights in the trees?"

"Mmhmm," Sage said, bussing his lips over Conrad's skin. "And lanterns over the dance floor. Fireworks sometimes. And a number of little nooks and crannies for salacious goings on."

"Sounds exciting."

Sage kissed him. Conrad wanted dearly to ask if they would still be pretending when they were in London, but he didn't quite dare. The whole scheme had been Sage's idea from the start. He was determined to let him be the one to change the rules when he was ready.

"So you see, nothing to mourn at the end of this party. I'd say your fun has just begun," Sage said when he pulled away.

"Quite right," Conrad replied with a grin. "Thank you for pulling me out of my brief spell of melancholy."

"You do melancholy very poorly."

He laughed. "Very true. Shall we go down to breakfast?"

Sage groaned. "I shouldn't have said anything at all."

Conrad traced his cheek with a fingertip. "I'll miss waking up with you beside me."

Sage sobered and then he nipped at Conrad's finger with his teeth before sitting up. "If you think I won't sneak into whatever bed you're renting, you're woefully mistaken. You won't get rid of me that easily."

Conrad beamed and hopped out of bed. "I'm delighted to hear it."

When they reached the breakfast room, they found Roger in an evident state of nerves and everyone else in an evident state of trying to soothe Roger's nerves while simultaneously pretending like they didn't know why he was so nervous. It would have been amusing if it wasn't so difficult to see Roger anxious.

Conrad and Sage took their usual seats and contributed to forcing an air of cheerfulness. Conrad was almost surprised by Sage's efforts until he remembered that the man had been helping Roger with the planning. He'd likely gained a great deal of experience in soothing the man's nerves in the past month.

When Roger's valet entered the room and leaned down to whisper in Roger's ear, Roger brightened, glanced at Conrad, and then left the room. He came back less than ten minutes later and said, "Conrad, there's someone here to see you."

Bemused, Conrad followed him down the hall and into a small sitting room. "Just be yourself," Roger whispered, before ushering him inside. Then he straightened and said in a more formal voice, "Father, I'd like you to meet Mr. Conrad Moore. Mr. Moore, please allow me to introduce my father, Mr. Norman Barnes. He's the Head of the Council for the human side."

Mr. Barnes stood, beamed, and held out his hand for Conrad to shake. It was more along the lines of how Conrad met people in his own station, which put him instantly at ease. When it occurred to him that this was likely the gentleman's intention, he relaxed even more. Roger excused himself and bustled out of the room, closing the door behind him with a quiet snap.

They both sat and Mr. Barnes turned his smile fully to Conrad. He looked very much like his son—the same light brown skin, the same dark eyes and dark hair, the same roundness of face and figure, and the same gentleness of spirit. Conrad recognized that this was what Torquil had been trying to tell him the previous day. If he could get along with Roger, he would likely get along just fine with Mr. Barnes.

"I'm told you wish to apply for the vacant position on the Council," Mr. Barnes prompted him.

"Yes, sir."

"Everything I've heard about you is very promising. Why don't you tell me a bit about yourself?"

Conrad launched into a brief summary of coming from Bristol, his work on the docks, his dream of doing more, how learning about the new rubrics gave him hope for families like his own, and how he had developed his plan to come and apply for the position on the human side of the Council. "I have a number of ideas. I've talked about them at length with Roger, Wyndham, Torquil, and Silas. I'd love to be a part of launching the rubric. I realize the Council is in a stage of change at the moment, what with a number of members leaving and another group joining; I'd very much like to be a part of that change and help to mold what we make of the future."

Mr. Barnes' smile grew. "That's exactly the sort of thing I wanted to hear. Anything else I need to know?"

Conrad hesitated. "I confess that my magic is not as strong as I'd like it to be. I was educated at home by my parents, so I had no formal training. My Hastings score was quite low, but there was nothing for us to inherit anyway, and the jobs we work don't require any particular score. When working with raw materials, my magic is stronger. And I've been experimenting with another fae in residence here—

under Roger and Wyndham's supervision and guidance of course—and my magic is significantly stronger when I do that. But I don't wish you to be under any illusions as to my magical prowess. Though I cannot sense magic like Roger, I am eager to learn whatever I can."

Mr. Barnes' expression sharpened at the mention of raw materials and the experiments with Sage, but he chuckled at the end of Conrad's speech. "I cannot sense magic either. And I would prefer to have someone of the right temperament and vision than simply picking someone with a certain level of magical power. Besides, having someone from a humble background is a good thing. You would provide a much needed perspective in terms of what ideas might be feasible for people in different financial situations. It didn't occur to me what a lack of inheritance might mean for a family with an informal education or low scores. We would need to take that sort of thing into account when we prepare the rubrics."

Conrad breathed out in relief. "I am glad I'm not alone in not being able to sense magic."

"Not at all," the other man said. "Truth be told, I'd be relieved to have another member on the Council who cannot. I am now decidedly in the minority where that skill is concerned."

Conrad beamed in response. "Is there anything else you wish to know?"

"I would like to hear more about your work with raw materials and this experiment with another fae, but that can wait. I've been impressed with you since my son wrote of how you traveled all the way from Bristol to inquire about the position. I was pleased to hear of your amiable disposition and how you seemed to get along with everyone you met. He is far more complimentary when discussing your magical skills, though I won't deny that humility is a good trait," he added with a wink. "I had honestly all but made up my mind before my arrival."

Conrad clasped his hands together in his lap, barely daring to breathe. "You had?"

"Oh, yes. A determined, intelligent, amiable, kind, and skilled young person such as yourself? One with a vision for a better future, who's willing to work for it? I couldn't ask for a better applicant." He held out his hand, "Welcome to the Council for Fae and Human Magical Relations, Mr. Moore."

Conrad grasped Mr. Barnes' hand with both of his own. "Thank you," he breathed. "I cannot tell you what this means to me."

Mr. Barnes gave a kindly chuckle. "After hearing what you went through to get here, I can imagine. As I understand it, you've been staying here until we could talk. So if you need an advance on your salary to tide you over in London, let me know."

"Thank you," Conrad repeated. "I may take you up on that. Torquil has offered for me to use their townhouse when I go, so that will help considerably."

"I imagine so. I'm glad to hear it." He stood. "I certainly don't want you struggling before you've even had a chance to start. And it's good to know that you have Torquil's good opinion. They are an excellent judge of character."

"They are quite wonderful," Conrad said.

"Indeed." Mr. Barnes flashed him a smile. "Now, unless you have any questions for me, I should sneak back out. Roger has been adamant that my arrival be a secret."

Conrad laughed. "Nothing comes to mind."

"I'll be at the..." He lowered his voice to a whisper for the next word, "...*party* tonight," he resumed at normal volume. "So if you think of anything, don't hesitate to ask." He shook Conrad's hand again. "It was a pleasure meeting you."

Conrad thanked him again. Mr. Barnes opened the door, greeted someone on the other side of it, and then left. Conrad stood in the center of the room, feeling dazed by how swiftly and easily his dream had come true.

"Conrad?" Sage's voice stirred him out of his thoughts.

"Hm?"

"How did it go?" Sage poked his head in the door, frowning with concern.

Conrad broke into a grin so broad it almost hurt. Sage was at his side in a moment, arms wrapping around his waist. "I knew you could do it," he whispered against Conrad's neck.

Conrad wrapped his arms around Sage's neck with another bright laugh, bouncing on his toes as he did so. "I can hardly believe it. It happened so quickly."

"You were the only one who doubted it would

happen," Sage reminded him. His voice lowered as he said, "I'm proud of you."

Conrad blinked away tears as he pulled away enough to frame Sage's face with his hands and kiss him.

Chapter 38
Sage

As gatherings between friends and family were wont to do, all of the careful planning Roger and Sage had done came to fruition with ease. After an enormous amount of help from the staff, the space between the ash trees had been transformed into a garden party that deserved to be written about, but only with the highest sort of praise.

Lanterns and candles flickered softly along the path to direct guests from the stables, where they'd all arrived from to keep their presence hidden until the time was right. More lanterns had been attached to the branches above, along with swags of sheer fabric and strings of colorful glass beads that caught the light in a fanciful way.

The tables were set with more candles and sprays of flowers that had been collected from the garden, just as Sage had suggested. He couldn't help but smile when Mrs. Wrenwhistle inspected one of the bouquets with an air of distaste that shifted into a nod of approval.

Wyndham's entire family was there, including his eldest brother Auberon, who had not removed his arm from around his wife, Rose, since they'd arrived. The way she kept her hand on the expectant curve of her belly was explanation enough. Wyndham's sister Aveline was also there, along with her husband Arlen, both of them still glowing and apparently unafraid to face society after their sordid elopement at the end of the Season.

Iris Wrenwhistle was resplendent as she sailed through the crowd, greeting everyone just as she always had. Sage supposed it was a hard habit to break after a lifetime on the Council. Slightly more surprising was the sight of Mrs. Leonora Pimpernel on her arm. The gesture was easy and natural, giving the impression of two ladies who had been friends for a very long time—until they shared a kiss that was decidedly *more* than what one might expect from friends.

Sage wondered absently how Emrys and Torquil felt about this connection, and then laughed at himself for how naturally he'd decided to tease them about it when he got the opportunity. It was perhaps the first time he had ever felt that he could do such a thing and expect a companionable response.

Like his mother, Emrys was not afraid to share his opinions openly. Upon entering the space, he had immediately made a comment about how dark it was and began calling on fairy lights with ostentatious snaps of his fingers. Along with the help of his grandmother and sister, the trees became beacons in the night. Sage privately hoped that Roger would be pleased when he saw it.

Roger's family was there, as well. Sage had never been properly introduced to any of them, but it was impossible to mistake how similar they were in appearance and personality. While half of them were speaking cordially with the other guests, the rest explored the space as though they were collecting information on everything they encountered: his father stared up at the fairy lights with his mouth open in awe while his brother inspected the wildflowers.

The rest of the party was made up of fellow councilmembers, including Keelan's mother, who was never one to miss out on a social event. Despite the relative quiet surrounding her son's brief and broken engagement before he quit London to run away with Silas and get married in the country, it had been a topic of heavy conversation before the Season ended. Sage wondered how she felt about being a part of the scandal for once, rather than simply spreading the gossip around as she was known to do. It was impossible to tell with her cool composure and diplomatic smile.

Drink in hand, Sage had been making his observations from near the edge of the clearing. A consequence of his reputation in London was that his name appeared on the list for all the best parties, but once inside, he often found that there were very few people who actually wanted to interact with him. Usually it was not until the early hours of the morning, when everyone had their fill of dancing and alcohol, that a gentleman would lock eyes with him across the room. So he was a bit hesitant when Harriet called his name and waved him over to join her and the others.

"Brilliant work on the party, my dear fellow," Cyril said, raising his glass of champagne in Sage's direction as Harriet patted his back.

"Did all of you know about it, as well?" Sage asked, scanning their faces.

"Roger is not exactly adept at hiding his emotions," Lady Anthea said, her arm looped with Lady Imogen's. "We knew he was trying to keep something a secret, especially when he started sneaking around with you of all people." Her wife gave her a strong look. "No offense," she amended quickly.

"You've mended the rift, haven't you?" Harriet smiled up at him. "Now we can all be friends." Her hand was still on his back. Sage swallowed at the tightness that formed in his throat.

"To friends," Fern said, holding their bowl of lemon ice up for a toast. The Ladies Fitzhugh put their glasses in, followed by Cyril and then Harriet. They all looked at Sage expectantly. With a huff of laughter, he touched his glass to theirs.

"To friends," he agreed.

Heavy footfalls came ripping across the grass from the direction of the garden. It was Keelan running and waving his arms above his head like a man unhinged.

"They're coming!" he whisper-shouted. "Everyone be quiet!"

A silence settled across the crowd as everyone turned to face the direction he'd come from. The only sound was Keelan's panting as Silas collected him into his arms, along with some of the delicate beads tinkling in the leaves on a gentle breeze. Harriet fidgeted with excitement beside Sage as Wyndham came into view with Roger holding one arm and Conrad holding the other, both carefully guiding him. Someone had tied a cravat around Wyndham's eyes. Roger looked as though he might burst with joy.

When they finally stopped, Roger took Wyndham's hands in his and gave Conrad a nod. Conrad went up onto his toes to untie the cloth covering Wyndham's eyes and wrapped it around his hand twice as he stepped back, smiling.

"All right," Roger said. "Open your eyes."

Wyndham did, blinking against all of the lights as an entirely unrehearsed chorus of 'surprise!' and 'happy birthday!' rang out in his direction. The color drained from his face, and for a moment he did look genuinely startled. But then, he donned his most dashing smile as he bent to give his husband a kiss while the onlookers applauded and cheered.

Still clapping, Sage watched as Conrad slipped away and left little room for wonder about where he was going. His magic lifted and swirled in his chest as

Cleaning Spells Before Courtship

Conrad approached him, looking devilishly handsome. After casting the cleaning spell together on Conrad's clothes to make sure they were extra bright for the party, Sage had demanded to dress Conrad with one of his own cravats and a pin to match. The jewels of it caught the twinkling fairy lights as they came together for a short embrace.

"That seems to have gone about as well as it could have," Sage said, giving Wyndham and Roger another glance where they were busy greeting all of the guests who had arrived in secret.

Conrad chuckled, accepting the glass of wine Sage offered him.

"I daresay it's a good thing Wyndham was not entirely unaware of what tonight was all about. You should've seen the look he gave Roger when he discovered I was going to cover his eyes with the cloth."

Sage laughed as he imagined how ridiculous Wyndham found it.

"The things you'll do to appease the person you love, I suppose."

Conrad winked at him after taking a sip of wine. "Indeed."

· ·. ·. ·

The party lasted for hours, as expected. Roger and Torquil took turns introducing Conrad to everyone, which meant that Sage also made several new acquaintances, for they did not spend a single moment apart. Sage noted the way both took care in how they presented them by name—Mr. Ravenwing and Mr. Moore—rather than by any sort of connection between the two of them. However, a couple of knowing looks and telling smiles were evidence enough that most came to their own conclusions on the matter. Sage was sure that the way he'd wrapped himself around Conrad's arm only aided in the process.

In truth, he found himself wishing for the others to see Conrad as his beau, or even as his suitor. If it had been anyone else making the introductions, perhaps the words would have come more freely, but Roger and Torquil were nothing if not discreet in the moments when it mattered most.

He knew he should be grateful for it. The brief lapse in reality he and Conrad shared over the previous several weeks did nothing to erase what awaited them in London. They had spoken at length about continuing to work together, especially since learning that Conrad had secured his position on the Council. Sage had also appointed himself as being responsible for showing Conrad around the city. But what of their connection beyond all of those things?

Just as he began to lose himself in his thoughts, the first dance was announced. Sage prepared to let Conrad go, as he recognized it as one that the other man was likely unfamiliar with, but he would still be expected to join. Instead, Conrad placed his hand over Sage's on his arm to hold it there and escorted him to the dance floor.

"Do you know this one?" Sage asked, trying not to sound too doubtful.

"Only a little," Conrad confessed. When they separated, he gave Sage a neat bow. "But I would like to share it with you regardless, if you'll allow it."

Sage was certain that his heart was melting in his chest faster than the ice cream Roger had been so worried about. He answered with a small nod and allowed himself to be swept up into what was the most wonderful dance he'd ever been a part of.

By the time supper was served, everyone was relieved to rest their feet for a while. The meal was a grand affair in its own right. Serving dishes overflowed with what turned out to be all of Wyndham's favorite foods, plus a few other items to fill in the gaps.

Across the table, Lady Anthea scoffed. "Harriet, what are you doing?"

She was shifting around in her chair with a disgruntled expression.

"I am attempting to remove my shoes," Harriet explained. "This bloody dress makes everything so difficult."

"Perhaps you should try trousers?" This was Lady Imogen's suggestion.

Harriet stilled. "That would be incredible."

Lady Anthea tutted. "Your poor mother would simply expire."

"First order of business when we return to London," Harriet announced, "we are all going shopping!"

Cyril gave her a long, assessing look and then returned to his meal. "You and Conrad are about the same size. It would do well for you both to find a tailor who can work with such petite measurements."

Harriet's eyes lit up. "Conrad, might I try some of yours on before we go?"

Lady Anthea nearly spit out her drink. It gained the attention of some of the other guests sitting nearby.

Conrad laughed and gave an indifferent shrug. "I wouldn't mind it."

Lady Anthea shrilled. "You cannot simply go around trying on someone else's clothes! Besides, I would hardly recognize you without a dress."

Unexpectedly, Emrys leaned his way into the conversation.

"And who gave you the authority to determine who is allowed to change their appearance to suit their fancy?" It was perhaps the most serious thing Sage had ever heard him say. On Emrys' other side, Torquil was speaking with someone else, a beautiful comb glinting in their dark curls and a most innocent sweep of rouge sitting on their high cheekbones. Vastly different from the dull print shop garb they'd worn not six months earlier.

Lady Anthea swallowed her words.

Emrys turned his attention on Conrad, expression softening.

"But she is correct," he said, signature smirk returning to his lips. "You'll have to find someone else's clothes to borrow. The only one getting into Conrad's trousers is Sage."

The end of their supper was marked with the reveal of a most sumptuous dessert table. Sage had seen what Roger spent on the display, but to see the entire contents of a patisserie uprooted and laid out for this simple garden party in the country was something else entirely. If there was one part of the planning Roger had been selfish with, it was this, and they were all the more fortunate for it. Tiers of pastries, tarts, and small cakes surrounded a larger cake decorated with icing and a few flowers that looked similar to the ones from the garden.

Organized chaos ensued as everyone scrabbled for a place in line. Wyndham and Roger stood beside the table and took turns forking mouthfuls off a shared slice of the lemon cake, pausing in between to thank everyone for coming and wishing them a safe journey back to wherever they'd arrived from. Somewhere behind the trees, the sky had started to lighten along the horizon.

After carefully filling a single plate between them, Sage and Conrad decided to take their spoils to the garden so that they might find some solitude. They exchanged a grin as they passed by the rickety bench beneath the willow and instead settled on one near some fragrant rose bushes. The light pink blooms watched as they took bites of each confection, both of them slowly coming to the conclusion that it would be impossible to pick a clear favorite.

When only one bite of a berry tart remained, Sage clasped his hands in his lap and leaned away slightly.

"You should have it," he encouraged.

"Absolutely not," Conrad challenged. "It's yours."

Sage shook his head. "I want you to have it."

"I will not." Conrad picked it up and brought it toward Sage's mouth. Sage turned his head away with a bubble of soft laughter, but Conrad went after him, leaning closer as he grasped the back of Sage's neck with his other hand to keep him from escaping. Sage yelped and grabbed his wrist.

"I relent!" he pleaded, opening his mouth so Conrad could feed him.

"So stubborn," Conrad grumbled, though it was laced with affection.

"I never promised you otherwise."

Conrad gave a gentle hum. "Only the mutual benefit of a temporary arrangement, if I remember correctly?"

Sage's grin fell as fast as his magic in his chest. "Yes."

"I suppose we both got what we were after," Conrad went on, moving their empty plate to his other side so he could slide closer to Sage on the bench.

Sage looked down as Conrad took both of his hands, wrapping his fingers around them on his lap. He noted how warm they always were compared to his own. "I suppose we did."

"I've something exciting to tell you."

Sage met his gaze, smiling bravely. "Oh?"

"Torquil has offered me a place to stay when I arrive in London. They said I'll be doing them a favor by taking up residence in their townhouse, which I'm not entirely sure that I believe, but I am not so proud as to pass up such an opportunity when it is given."

As heavy as the moment felt, Sage could not deny the relief that washed over him. He would've been willing to find Conrad no matter where he settled, even if it meant visiting the worst parts of the city. The street Torquil's townhouse sat on was a far cry from the docks.

"Apparently they are eager to see Mrs. Pimpernel removed from the difficult memories there."

Sage thought of the affection he'd seen her share with Iris Wrenwhistle.

"It will be no hardship for her to find a soft place to land," he guessed.

"An ideal situation for all parties," Conrad said, giving Sage's hands a gentle squeeze. "I'm to travel with her to London so that she might instruct me on running the household. It will make for a smooth transition, and it will give me something to do until the Council reconvenes."

The news left Sage unable to take a full breath.

"You're leaving...tonight?"

"Yes." Conrad flashed a mischievous smirk. "Fortunately, it will not take me long to pack."

Suddenly, Sage was angry. How could he find humor in a moment like this? As the emotion took over his features, brow furrowing and lips curving into a frown, Sage pulled his hands away and stood up.

"You cannot leave now," he said weakly.

Conrad's surprise was evident. He reached after Sage as he got to his feet, reclaiming both of his hands. "What's the matter?" he asked. "We both knew I would have to leave eventually."

"But not like this!" Sage felt them then, all of his unspoken words, rising up to be heard even if he did not feel entirely prepared to say them. The man had that effect on him from the very beginning. "I—" he tried, before letting out a huff and staring at their joint hands, unable to look Conrad in the eye. "I do not want to be apart from you. The trifling idea of it is enough to put me out of sorts."

"Sage," Conrad breathed, reaching to cup his cheek. Sage wished he hadn't. It only made it harder to continue without more emotion creeping into his voice.

"I meant to ask you to come with me instead," Sage went on, thoughts a tangle even as he said them. "You could spend the rest of the summer with me. You could meet my family." He was certain that they would all adore him.

Conrad's answering smile was steady, if not a little sad.

"I would love nothing more than to meet your family," he said, thumb stroking Sage's cheek. "And I fully intend to do just that, once we're all back in London." A pang of hurt in Sage's chest made him wince. "It will give me the time I need to settle. A shopping trip with Harriet sounds like great fun, but I suspect I'll add a few pieces to my wardrobe before then. Perhaps I'll buy a pair of shoes that do not smell like lake water." Sage was able to manage a pitiful, slightly wet laugh at that. "By the time you see me again, I'll look like a true gentleman."

Sage leaned into his palm. "I like you just as you are."

Conrad's smile grew. "I was hoping you'd say that. It will make our courtship far easier, from what I understand."

Sage's entire world slowed to a stop.

"Our what?" he whispered.

"It wouldn't do for me to show up at your family's estate looking like this and expect to make a good impression. I am only a simple man from Bristol, but I know that much. I want your parents to feel confident that I will be able to look after you when I ask for your hand." He gave a small shrug.

Sage blinked once, twice, vaguely aware that his hands were shaking.

"Are you asking me to marry you?"

Conrad's brows went up. "Oh, er...yes. I thought you realized."

Sage's jaw dropped as his magic twirled. "You," he said with slow emphasis, "want to marry *me*?"

Conrad nodded eagerly. "Wasn't it obvious?"

"I—" Sage wheezed. "I need to sit down."

They found the bench again together. Sage stared intently at his shoes while Conrad rubbed a hand on his back. How many times had he dreamed of this exact moment—being proposed to in a lush Wrenwhistle garden by the man that he loved. When he finally managed to collect himself, he turned slowly to find Conrad's waiting grin.

"This was...a dream. A fantasy. Life is not like this in London."

"I am not afraid of working hard to make my dreams come true," Conrad reminded him. "Is this not what you want?"

"It is everything I have ever wanted," Sage said, a little breathless.

"Then you shall have it."

Sage studied his face for a moment in the earliest morning light, searching his eyes for something he already knew he would not find. There was no uncertainty. No hidden emotions whatsoever. Conrad was exactly as Sage had ever known him to be—confident, hopeful, and wholly himself. As he wrapped his arms around Conrad's neck, he set his magic free, allowing himself to be all of those things too, in a way he never felt that he could until now.

"You strange creature," he whispered against Conrad's lips just before he kissed him.

Epilogue
Conrad

Conrad awoke to the sound of London traffic outside and the sunlight streaming through the lace curtains on the window. He smiled and glanced at the man curled up at his side. Sage was sleeping in his usual way, nestled close, with his cheek on Conrad's shoulder, their legs tangled together, and one arm draped across Conrad's chest.

He had shown up on Conrad's doorstep the evening before, still wrinkled from traveling all day. Sage assured him his family wouldn't miss him that night and then promptly enveloped Conrad in an embrace and a kiss. Conrad had been surprised that the man hadn't changed from his traveling clothes first and found himself noticing different perfumes— hints of family members who had sat beside him— before he caught the familiar scent of rose and almond and kissed Sage back with a little more fierceness than usual. Sage had moaned against him and Conrad laughed and pulled away.

"Is that a hint for what you're wanting tonight?"

Sage had smiled and shook his head. "No. I just want you."

They'd stayed up late, catching up on the past couple of months—Sage talked about his time in the country with his family and Conrad described what his time in London had been like. Sage had fallen asleep first, weary from travel and attempting to continue speaking between yawns as Conrad pulled him close.

Now, Conrad was at liberty to once again study Sage's face, softened as ever in sleep—the dark curling lashes, strong cheekbones, pouting lips, olive complexion, and black hair that splayed out over the pillow and Conrad's arm. He sighed and traced a finger across Sage's cheek. He'd missed waking up beside him. The days had been busy yet strangely empty in a new house, a new city, and with new responsibilities to keep him occupied.

But in that time, he'd made plans. Now that he had managed his first impossible dream, the time had come to work on his next one. He'd received a great deal of advice from Leonora on the subject and, surprisingly, from Wyndham, Roger, Emrys, and Torquil as well. A ring had to be considered, and the right question to ask Sage's parents. Furniture had to be arranged so that the nicest vanity was placed in the largest bedroom.

Sage nuzzled against his shoulder when he woke

and smiled, his eyes still closed. "You made me a morning person and I'll never forgive you."

Conrad laughed in surprise. "My apologies."

"I've woken up every morning for months feeling like something was missing." Sage's arm wrapped around Conrad's chest. "Now I have it back."

Conrad smiled too and curled his fingers to brush against Sage's cheek. "That you do. And if all goes according to plan, we won't have to spend so long apart again."

Sage's eyes flew open. "You have a plan?"

"Of course."

Sage rolled his eyes, but there was a grin tugging at his lips as he repeated, "Of course. Are you going to tell me what it is?"

"Well, the first part is to make sure we eat breakfast."

Sage groaned. "Absolutely not. I've waited this long. The least you can do is stay in bed with me."

Conrad chuckled and mentally reorganized the list in his head. "You'll note that I never said what time breakfast would be."

Sage closed his eyes and pulled close again. "That's more like it. And then what?"

"And then I need to show you my new clothes."

Sage made a sound of interest but did not move. "You bought new clothes?"

"I told you I would. I want to do you proud. And if I'm going to do that, I'll need the most fashionable person I know to give his approval."

"I hope you got some colorful items. Human men tend to wear such drab and plain clothes. It's absurd."

"Cyril doesn't."

"A rare exception."

"And yes, of course I did. Wyndham sent me a recommendation for his favorite tailor. He even had a few of my first pieces credited to his account, the sneak. So my wardrobe has grown significantly since you last saw me. Nothing to rival yours, of course." He paused, considering. "I'll need to make a note to add wardrobes to this bedroom. It can't be good for your clothes to be all stuffed together like they were in the country."

Sage's expression softened. "That's very considerate."

"And then, after you've looked over my clothes, and we've had breakfast, you're going to give me your London address so I can invite your family over to dinner. That will likely have to happen on a different night, of course. And I'll ask them for your hand. And then all we'll have left to do is plan the wedding."

Sage gave a snort. "You've clearly never been to a fae wedding if you think that will be the easy part."

Conrad shrugged as he relaxed against the pillow. "Well, I'm content to let you handle most of that. I'm impartial to the dates. Although Wyndham suggested I keep in mind what colors will be in fashion for the season. So I think autumn or winter might be best as you seem to favor those richer shades and—"

He broke off as Sage kissed him. "You really have thought of everything, haven't you?"

Conrad grinned at him. "I do my best. I still have a number of details to work out. As you can imagine, I've been quite busy becoming a gentleman of London."

"Did you get lost yet?"

"Multiple times."

"It's a rite of passage. Have you gone riding in the Park?"

"Not yet. I was waiting for you. But I did go shopping for some basic spell ingredients, and I bought a few books, and Iris kindly gave me a tour of the Council chambers." He reached for the nightstand. "I also subscribed to the best gossip column in town. I've been told it's a necessity for city life."

Sage grunted. "Ah, yes. The *Tribune*. Anyone who's anyone reads it."

Conrad caught the wary tone in Sage's voice. He said gently, "I think you'll enjoy this edition. Shall I read it to you?"

"If you like."

Conrad held it up and cleared his throat:

"Greetings returning readers,

Life has been exceedingly dull here in London with the ton spread out across the country for the summer. But we anticipate an exciting Season ahead.

First, the Council for Fae & Human Magical

Relations has finally filled the remaining gap in their numbers with a third human member. Little is known about this person. All we know is that he is acquainted with a number of notable members of society, including several of the other councilmembers. We are sure the gentleman will be met with eager curiosity and, hopefully, congeniality upon his entry into society.

The Wyndham Wrenwhistles hosted their first house party over the summer. To all accounts, it was an enormous success. Many anticipate this couple to be leading figures in fashionable society. The event ended with a celebration of Mr. Wyndham Wrenwhistle's birthday. Family and friends were invited. According to sources, noteworthy guests include Mr. Sage Ravenwing, who sported a gorgeous plum waistcoat, Mr. Cyril Thompson, who looked very fine in a subdued green suit, and Mrs. Aveline Buckthorn, who was lovely in peach.

As people trickle back to our fair city, we are already hearing whispers of potential matches. Will this be the year that Mx. Hillcrest, Mr. Thompson, and Miss Thackeray finally head to the altar? Will Miss Gloucester-Stone stun society with her ready smile and quick wit? Will the mysterious new councilmember catch anyone's eye?

One member of society who seems to be

spoken for at last is Mr. Sage Ravenwing. We are sure this news will be met with dismay as the gentleman has brightened many a salon in recent Seasons. According to sources, Mr. Ravenwing found love over the summer. Was it during the Wrenwhistles' house party? Or perhaps a friend near the Ravenwing estate? Mr. Ravenwing has graced the pages of this column ever since his debut. We are delighted that he should find someone worthy of him at last.

If there's anything this humble writer believes in, it is that everyone is deserving of love, friendship, and happiness. We hope you all find it, gentle readers, whether it be in this Season or the next. Whatever shape that love may arrive in, we hope that it fills your heart with joy and your magic with sparkle.

In the meantime, we look forward to a most eventful Season,

Your winsome writer,

Sal Bailey"

Sage was unmoving beside him as he laid the column aside. Conrad ran fingers through his hair. "I wonder how they shall describe us when we first appear in public together? The illustrious Mr. Ravenwing and the mysterious Mr. Moore?"

"Tell me the truth," Sage said, looking up at him. "Were you their source?"

"I was not."

"Truly?"

"Upon my honor."

Sage frowned. "That's the nicest the *Tribune* has ever been about me. I felt sure it was you."

"Then it must have been one of your other friends. Someone who wanted to make sure the rest of London recognized how wonderful you are."

The corner of Sage's mouth ticked up. "Someone wrote about you too, from the sounds of it."

"Hm. Everyone will be very disappointed when they discover how much I lack mystery and intrigue."

Sage laughed and then pressed a hand to his mouth. "I doubt disappointment will be on their minds after meeting you."

"How kind of you to say." Conrad cupped his chin and pulled him close for a kiss. "So, what do you think?" he asked when he broke off. "Will the elegant Mr. Ravenwing find love this Season?"

"Of course not. He already found it."

"Oh? At this famous house party that everyone will be talking about?"

"Most specifically, at the lake, when he kissed a sweet and cheerful man and it felt so magnificent that his magic swept around them in a whirl."

"And ruined our clothes."

"No one needs to know about that."

Conrad smiled against his lips. "It makes for a very romantic tale. I'm afraid Mr. Moore's story will not be nearly as interesting to readers."

Sage stroked his temple with his thumb. "Why not? When did he fall in love?"

"In the quiet hours of the morning. It happened slowly, softly. When he realized that he liked the smell of roses and almonds best of all, and the way his legs tangled perfectly with one particular man, and the way they taught each other so many things, and the way their secrets always felt sacred when spoken together. And when he realized all of that, Mr. Moore found that he was in love with one of his dearest friends. It's not as thrilling a tale as wind whipping across a lake."

"Nonsense," Sage breathed, as his arms slowly wrapped behind Conrad's neck. "It's the most beautiful story I've ever heard."

"Would you like to hear it again?"

"Yes."

Then Sage closed the distance and kissed him and all Conrad could think of was the softness of his lips, the warmth of his skin, the joy in his own heart, and the scent of roses and almonds in the air.

The End

Note from the Authors

Greetings, radiant readers,

Sage started out as a one-scene character in *Breeze Spells and Bridegrooms*. In fact, when we put together our character list for the book, he was described as "Random Fae #1." But as soon as Shannon wrote Sage's devastating Vauxhall scene, Sarah began campaigning for him to get a redemption arc. After the book was published, we learned that our readers were hoping for more of Sage, too. Thankfully, his story had already been written by the time they met him.

Conrad's inspiration was drawn from a viral video of two men dancing West Coast Swing together. Shannon sent it to Sarah and Sarah immediately saved the video and watched it approximately a million times. While Conrad's character transformed into his own personality, we will forever be grateful to the cheerful, buff, and short king who won our hearts.

This story brings the Fae & Human Relations series to a close. It's a bittersweet thing, bidding goodbye to a world and a set of characters. These books brought us together. We grew as writers and as friends. It's not hyperbole to say this series changed our lives. We couldn't have done it without you sticking with us, dear readers. Thank you for reading our stories, for supporting our work, and for loving our characters.

We are looking forward to taking you on more adventures to come!

In the meantime, we remain,

Your winsome writers,

Sarah & Shannon

Acknowledgments

This book wouldn't be possible without our network of support. Thank you to our alpha and beta readers, Bronwyn, Anna, Alexis, Kayla, Meg, and Becca. Thank you to our amazing editor, Mackenzie! Thank you to our wonderful proofreader, Ashley. Thank you to our fantastic narrator, Maxwell. Thank you again to all of our cheerleaders who encouraged us throughout the process, especially John, Ashley, and Bronwyn.

Cover art: Caras Alexandra
Editor: Mackenzie Walton
Proofreader: Ashley Scout

Also by Sarah Wallace & S.O. Callahan

Also by Sarah Wallace

Letters to Half Moon Street

One Good Turn

The Education of Pip

Dear Bartleby

The Spellmaster of Tutting-on-Cress

The Viscount Says Yes

Free to Sarah's newsletter subscribers:

The Glamour Spell of Rose Talbot

Also by S.O. Callahan

Fella Enchanted

Fella Ever After

About Sarah Wallace

 Sarah Wallace lives in Florida with
their cat, more books than she has
time to read, a large collection of
classic movies, and an apartment
full of plants that are surviving
against all odds. They only read
books that end happily.

About S.O. Callahan

S.O. Callahan has always been fond of sweet things, namely chocolate and love stories. When she's not writing or reading, she enjoys baking, visiting National Parks and Historic Sites, and traveling with her husband. They live in Chicago and have two very spoiled cats named Ozzy and Beau.

www.ingramcontent.com/pod-product-compliance
Lightning Source LLC
Chambersburg PA
CBHW020836020726
47497CB00005B/1127